YULETIDE WISHES

A REGENCY NOVELLA DUET

GRACE BURROWES
CHRISTI CALDWELL

Ebook ISBN 978-194-141-9885

Print ISBN 978-194-141-9892

Grace Burrowes Publishing

LADY MISTLETOE'S HOLIDAY HELPER

BY GRACE BURROWES

CHAPTER ONE

"The decorations must be exquisite, Lady Margaret. Beyond perfection, though within the bounds of good taste, of course." Lord Marcus Bannerfield paused on the landing, and Meg had no choice but to pause with him. "Do I make myself clear, my lady?"

Lord Marcus was Meg's most prestigious customer thus far, meaning his budget for holiday decorating would also be the most prestigious, if Meg had anything to say to it.

"I do understand, my lord. Lady Mistletoe's Holiday Helpers take great pride in delivering not simply satisfaction, but *magic*. Your Yuletide decorations will outshine anything ever to grace this house."

Meg made the standard claim in her standard cheerful-but-brisk tones and proceeded down the steps. Lord Marcus's home was large, as befitted the second son of a marquess, and touring the premises had nearly put her behind schedule. The house was immaculately maintained. The sconces gleamed, every pair of curtains hung in symmetrical folds, even the wainscoting bore a patina of beeswax and elbow grease worthy of a royal domicile.

His lordship remained on the landing, hands behind his back, like a ship's captain gazing out to sea on a fine, breezy day. The ocean before him was a soaring domed foyer complete with a black and white marble parquet floor, enormous potted ferns, and a slight, churchlike echo. The circular skylight at the top of this architectural marvel should have provided at least one beam of golden sunshine, but the weather refused to oblige.

"Magic is the invention of an overactive imagination," Lord Marcus said, "but a decree has gone forth from Lady Elizabeth Hennepin that I must decorate the house, so decorate the house, I shall. I ignore my sister's proclamations at peril to my domestic tranquility. Where do you propose we hang the mistletoe?"

His expression held a hint of belligerence, as if this sororal decree was a challenge of some sort. Lord Marcus managed the marquessate's business for his father, and he had also recently taken on the raising of his late brother's orphaned children. Meg had done her usual research and been surprised that a man carrying that much responsibility had time to consider a task that usually fell to the servants.

Lord Marcus was shaping up to be that most vexatious of all holiday curses—the meddling client.

"We have time to ponder where the kissing boughs should go, my lord. I shall have an estimate to you by noon tomorrow, complete with sketches."

Meg expected him to direct her to send the estimate to his man of business, his solicitors, some earnest, overworked minion who would let her careful figures and drawings sit for at least a week.

"That's the soonest you can send it along?" His lordship came down the steps, a powerful, graceful man prowling confidently through his own domain. He topped six feet by an inch or two, wore his brown hair in an old-fashioned unpowdered queue, and had brown eyes, probably courtesy of his French mother.

He was a departure from the usual Saxon lordling, all blond, blue-eyed breeding with a solid oxlike build. Lord Marcus had plenty of muscle, but his physique was that of a fencer or an equestrian rather than a pugilist. For his house, the decorations should emphasize light and elegance, rather than an overabundance of greenery.

And he would doubtless, *doubtless*, oversee every bit of the setting up and taking down, because a peer's heir had nothing better to do than quibble over the location of his kissing boughs.

"I have other appointments this afternoon, my lord, else I should have your estimate completed by the end of the day." Meg pulled on her gloves and stuffed her sketchbook into her satchel, barely resisting the urge to consult her watch. Papa's timepiece was the only possession of his that Lucien had allowed her to keep. Meg liked to hold it and to look at it. She did not like to feel another day slipping past with no signed contracts to show for her hard work.

Lady Mistletoe's Holiday Helpers, some of whom were barely old enough to know their letters, depended on her.

As did Charlotte.

"We're in for snow," his lordship said, peering through the window beside the imposing front door. "I have a few more ideas regarding the nursery decorations. They will affect the budget." He took Meg's cloak down from a hook. "I don't suppose you'd consider sharing your midday meal with me so we could discuss my suggestions?"

Meg moved around him to glance at the street and bit back an unladylike observation. A few lazy flakes drifted from a pewter sky.

"I do not care for snow." She hated snow, hated the glee clubs cluttering up street corners with their yodeling and bell-ringing. Hated the cold and darkness and the whole holiday season. "If the weather is turning foul, my lord, all the more reason I should be about my appointments. One's progress is slowed by disobliging precipitation."

"Disobliging precipitation?" He enunciated each syllable, as if the phrase were a new addition to his French vocabulary. "Ah, you came on foot rather than force a team to wait about in the cold. I do understand, and I propose a compromise. You bide here for another thirty minutes to share my luncheon and resolve my plans for the nursery, and I will put my second town coach at your disposal for the remainder of the afternoon. Have we a bargain, Lady Margaret?"

Had he made that offer with a smile, a leer, or a hint of innuendo, Meg would have turned him down flatly and accounted the last hour entirely wasted. But he'd posited sharing a meal with her as a means of continuing a business consultation, and she was so very hungry. Cold weather did that and left her with blocks of ice where her feet should be, and with nothing but cross words for Charlotte, who deserved all the good cheer in the world.

Then too, Meg's next appointment was halfway to Chelsea, a substantial hike while toting a heavy satchel. "I cannot tarry long, my lord."

He replaced her cloak on the hook and set her satchel on the sideboard. "I am rather pressed for time myself. My sister has also reminded me that children still require a holiday token on Christmas Day. I must brave the mercantile establishments in hopes of procuring these gifts, for nothing will do but I choose them myself."

He offered his arm, something he'd not done previously. One did not refuse such a courtesy from a marquess's heir.

Meg laid her gloves on the sideboard and accepted his escort. "Is that another edict from your sister?"

"Not from my sister, from my own upbringing." His lordship led Meg down a corridor lined with Dutch landscapes, gleaming pier glasses, and exquisite porcelain. The claret-colored carpet—easy to embellish such a shade with holiday flourishes—looked to have been woven for the exact dimensions of the corridor, the hues chosen to complement the paintings.

His lordship had good taste, which made decorating his house at once a greater challenge and greater delight.

"Papa stood back from the holiday madness," he went on, "allowing my mother enormous latitude with decorations, entertainments, and menus, but he insisted that his imprimatur be on the presents bestowed in the nursery on Christmas morning. I expect my father will pay a call here on Christmas Day, and I refuse to be bested by the old fellow simply because he has a thirty-year start on a family tradition."

Male competition made perfect sense to Meg. That Lord Marcus referred to the Marquess of Innisborough as Papa was harder to explain.

"You aren't concerned about spoiling your nieces?" she asked.

He opened a door for her, warmth and the scent of good food gusting into the corridor. Meg scooted into what was probably a breakfast parlor, for the windows faced east and showed a garden already dusted with snow.

"My nieces have lost both parents, my lady," Lord Marcus said, holding a chair at the right hand of the head of the table. "A mountain of gifts would not give them what they truly long for, would it?"

"I suppose not, so why trouble over a holiday token?"

A procession of staff arrived—two footmen, two maids—all carrying dishes placed over warming trays. One of the maids set a serving of silver utensils before Meg, and she was assailed by memories of the years when this scene could have been taken from her own upbringing.

Lord Marcus excused his domestics with passing thanks. "I prefer to serve myself," he said. "Less food goes to waste that way, and I have more privacy. Would you care for some soup? Looks like a humble pepper pot today."

"On a day such as this, nobody with sense refuses a steaming bowl of pepper pot." Meg took good portions of the bread and butter, too, though she did feel guilty. Charlotte would relish such a meal and would delight in the heat thrown out by the fireplaces bookending the room. A little girl should not have to spend her entire winter swaddled in two of her mother's shawls.

Lord Marcus took his seat at the head of the table and served the soup. Meg passed him the bread and butter, realizing she should have waited for him to be seated before helping herself.

If he noticed that faux pas, like a gentleman, he pretended to ignore it. He took up his soup spoon, so Meg did likewise.

"How do you celebrate your holidays, Lady Margaret? Surely a woman who has raised Yuletide decorating to a professional art must delight in every little detail of the season?"

"Oh, I do enjoy Yuletide." She offered that bouncer just as something—a peppercorn?—went down the wrong way and sent her into a most unladylike fit of coughing.

~

LADY MARGARET ENTWHISTLE WAS A PRETTY, prim puzzle, and Marcus was more than willing to be distracted by the conundrum she posed.

She wasn't impressed by his rank, though as the daughter of an earl, she'd doubtless met many men with titles or expectations of a title. She also wasn't overly concerned about her appearance. Her dress, while made of good-quality green velvet, was at least two years out of date. She wore her dark hair in a severe bun and eschewed jewelry of any kind.

No woman could have signaled less of an interest in Marcus as a man or as a marital prize. She'd marched about his house, scribbling notes, making quick sketches, and peering out of windows as if she were considering purchasing the property. That experience, of showing his entire home to a woman he barely knew, had been oddly intimate.

When Lady Margaret set down her spoon and began coughing, Marcus rose to thump her gently on the back. The woman responsible for decking his damned halls could not be allowed to expire before the project was even begun. Eliza would never let him hear the end of such a misstep.

"Would you like some water?" he asked as Lady Margaret's coughing fit subsided.

She nodded, pressing her table napkin to her lips. "Peppercorn," she said, "down the wrong way."

He poured her a glass of water from the carafe on the sideboard.

Outside, the snow was thickening, from a flurry of wispy flakes to a steady white cascade. That was all to the good—fewer patrons cluttering up the toy shops—but had Lady Margaret truly intended to hike across Mayfair in this weather?

"I'll have a word with Cook," Marcus said. "Can't have one of the children choking on a stray peppercorn, can I?"

"I should have been more careful. Tell me about the children, my lord."

While her ladyship made short work of her soup, Marcus resumed his seat and passed along what little he knew of his nieces.

"Two females aged eight, though they are not twins. One will shortly turn nine, her sister not until next year. Their names are Amanda and Emily, and they should arrive next week, weather permitting."

Lady Margaret looked up from her soup. "Surely you do not expect the house to be decorated by next week, my lord? Christmas is more than a month away."

Surely he had been hoping for that very thing. "Perhaps not the whole house, but at least the foyer. Lady Eliza insists that the children's first impression of their new home be welcoming. You asked me earlier why I intend that the girls have gifts on Christmas Day. They have lost their parents, and no doll or storybook can replace that loss."

"But you will give them dolls anyway?"

Well, then. No dolls. "They likely already have entire ballrooms full of dolls, but I want them to have *something*. Their father doubtless carried on Papa's tradition, and that tradition matters. Their mother made a great to-do over the holidays, as my mother did, and if I can maintain that emphasis for the girls, they will know I valued their parents and share those traditions. You look at me as if I've taken leave of my senses." Even Eliza approved of this reasoning, though she pronounced it a convoluted excuse to celebrate the holidays.

Lady Margaret set aside her empty soup bowl. "I very much doubt that you and your senses ever part ways, my lord. Children are perceptive. They grasp when we deal with them in good faith and when we're putting on a show. That you want your nieces to be welcome and comfortable will mean more to them than any set of fancy hairbrushes or box of paints."

"*Paints?* Isn't nine a bit young for paints?" Hairbrushes sounded entirely manageable.

Lady Margaret smiled, the first smile he'd seen from her. "Nine is not too soon for paints if the child is artistically inclined. I was using watercolors by then and demanding oils by the time I was twelve."

"And you were *allowed* to work in oils?" How... odd.

The smile, so unexpected and mischievous, winked out. "I was, which my brother still thinks was a signal error on the part of our parents. Your soup will get cold, my lord."

"Your brother would be the Earl of Webberly?" Marcus had glanced at DeBrett's, finding it curious that a titled widow would engage in any sort of commerce at all.

"My brother is the twelfth Earl of Webberly. That ham looks delicious."

Her ladyship was hungry, in other words, and intent on arriving to her next appointments on time. Marcus appreciated punctuality, but was his company really of so little note compared to a boring old ham?

"Will you celebrate the holidays with your brother's family?" Marcus asked, taking up the carving knife.

"Certainly not. My business is at its most frantic over the next six weeks, and traveling to the family seat is out of the question."

He passed her a plate bearing two slices of ham. "Did your late husband approve of a venture that demands so much from you at a time of year usually reserved for family gatherings?"

Her ladyship rose, taking her plate to the sideboard. "Major Entwhistle would well understand why I have taken on the Lady Mistletoe business. Would you care for mashed potatoes, my lord?"

What sort of answer was that? "Please."

She served herself a generous portion of potatoes. "What day are your nieces scheduled to arrive?"

"Wednesday."

Her ladyship sat back down with less than studied grace. "You want the foyer decorated by *Tuesday*?"

"Is that a problem?"

She stared at the meat and potatoes before her. Marcus imagined the sound of gears whizzing and the beads of an abacus clicking back and forth.

Her ladyship took up her knife and fork. "I can have the foyer looking festive by Tuesday evening, though, mind you, the job will be only halfway complete. I will rob Peter of his gold ribbon and Paul of his fresh oranges. Your cook will mutter foul oaths at the mention of my name, and your housekeeper will have worse than that to say about me."

Cook likely uttered foul oaths regarding her employer. "You sound pleased, my lady." She looked pleased too. Her gaze, usually a steady blue-eyed regard, had taken on a gleam of ambition.

"When I contemplate what your lordship will pay for expedited service, I am very pleased indeed. This is good ham."

Of course it was, and yet... she went after her victuals as if she'd meant the compliment sincerely. Perhaps her kitchen wasn't properly staffed. Good help was hard to find and harder to keep.

"I'm glad you're enjoying it." Marcus took a bite and found the ham a bit salty. "If you were purchasing presents for two little girls, what would you buy them?"

"That depends on the girls. Tell me more about your nieces."

"I hardly know them. My brother preferred to raise his family at Banner Hall, and I seldom had enough leave both to visit there and to see my parents here in London."

Lady Margaret paused, her hand upon her wineglass. "You were in the military?"

"For ten years."

"Did you know my husband? Major Peter Entwhistle? 52nd Foot?"

"I am sorry. I did not."

She took a sip of her wine. "What fine libation you serve, my lord."

That was as awkward a change of topic as he'd heard her make, and her conversation generally leaped about a good deal. Perhaps she still grieved for the major?

"I have had good luck with Rieslings of late. Now, what do you advise regarding gifts for my nieces?"

"You might consider asking them what catches their fancies."

Ask them? Ask *small children* regarding holiday wishes? "And if they want a coach and four? A trip to Paris? A yacht? Matching pink unicorns?"

Lady Margaret gazed out at the garden rapidly disappearing beneath a blanket of white. "What any grieving little girl would want, more than a coach and four, would be to make happy memories to balance the sadness filling her heart. Take your nieces to walk in the park on a snowy day, show them how to aim a snowball at a tree trunk. Read to them, let them join you at breakfast if their manners are up to that challenge. Spend time with them, because one day, they will lose you too."

At some point in that diatribe, Lady Margaret had ceased making a suggestion regarding Marcus's nieces and instead offered a confession of sorts.

"How long has your husband been gone?"

"Four years. He loved the military. He was never in England for very long, and he would not hear of me following the drum."

"I am sorry." Had Major Entwhistle bothered to make happy memories with his wife? Marcus suspected he had not. "Our discussion has ranged far afield from dolls and mistletoe. Perhaps we should sample the apple tarts?"

Lady Margaret took two from the basket he held out to her. She did equal and thorough justice to both, while Marcus contented himself with one. The meal had not been as enjoyable as he'd hoped, though the food was, as always, plentiful and good. He wasn't sure what exactly about the shared repast disappointed him, but then, what had he expected?

Lady Margaret was a busy woman, and Marcus was... a busy man? He rang the bell-pull, signaling that the table could be cleared, and when the tea had been brought in, he poured out for his guest.

"I wish you did not have to brave the elements," he said. "This afternoon would be best spent before a roaring fire with a good book."

"I will leave the roaring fire and good books to you, my lord. I have two more calls to make, and the use of your coach will be much appreciated."

"Why do you do it?" he asked. "Why spend your holidays prettying up other people's houses?"

She dusted her hands over a plate that held only apple tart crumbs and aimed a bright smile at him. "I simply enjoy decorating for the holidays. For a few weeks of the year, we are encouraged to make our dwellings as cheerful and inviting as possible. I have a knack for it, so why shouldn't I put my skills to use for others?"

Why? Because the daughter of an earl had no business dealing in trade, and yet, Marcus admired a woman willing to demonstrate initiative and ingenuity. Heaven knew he had no idea how to make a house *cheerful and inviting*.

"I must be on my way," her ladyship said, rising. "My thanks for a splendid meal, and I will have my estimate to you by noon tomorrow."

Marcus got to his feet and held the door for her ladyship. He murmured a brief instruction to the footman tidying up at the sideboard, then escorted Lady Margaret to the front door. The lingering sense of something lacking about what should have been a sociable meal on a winter day would not leave him.

"A week from now," her ladyship said, "this foyer will look very different. The air will be laden with cloves and cinnamon, the bannisters wrapped in red velvet ribbon."

Marcus draped her cloak over her shoulders and smoothed the fabric out from the collar. "You even plan the scent?"

"Of course. When you walk into a beautiful old home, then catch a whiff of mildew, your impression of the place is unalterably diminished. Your abode will be fragranced with seasonal joy, my lord. Depend upon it."

She pulled on her gloves—mere kid, and in this weather—and tied her bonnet ribbons beneath her chin. The figure she cut was stylish, though Marcus noted a bit of darning on her right middle finger.

"I will look forward to our next meeting," he said, though he wasn't sure that was true. He had never met a woman less given to seasonal sentimentality. As his own stores of that commodity were thin indeed, he and her ladyship should have got on famously.

Marcus's guest cast a weather-eye around the foyer. "Before I am through, you will probably dread the sound of my voice, but you will love the impression your home makes on your holiday guests."

Holiday guests. Marcus mentally shuddered at the very notion.

Her ladyship squared her shoulders and stood back for the butler to open the front door. The town coach sat at the foot of the steps, and Marcus had ordered the floor bricks heated, but he still didn't like to send her out in such weather.

The footman from the breakfast parlor passed him a paper-wrapped parcel, which Marcus held out to the lady.

"Take a few apple tarts, please, Lady Margaret. Your day is long. Bustling about must be hungry work."

She looked at him, then at the apple tarts. Some impossible longing flickered in her gaze, and he thought for a moment she'd refuse his gift.

"That is very thoughtful of you, my lord. Thank you." The tarts went into her satchel, and then she was out the door.

"Shall I build up the fire in the library, my lord?" the footman asked.

A sensible request on such a day. The coach pulled away from the steps, the jingling of the harness muted by the falling snow.

"No, thank you," Marcus said. "Duty calls, and I am its willing vassal. I am off to practice pitching snowballs at tree trunks."

"Very good my—my lord?" The footman was young and too new to his livery to hide his consternation.

"The children will be here next week, James. I have just been informed that my pitching arm may be my greatest asset in their eyes."

"If you say so, my lord." He bowed and withdrew, leaving Marcus to puzzle over Lady Margaret Entwhistle. She'd been singularly uncharming, as ladies went. Most unmarried women, and a few of the married ones, were bold in their appreciation for his company. Lady Margaret had been appreciative of the soup, the ham, the wine, and the tarts... but she'd assayed not a single flirtation in his direction.

More to the point, she'd made it very clear he need not attempt any flirtation in her direction either.

Which should have been a very great relief indeed.

CHAPTER TWO

Thank God for Lord Marcus's coach, because Meg's spirits had sunk lower as the snow had deepened. Neither of her afternoon appointments had shown enthusiasm for her services, but they had both wanted estimates on the spot.

She knew better than to toss out numbers off the top of her head. Her written estimates listed exactly what she was obligated to do, when she'd have it done, and for how much coin. Too many customers expected an extravaganza worthy of the Prince Regent, and then they followed up with a similarly royal inability to pay the resulting expenses.

Since one of her early customers—an older gentleman who owned several coaching inns—had suggested that she have clients countersign a documented estimate, she'd had far fewer "misunderstandings" with pinchpenny beer nabobs.

The coach rocked to a halt at the corner nearest Margaret's rooms, and she braced herself for another trudge through cold and slush.

The footman opened the door, lowered the steps, and offered her a hand. "Careful, my lady. The snow is piling up."

She descended, the casual courtesy giving her a pang. Once upon a time, her father's footmen had treated her with similar care. She'd known them by name, and they'd kept her and Aunt Nan company on every shopping expedition.

Aunt Nan was dead these eight years, and Meg missed her most as the holidays approached.

Another footman in different livery approached Meg as her escort was bowing his farewell. Lord Marcus's man stepped in front of the newcomer, though Meg recognized the livery all too well.

"Have you business with her ladyship?"

The other fellow bristled like an outraged dowager. "Happen I do. Lord Webberly would like a word with his sister."

Across the street sat a crested vehicle finished in gleaming black lacquer with red and gold trim. Lucien did like to travel in style. His coach was pulled by four matched blacks, snow melting on their backs and matting their coats with damp. They had apparently been waiting for some time, for the snow at their feet was churned and stomped to mud.

"My lady?" Lord Marcus's footman remained between Meg and Lucien's lackey. "What say you?"

"I say, please thank Lord Marcus for his consideration, and thanks to you and John Coachman as well."

Lord Marcus's footman took her satchel from her hand and shoved it at the other fellow. "Mind you offer her ladyship an arm crossing the street."

Meg took the fellow's arm before fisticuffs erupted, though she was not in the mood to deal with Lucien. Anymore, she was never in the mood to deal with him.

The footman opened the door to Lucien's coach, and Meg climbed in. The scent inside was leather and damp wool overlaid with clove. Meg had taken her idea for Christmas sachets from Lucien's fancy carriages, for if anything confirmed an impression of tasteful wealth, it was a coach that smelled like a spice shop.

"My lord, to what do I owe the honor?"

The problem with Lucien was that he still looked like the brother she'd grown up with. Sandy-blond hair, angular features, blue eyes, and a serious nature. Since marrying Lady Evelyn Parmenter, his nature had gone from serious to sour. Lady Evelyn's settlements had apparently been her most endearing feature, and an earl must have an heir. Marital martyrdom had followed on all sides.

"Do you ride about Town in fancy coaches now, Margaret?"

"You certainly do. Why shouldn't I?"

He sighed and glanced out the window as if importuning the gray sky for strength. "I am not here to bicker."

"You aren't paying a social call either, Lucien. I would receive you, you know. I'd even offer you hot tea and apple tarts." The tea leaves would be reused, but only once. Or twice. And Meg would begrudge him every tart he condescended to eat.

He rested his gloved hands on a gold-handled walking stick. "I am here to make an offer, Sister. A most generous offer that I extend despite our differences. My lady wife and I have decided on this course out of Christian duty to Charlotte as her aunt and uncle. You may choose to make a spectacle of yourself, engaging in trade, borrowing some cit's coach in exchange for heaven knows what favors, but I hope you will allow Charlotte some charity from her proper relations."

The apple tarts had been calling to Meg all afternoon, but her devotion to Charlotte called more loudly. Charlotte was why Meg worked until all hours, why she bore the malicious pity of her peers, why she maintained a semblance of civility with Lucien and Evelyn.

"Charlotte does not need your charity." She needed new boots, she needed books to read, she needed friends who did not make sly jokes at her expense.

"Charlotte's antecedents are irregular," Lucien retorted. "Her mother has fallen from the notice of polite society and rightly so. In ten years, Charlotte will be of marriageable age and will need all of her aunt's influence and goodwill. Let Charlotte spend the holidays with us."

Margaret sat calmly in Lucien's lordly coach, but in her heart, in that place reserved for her most-honest feelings, she fell howling to her knees.

"You mean well," she said slowly.

"Of course I mean well. We have our differences, Margaret, but I don't hold Charlotte accountable for your errant ways. The longer she's associated with you, the harder her path in life will be. Soon, she can be made to understand that, and though you love her—Evelyn insists that you love your daughter—you cannot provide for her as we can. Unless you want that child to make the same mistakes you have made, you will put your selfish needs aside and appoint me as her guardian."

Meg made a fist, rather than chance Lucien noticing the darning on her gloves. "And if I remarry?" How calmly she posed the question, when her heart was breaking in the loud, angry cracks of a frozen lake casting away winter's cold.

"I have ever and anon advised you to remarry. All widows should remarry, for the sake of their own well-being and the good of the realm. You aren't bad-looking. Find a decent fellow from a good family who can provide adequately, explain to him the follies of your youth. Charlotte is a girl child. It's not like she's a son. Present me with a groom from a proper family of means, and you will have my blessing."

Would a marriage into a proper family of means inspire Lucien to withdraw this threat to snatch Charlotte away? Was that what his almighty *blessing* amounted to?

"I must think on this," Margaret said. "The holidays are still some way off. How much longer will you be in Town?"

"You must *think on* the only opportunity your daughter will have for a decent life among decent people? I do not understand you, Margaret. A child is not a possession or a pet to be hoarded away for when you are in a low mood and want to jolly yourself out of it by playing mama. A child is a responsibility."

Meg took a slow, deep breath. She was cold, tired, and hungry.

Lucien had ambushed her, rather than send her a note or even knock on her door. Between his insults and his lordly scruples, he made a rotten kind of sense, but this was not a commitment to make without weighing every possibility.

The heir to the Innisborough marquessate was on the verge of retaining Meg's services. She had apple tarts in her satchel, and as surely as Lucien attended services every Sunday, if Meg sent Charlotte to bide at Webberly Hall, Lucien would feel it his duty to blacken Meg's standing with her own daughter.

"I appreciate that you mean well, Lucien, but what is Charlotte's favorite book?"

"How should I know?"

"What sort of pet does she long to have?"

"She's too young for a pet, and pets do not belong in the house."

Lady Evelyn had her husband firmly on a leash. What need had she for a pet? "Is Charlotte better at French or Latin?"

"Why teach a female Latin in any case?"

"You do not *know* your niece. She might as well be an alien species to you. We cannot love whom we do not know. You can provide in many important regards—connections, standing, material goods—but children need love as well."

Lucien reached across the coach to unfasten the door. "Every gin-soaked streetwalker in London loves her children. Love will not see Charlotte settled into a happy adulthood. Love will not introduce her to honorable men. You loved Entwhistle. Look where that led. A good man gone astray, a family's name tainted with your thoughtless behavior."

"You called Entwhistle your friend once." *You introduced him to me.*

"And because he was a friend once, I will not disrespect his memory by allowing this conversation to descend into bickering. Think about your daughter, pray on this matter if your conscience allows you that comfort. You are behaving as little better than a strumpet, flouncing about Town with some man's liveried servants in train, and that will reflect on your daughter."

The cold air gusted in, and fatigue all but smothered Meg's self-control. She remained on the velvet-cushioned seat long enough to fire off one more broadside.

"Lord Marcus Bannerfield offered me the use of his second coach because the weather was turning inclement and our appointment ran long. I am in nobody's keeping, Lucien, and I'll thank you not to repeat that insult."

"Marcus Bannerfield? Innisborough's heir?" Lucien's air of affronted impatience faltered, and a hint of surprise colored his tone.

"The very same. I wish you good day and offer my regards to Evelyn and the children. I'll let you know what I decide for Charlotte."

Meg ducked out of the coach, mindful of her steps, because Lucien's footman stood staring straight ahead as she descended, the snow falling on his shoulders and hat. Margaret didn't recognize him, but then, in recent years she hardly recognized her own brother.

She took up her satchel, trudged around the corner, and climbed the stairs to the apartment she and Charlotte called home. No sooner had she set down her burden than Charlotte came rocketing out of her room, shawls flapping.

"Mama, do you know what Sunday is?"

Margaret snatched up her daughter and hugged her stoutly. "A day of the week?" Charlotte was growing too old to be hugged like a toddler, but particularly after that exchange with Lucien, Meg needed to hug her.

"Not merely a day of the week." Charlotte wriggled to her feet. "Not this Sunday, but the next Sunday is Stir-Up Sunday." She adopted a thespian's pose, hands folded at her breast. "'Stir up, we beseech thee, O Lord, the wills of thy faithful people!' We can make a Christmas pudding, and play snapdragon, and make wishes and everything!"

Charlotte's braids were coming undone, a casualty of fine blond hair and the child's tendency to gallop from one end of the apartment to the other. She wore a pair of knitted stockings, the ends of which were flapping several inches beyond her toes, and the older of Meg's shawls was now dragging on the floor.

But Charlotte's smile, oh, her smile. Such glee and joy, such merriment and hope. Such trust.

"Christmas puddings are very dear," Meg said, unbuttoning her cloak. "We might have to make do with hot buttered gingerbread from the bakeshop, but do you know what we're having for supper tonight?"

Daisy, the girl who watched Charlotte on days when Meg had to go out, took Meg's cloak. "We're having a snowstorm, apparently. Hasn't let up all afternoon."

"You can't eat a snowstorm," Charlotte said, twirling and making her shawls bell out. "Not unless you're in a Greek myth or a titan or something."

"We're having apple tarts and cheese with a fresh pot of tea."

Charlotte came to a halt. "Apple tarts for dinner?"

"A special treat for my special girl."

Charlotte squealed, Daisy scolded her, Meg took the chair near their tiny parlor stove. Her feet were frozen, her heart leaden, and she would have to go back out tomorrow to deliver Lord Marcus's estimate, but tonight, she'd made her daughter happy, and that would have to be enough.

"LADY MARGARET ENTWHISTLE *AND FRIEND*, to see you, my lord." Nicholas, the butler Marcus's mama had chosen for his London house, made this announcement as calmly as if some old army comrade had dropped by.

"Her ladyship came in person, in this weather?" Outside the library, the day was gray, frigid, and windy, the sky still spitting intermittent snow. Marcus could not imagine more wretched, dreary weather.

"I believe her ladyship came on foot, sir. She says she needn't trouble you, she's only delivering a document for your consideration."

Lady Margaret *had* been troubling Marcus, troubling his sleep and his curiosity. His shopping expedition yesterday had been entirely fruitless—this was somehow her fault—and Marcus had been certain she'd miss her noon deadline, given the foul weather.

"Show her and her friend in." Marcus capped the ink, sanded the letter he'd been composing, and rose. "And a tea tray would be appreciated, all the trimmings, and three cups." If Lady Margaret had brought a companion of any standing, then that lady should be included in the civilities.

Nicholas bowed and left Marcus to examine his reflection in the mirror opposite the fireplace.

Simon, the firstborn and original heir to the Innisborough title, had been handsome, witty, charming, and a tailor's delight. He'd had the sense to stop growing just before he'd topped six feet, and his eyes had been the traditional Bannerfield green. Compared to him, Marcus had always felt like exactly what he was—a spare. Serviceably intelligent, tolerably well put together, unobtrusively competent.

He'd been a good officer, and he was a dutiful son, but he had no earthly idea how to be a proper uncle to two little girls. He was thus entirely unprepared for Lady Margaret's *friend* to be a small girl who clung to her ladyship's hand and gawked alternately at the library and at her own booted feet.

"Ladies, good day." He bowed to Lady Margaret and then to the girl. "I believe an introduction is in order?" Or perhaps it wasn't, but one couldn't entirely ignore a child standing right before one plain as day.

Lady Margaret curtseyed, her enormous satchel bumping against her skirts. "My lord, may I make known to you Miss Charlotte Entwhistle. Charlotte, make your curtsey to Lord Marcus."

The girl's curtsey was a small replica of Lady Margaret's, though the child bore little resemblance to her ladyship. Perhaps Miss Charlotte was a niece?

"Pleased to make your acquaintance, Miss Charlotte. Shall we be seated, Lady Margaret? I've ordered a tea tray, and I understand you have an estimate for me to peruse."

The girl watched him as if he were an exotic beast given powers of speech. He felt rather the same about her, though he doubted she would dare speak up in the company of adults.

"We need not trouble you for tea, my lord." Lady Margaret opened her satchel and passed over a rolled document tied with a red ribbon, like a legal brief. "I promised you an estimate by noon, and that hour approaches in fifteen minutes."

"So it does," Marcus said. "Nonetheless, I am overdue for a cup of tea, so you will simply have to join me. The chairs by the hearth are the most comfortable." He led the way across the room, the ladies trailing him.

"Mama, he has a *lot* of books!" The girl—Lady Margaret's *daughter*—stage-whispered that observation.

"Charlotte," Lady Margaret murmured, "*manners.*"

"My mother used to do that," Marcus said, "pack a whole lecture into a single word. I daresay she perfected the art on my father before turning it on her sons. I do have a lot of books, Miss Charlotte, you are quite right." He cast around for a question that might appeal to a small child. "Do you read?"

"Yes, sir, though Mama says my French is the despair of her waning years. I'm much better at Latin. Latin is better organized than French."

Lady Margaret closed her eyes. "Charlotte, you promised. Not a word."

"But, Mama, I would be rude to ignore his lordship's question."

The child was blond, whereas Lady Margaret was dark. The girl was robustly rounded, her mother trim to a fault. They were different sorts of females, and yet, they each had a well-defined jaw and a chin that looked prone to jutting in certain moods.

A soft tap on the door gave the child a reprieve from further maternal remonstrations, though Marcus rather agreed with Charlotte—Latin was much better organized than French.

"Come in," Marcus called, though why his butler was standing ceremony today, he did not know. "Nicholas, please set the tea tray by the hearth." When Nicholas had withdrawn, Marcus joined the ladies as they took chairs near the fire's warmth. "Lady Margaret, would you pour out?"

"Mama and I had a fresh pot of tea last night with our apple tarts and cheese." The child bounced a bit on the seat cushions, delighted with her own recitation. "The tarts were dee-lish-us!"

Lady Margaret busied herself with untying the bow to the child's cloak. "Charlotte, enough."

"But, Mama, the tarts were wonderful. You said so."

Her ladyship sat back when the child was free of her cloak. "My lord, I apologize. Charlotte's minder came down with a head cold, and I did not want to miss my promised delivery to you. I thought I could drop off the estimate without..."

Charlotte watched her mother make this apology, her expression puzzled and wary.

"Without joining me for tea?" Marcus asked. "Is my company so objectionable as all of that? Charlotte, are your hands clean?"

She held them out. "Mama is a demon when it comes to washing, sir. Dirt is the mortal enemy of good health and decorum."

Lady Margaret was now staring at her lap, her cheeks aflame, and Marcus was beginning to enjoy this dreary, miserable day.

"Conscientious mothers the world over would agree," he said. "Lady Margaret, would you be very offended if I glanced at your estimate while we enjoyed our tea?"

"Not offended at all, your lordship. How do you take your tea?"

They got through the ritual of the tea tray, the child sitting up very straight. Her mama put two biscuits on a plate and passed them over, then fixed a cup of tea composed more of sugared milk than tea.

"I'd forgotten that," Marcus said, setting the estimate aside. "How one fixes tea for a small child. Charlotte, would you like to explore the library while your mother and I chat for a moment?"

"Mama?"

"If you climb on anything, *anything* at all, Charlotte Marie, you will subsist on prayers and porridge for a week."

Charlotte was out of her chair like a liberated puppy. "Yes, Mama!"

"My lord, I do apologize for all this bother."

"To have company as I enjoy a cup of tea is no bother. I've asked my father if he and I might combine our households, but he refuses to leave the quarters he long shared with my late mother. His town house hasn't room for me, plus two little girls and their nurses, governesses, and so forth."

Lady Margaret sipped her tea, cradling the cup in her hands as if hoarding the warmth. "The marquess lives alone, then?"

"With his retainers of longstanding, but yes, Papa is alone. My sister and I look in on him as often as possible. My brother's death was a blow, and Papa is no longer the man who raised me."

"It's not good for the elderly to face the holidays alone."

Was it good for Lady Margaret and her daughter to face the holidays alone? Marcus might ponder that conundrum late into the night, but another thought seized his present awareness.

"Would you be willing to join me on a reconnaissance mission to the marquess's house? My sister could lure him away for supper, and you and I could reconnoiter."

"Reconnoiter, my lord?"

"Papa's house needs some holiday cheer, my lady. The servants won't ask him for permission to decorate, and he won't suggest they bother with the folderol lest he add to their burdens. The lot of them are quite venerable, but as you say, the elderly should not be left out of the holiday festivities."

Papa would probably disown him for this, but Marcus liked the idea more the longer he pondered it. Eliza should have proposed such a project, but for once, Marcus could beat her past the post.

Lady Margaret set aside her empty tea cup. "Have you considered my estimate for this household, my lord?"

Her estimate was a quartermaster's delight, every item noted, priced, totaled, and scheduled. The sum was considerable, but included taking down all the decorations as well as setting them up.

"I notice you have everything scheduled except when you'll remove the decorations." An odd oversight, given how thorough she was in every other regard. "Have some more biscuits."

She took one more. Only one. "I will remove the ribbons, cloved oranges, kissing boughs, and satin runners within one week of Twelfth Night, sooner if you contract for it."

"And the greenery?" She'd proposed a Bavarian forest worth of Christmasing—swagging, wreaths, and table trees.

"That's on page two, sir. I remove the last of the exterior decorations when you make the final payment. Not before."

"Because some people try to avoid paying you altogether?"

She spoke very quietly. "Most households pay merchants and shopkeepers for the entire year in December. Then there are gift baskets for the servants and neighbors, holiday meals and celebrations, charitable projects, and the like. Trying to collect a substantial sum in January can be frustrating."

Charlotte appeared at her mother's elbow. "May I please have another biscuit?"

"One more," Lady Margaret said, "and then we must be going."

The child plucked a biscuit from the tray as nimbly as a pickpocket lifting a watch, then darted off again. To eat a treat while wandering about the library was poor manners, but Marcus was beginning to suspect that many varieties of poverty afflicted Lady Margaret and her offspring.

"Have you any questions regarding my estimate, your lordship?"

"I do not." Even Eliza would have been hard put to find fault with Lady Margaret's work. "You sent two copies, and I gather we sign them to memorialize the terms of our agreement."

She looked pathetically relieved. "Just so. And the first payment—"

Marcus held up a hand rather than allow an earl's daughter to discuss money before her own child.

"I will write out a bank draft for the entire project. As you say, the holidays can be hectic, and a single payment is less bother than several installments. When will you begin your work here?"

"Tomorrow." Her gaze strayed to the basket of biscuits. "Nine of the clock, sir, and we will make a deal of noise."

The child, by contrast, was silent somewhere between the shelves of books.

"I will look forward to seeing my house transformed, Lady Margaret." He wrapped up the remaining biscuits in a linen table napkin, passed them to her, and put a finger to his lips. "And perhaps on Friday, we can find a time to take a peek at my father's house."

"That depends on how much progress we've made here, sir." She slid the biscuits into her satchel and rose, gathering up her daughter's cloak. "Charlotte, come along. It's time we were leaving."

"In a minute, Mama. I just want to—"

A loud crash came from the direction of the globe, then a beat of silence, followed by a hearty wailing.

CHAPTER THREE

Charlotte's manners were disgraceful, but then, what had Meg expected? One did not take children on business or social calls. Charlotte had only Daisy to mind her, and Meg was too busy earning a living to impart to Charlotte more than casual lessons in deportment.

Tea with Lord Marcus had thrown the shortcomings of that arrangement into stark relief. Charlotte fidgeted, she interrupted, she stared like a bumpkin, she was impertinent and boisterous, and now this—outright disobedience.

"Dear me," Lord Marcus said with admirable calm. "Somebody has taken a spill."

Charlotte was on her back, half braced on her elbows, waving one booted foot about and howling as if possessed. Around her lay the shattered remains of a globe, suggesting Charlotte had been *climbing the bookshelves* and had fallen onto the sphere from above.

"Charlotte, stop that racket," Meg said, kneeling beside her daughter. "You have destroyed the world, and you can claim all the affliction you want, but you disobeyed a clear instruction."

The wailing ceased as if a tap had been shut off. "I fell. My knee hurts."

Lord Marcus knelt on Charlotte's other side. "Shall we have a look at the injury?" No censure colored his question, suggesting small children smashed his possessions regularly.

"Charlotte, if you are shamming, the consequences will be dire."

"My knee hurts. I banged it on something."

I can ill afford to take you to a physician. Lord Marcus had not yet written out his bank draft, and physicians expected payment for services rendered.

His lordship scooped Charlotte into his arms and carried her to a velvet-upholstered sofa. "I will leave your mother to examine your wounds while I see about procuring some ice."

The sofa was some distance from the fire and thus not exactly cozy. Meg fetched Charlotte's cloak and spread it over her, then dealt with Charlotte's boots and stockings while Lord Marcus absented himself. An angry red weal was already rising above Charlotte's right knee, and another bruise was forming on her shin.

"You will suffer for your transgression," Meg said, but because that sounded too much like something Lucien would say, she also smoothed a hand over Charlotte's hair. "Was it fairy tales that led you astray?"

"His lordship has a whole shelf of fairy-tale books, but I had to climb to read the titles. I tried to reach for Aesop, but I could not hold on tightly enough. Are you angry, Mama?"

Charlotte had her father's store of guile, but she wasn't crafty with it—not yet. "I am disappointed because you disobeyed me, but I also realize you have never seen such a library before. To allow you to roam here was like inviting a hungry cat to explore a fish market unsupervised."

Though at Webberly Hall, Charlotte would have access to a library nearly as grand as this, and the girl did love books.

"A cat would not have fallen like I did," Charlotte said. "My knee really hurts."

"Ice will help, my dear." But what antidote could Meg prescribe for Charlotte's lack of decorum? Her ignorance of proper manners?

Meg had sold her only formal tea tray years ago. How was Charlotte to learn how to comport herself when taking tea when Meg had only cracked mugs and mismatched saucers for Charlotte to practice on?

Lord Marcus returned, bearing a basin full of chipped ice and several linen cloths. "I regret to inform you, Miss Charlotte, the housekeeper is brewing up some willow bark tea. I've seen battle-hardened soldiers cry at the prospect of a single serving."

"Is it truly awful?" Charlotte asked.

He passed Meg the basin and pulled a hassock up to the side of the sofa. "That depends. I might be able to bribe Cook to add a dash of honey, and then the trick is to drink it all at once. Down the hatch, rifles at the ready. Ye gods, child, that is a mortal wound. You have given your knee a black eye."

Meg took the cloths from him and fashioned an ice pack for the mortal wound. "It's a mere bruise, and one that resulted from disregarding the rules."

Lord Marcus appeared to inspect the injury, which meant he leaned nearer to Meg's chair. On a man of such unrelenting dignity, she expected a traditional masculine fragrance—bay rum or lavender. Instead, his scent brought to mind the warm spices—cinnamon and ginger, with a hint of citrus.

"Miss Charlotte, you surely did disregard the better angels of common sense," he said, sitting back. "See what comes of such lapses? We will bind up the knee when the ice has reduced the swelling, and you will hobble quite pathetically for days, if not weeks."

Charlotte clearly wasn't sure whether his lordship was teasing or not. Neither was Meg.

"I am sorry, my lord," Charlotte murmured. "I will not disregard the whatever-you-said again. The good angels."

"See that you do not, child. Your mama will consider me a bad influence, and I pride myself on never having earned that dubious distinction heretofore."

His lordship's expression put Meg in mind of the patriarchs of the last century, despite his hair being unpowdered. Long chestnut locks in a tidy queue put him in the category of people who disregarded fashion in favor of personal preference. Nonetheless, Meg doubted he would disregard the cost of a shattered heirloom.

"I will repay you for the damage," she said, applying the ice pack to Charlotte's knee. "That is the least I can do." Though an antique globe might be worth the entire profit on the decorating project... if not many times that amount.

A dire thought followed that realization: Charlotte might be forced to live at Webberly Hall simply because Meg hadn't the means to support her.

"That globe graced my father's schoolroom," Lord Marcus said. "Papa inflicted it on me because he doesn't like to toss out what needs tossing. The world has changed immensely in the past hundred years, and the globe had become all but useless."

He seemed to mean these words, but they offered Meg little comfort.

"I will buy you a new one, then," she said, "or you can subtract an appropriate sum from my invoice." She had no idea what a grand globe cost, complete with a mahogany stand, for Charlotte had shattered the stand as well.

The butler arrived with a pot of willow bark tea, and Charlotte dutifully swilled an entire cup. Her knee was swelling despite the ice, and the bruise on her shin was turning blue.

How am I to get her home? The way was long enough that Meg doubted she could carry Charlotte the distance, and the snowy, slushy streets would be treacherous even if some crutches could be found sized for a child.

"The physician will be along any minute," Lord Marcus said, "and lest you entertain daft notions about traversing the streets with an injured child, Lady Margaret, I've ordered the housekeeper to make up a guest apartment for your use."

His lordship spoke as if this magnanimity solved all difficulties, while Meg heard her brother's voice accusing her of riding around in fancy coaches like a kept woman. What would Lucien say about biding under the roof of an unmarried man without a chaperone or social connection to afford even a pretense of propriety?

Meg rose and set aside the basin. "My lord, might I have a word with you in private?"

"Mama's angry," Charlotte said. "When she talks like that, she wants to yell, but a lady doesn't raise her voice."

Charlotte chose a fine time to recall the dictates of ladylike deportment, for all she was telling the truth.

Meg *was* angry, also tired, overwrought, and frustrated, but Lord Marcus was trying to be helpful. Even if his kindly suggestion would ruin what was left of Meg's reputation, he did not deserve to have a basin of ice dumped over his head.

LADY MARGARET PACED BACK and forth before the hearth in Marcus's office. This was his favorite room in the house, being on the garden side and therefore private, and also cluttered with books, newspapers, letters, and other comforting indicia of a busy and meaningful life.

The office was, though, something of a mess, viewed through a visitor's eyes. Marcus could only hope Lady Margaret was too focused on composing her tirade to notice the untidiness.

"I am a lady by title and by birth," she began, swish-swish-swish-pivot. "My circumstances in recent years have become humble, but my standards of behavior remain fixed." Swish-swish-swish-pivot. "I expect of myself the proprieties an earl's daughter must observe if she is to uphold the promise of her upbringing."

A great clattering crash followed these opening remarks, for her ladyship's skirts had knocked the iron hearth set onto the bricks before the fireplace.

"Dash and blast," she muttered, hands fisting at her sides. "I cannot even deliver a proper defense of my own good name."

Marcus knelt to help her gather up the pokers, pincers, broom, and ashpan. "Is your good name under attack, my lady? I certainly hope not."

This close, he could see the fine lines radiating from her eyes, the slight shadows beneath them. Her gaze gave away more than that, a sort of weary exasperation bordering on defeat.

"I cannot bide here with you, my lord. Not if Charlotte were mortally ill, which she is not, could I tarry under this roof overnight unless a proper chaperone remained here as well."

"Come," Marcus said, offering her his hand and leading her to the sofa. "I am remiss for not acknowledging the obvious. You are concerned for Charlotte, and she is in no condition to travel. I could lend you my coach, but even going a short distance on foot might be too much for Charlotte's knee. You intended to be back here tomorrow morning in any case, so why not spend the night? I will fetch my sister, and propriety will be appeased."

Her ladyship settled slowly onto the cushions. "Fetch your sister?"

"Lady Elizabeth Hennepin. She likes children, and I dare to hope Eliza sometimes likes me." Marcus took the place beside Lady Margaret, and for reasons not entirely clear to him, he also kept her hand in his. "Whatever preparations you intended to make for tomorrow's efforts, you can make them from here."

Lady Margaret hung her head, an alarming lapse of her usual dignified posture. Marcus was in no wise prepared to deal with tears, whatever the provocation.

"I have much to do," she said, turning to regard him. "*Much.* Shops I must visit, supplies to assemble, staff to notify. The longer I tarry here, the later I must work this evening."

Any fool could see she was already short of sleep. "How many estimates did you prepare last night?"

"Three. I delivered one before coming here to present yours. I sent the third by post, because I could not drag that poor child halfway to Chelsea on such a day. I have two more to do tonight."

This degree of effort, this tenacious pursuit of every possible economy and client, did not portend a lady indulging a penchant for decorating in her ample free time. Something desperate was afoot. Perhaps Eliza would know exactly what.

"Fortunately for all concerned," Marcus said, "I have footmen idling below stairs, a secretary lazing about the premises somewhere, and grooms dicing away the day in the carriage house. While I call upon my sister, you shall give my staff something to do. Charlotte is already ensconced in the library, which you will find a commodious headquarters for the nonce."

Such a battle raged in her eyes. This woman would never take charity, never give quarter, and yet, she put Marcus in mind of his men when they'd endured one forced march, one winter storm, and one siege too many, all in the same fortnight.

"If I do this," she said slowly, "if I bide here, then I will decorate your father's home without compensation for my time. You may reim-burse me for materials, but not for my labor. That assumes your sister is willing to chaperone my visit."

The relief Marcus felt was out of all proportion to the situation, for it wasn't as if he *wanted* houseguests underfoot. Not at all, much less at the tedium of putting up with Eliza at the same time.

"We have a bargain, my lady. Now, as I am about to pay a call on Lady Elizabeth, and you are to take up your responsibilities in the library, I must complete your bank draft. If you endorse it, I can deposit the sum for you while I'm out and about."

She sat up straight, like Charlotte beholding the daunting prospect of a gleaming tea tray. "You are being kind." Her ladyship's tone suggested this offense surpassed felonies of any description.

"I am being expedient," Marcus said, rising and offering her lady-ship his hand. "A commanding officer learns to delegate as much as possible, my lady. Footmen are supposed to hare about, secretaries are to attend to documents for us. Why deprive them of their appointed tasks and deprive yourself of sleep?"

She rose, expression disgruntled. "That does not explain why you have promoted yourself to the ranks of my errand boys."

"I do so because your daughter needs her mama by her side this day, and that is not a role anybody else can fulfill, is it?"

He'd meant that observation as a placatory generality, but it was apparently the right thing to say. Lady Margaret's posture relaxed, and her expression acquired a hint of good humor.

"You are correct, my lord. You are absolutely correct. I will see to the patient now, and you can stop by the library before you leave."

Then she did the most extraordinary, unexpected, indecorous thing: She kissed Marcus's cheek, patted his lapel, and marched off, leaving him—scowling in utter consternation—amid the disarray of his office.

"WILL GRANDFATHER ENTWHISTLE send us a box at Christmas?" Charlotte asked from her perch on the library sofa. "He sent us a pudding last year."

Meg refused to look up, refused to put down her pencil. "I don't know, Charlotte, but you could write to him wishing him the joy of the upcoming season." Lord Marcus would not miss another sheet or two of paper, but Meg would soon go mad from Charlotte's attempts to distract her.

"I could ask Grandfather for a pudding," Charlotte mused, smoothing her hand over an embroidered pillow. Two other pillows bolstered her ankle and knee, and she was swaddled in quilts as well. "If I find the sixpence again, I will be *rich*! I will have new boots and new mittens. I can have a kitten, and even my kitten can have mittens. I will be smitten with a kitten wearing mittens!"

"That tears it." Margaret gathered up her lists, instructions, and schedules, tapped her papers into a tidy stack and rose from the reading table. "What you *do* have is a mother who needs peace and quiet. Read your books, Charlotte. Make some sketches, draft a note to Grandpapa, write to your cousins at Webberly Hall. I shall accomplish nothing while you prattle without ceasing."

Meg suspected that Charlotte needed a nap. She'd roused Charlotte quite early, tramped with her across half of Mayfair, and subjected her to the excitement of Lord Marcus's opulent library. Charlotte had been rubbing her eyes for the past half hour, a sure sign she was growing sleepy.

"Where are you going, Mama?"

"I will be right across the corridor in his lordship's office. If you bellow, which I well know you are capable of doing, I will hear you. You could also ring the bell sitting immediately beside you, and a maid or a footman will fetch me. I will send a maid to sit with you, if you like."

"I am nearly grown up," Charlotte said, abandoning the fidgety, whiny tone she'd been working up to. "I do not need a nursery maid."

"Very well, I will leave you to entertain yourself."

Meg did ask the butler to send a maid to the library to tidy up. The shattered globe had long since been dealt with, but Charlotte had a talent for creating disorder.

"I could play a hand or two of cards with the child," the butler said. "Old bones can use an excuse to sit in the middle of a chilly afternoon, my lady. His lordship specifically charged me with seeing to his guests' every comfort."

The butler was older, balding, and quite dignified, but his eyes also held a twinkle.

"Your offer is very kind, though one wouldn't want to impose."

"Your ladyship, it's no bother a'tall. I don't join in the card games below stairs because it would reduce my consequence to lose to the boot-boy. I can, with no harm in the consequence of my exalted office, take pity on a bored child who has had a mishap, can't I?"

He winked and sauntered off, putting Meg in mind of the butler she'd known at Webberly Hall growing up. Mr. Holcomb had had the same subtle good cheer, the same self-possession. She missed him, missed her parents, missed the Hall itself, truth be known.

"Which is neither here nor there," she muttered, letting herself into Lord Marcus's study.

This room broke the household pattern of spotless order, which—oddly—made Meg feel more comfortable. The office was organized—incoming correspondence here, pamphlets there, newspapers on the sideboard—but everything of immediate interest lay in plain sight. Meg worked well with such an approach, everything to hand, everything visible to remind her of what remained to be done and what tasks had been accomplished.

"Like an officer's tent." Peter had made that observation about Meg's private parlor on one of his rare leaves. "Set up for efficiency, rather than to impress."

She placed a pillow on the seat of his lordship's capacious chair and took the place behind the desk.

The view was intimate, not that Meg would snoop outright, but a man's penmanship said a lot about him. Lord Marcus's script was legible, confident, and free of unnecessary flourishes. He apparently composed his thoughts before putting pen to paper, for his penmanship was exceptionally neat. His pamphlets dealt with vice among the idle poor, temperance, the spiritual poverty of the merchant class, and other improving themes.

Meg set them aside, more than a little disappointed at the sanctimonious tone. Lord Marcus was clearly a decent man, but then, Lucien was considered a paragon of rectitude, even if he was vain about his conveyances and his cattle.

Also his tailoring.

And his servants' livery.

"Get to work," Meg murmured, fishing through her stack of papers to find tomorrow's schedule. The swagging on the house's exterior had to go up last, which meant finding tasks to keep her climbing boys out of mischief for the first part of the day. Phineas was a clever lad and happy to help with the indoor work, but his younger brother Caleb left a wake of chaos wherever he went.

What to do with them? Meg was jotting down the words *harness bells* on the side of her schedule when a wave of fatigue landed on her like a load of snow cascading from a steep roof.

"Nap," she muttered, scooting on her pillow and turning the chair so she could put her feet up on a hassock. Lest she become chilly, she appropriated a jacket hung over the back of the chair, folded her arms, closed her eyes, and prepared to rest her eyes for ten short minutes.

∾

MARCUS PUT off calling on Elizabeth by tarrying in three different toy shops, then chatting up his banker—who also happened to be Lady Margaret's banker—and dropping by to have a word with Papa, though Papa had been out. By the time Marcus made his way to the Hennepin town house, Elizabeth was out as well—a bad moment, that—but Aunt Penny came to his rescue.

The time Penelope Hennepin required to pack a bag would have been sufficient for a regiment to set up camp.

As soon as Marcus and Aunt Penny arrived home, she left him at his own front door and bustled off to conspire with Nicholas about heaven knew what. Aunt's favorite pastime was rearranging furniture in other people's houses, which had occasioned more than one profanity as Marcus had gone top over tail late at night in his own library.

The dictates of hospitality demanded that he stop by that library to look in on his guests, but the dictates of duty lay across the corridor, in his office. He'd let his correspondence slip the past few days, and no less authority than his father attributed the fall of Rome to slothful administration.

To the office, Marcus did go, intent on reading two pamphlets, writing two letters, and at least sorting the morning post before allowing himself his one brandy for the evening. He lit a carrying candle from the sconce in the corridor and opened the door to his office. Darkness had fallen, and the only light in the room came from the hearth, where a low fire awaited another scoop of coal.

The first indicator that his *sanctum sanctorum* was occupied came from the scent of the room. The usual leather, wool, and coal smoke were laced with... something pretty. Flowers of some sort. The only flower Marcus knew by scent was the rose, and this was not a rose.

Then he spied the lady slouched in his chair, her chin sunk upon her chest, his natty old morning coat draped over her, her feet on a hassock.

The Christmas angel has fallen. She slumbered on while Marcus debated his options.

He could retreat, rap on the door, and pretend he always knocked on the door of his own office... which Lady Margaret would know to be untrue.

He could have the housekeeper wake her, but he sensed that Lady Margaret would consider being caught *in flagrante somnum* by a servant a worse mortification than being found asleep by her host.

Or, he could build up the fire and hope the noise woke her.

He rattled a scoop of coal from the bucket. He poked at the embers on the grate. He let his cast-iron implement clatter against the bricks. He all but yodeled up the chimney, and her ladyship barely stirred.

"Lady Margaret."

She snuggled deeper under his coat. "In a minute."

"*Lady Margaret.*"

She opened her eyes, then closed them again. "Go away."

Soldiers on campaign had this ability to sleep through cannon fire and stampeding horses. The poor woman was exhausted, but she would not thank him for allowing her to slumber on.

"My lady, you have appropriated *my* chair, at *my* desk, in *my* office. I beg you to vacate same that I might tend to my correspondence." Marcus used his commanding-officer voice, and the result was a scowl worthy of a cat shoved out into a snowy backyard.

"You needn't shout, sir. I was merely resting my eyes."

"You were lost to the world, madam. Are you so enthusiastic about Christmas decorating that you neglect your rest?"

She pushed herself upright and passed him his morning coat. "I am no great admirer of Christmas. I do like to pay my bills. Lord help me, I've napped away my afternoon."

Marcus draped the coat over the chair opposite the desk and took the seat. "The woman who prides herself on creating exquisite Christmas decorations has no affection for the season itself?" And she napped in chairs and appropriated a man's old jacket too. Interesting.

Her ladyship rose—stiffly, he thought—and took a taper from the spill jar on the mantel. "My mother died at Christmas, my favorite aunt as well. I became engaged at Christmas, and Charlotte was conceived immediately thereafter." She lit the candelabrum on Marcus's desk and moved on to the tapers on the mantel. "Her father was home on winter leave, and he was so dashing in his regimentals..."

"You are sad, then, at this time of year." Understandable, though she didn't appear sad.

She lit the candles on the mantel, which cast her profile in half shadow. Her features were angular now, though as a younger woman, she'd likely been stunning.

"I am bitter, my lord. I was not married when Charlotte was conceived. You will hear the talk, if you haven't already heard it from your sister."

Lady Margaret glanced at him over her shoulder, her expression half defiant, half uncertain. Marcus remained seated, which, strictly speaking, was poor manners on his part. He sensed that her ladyship would rather he stay in a fixed location, while she went about chasing off the darkness.

His office, with its comfortable furniture and business clutter, was nonetheless a quiet room, and when its only illumination was candlelight, the space took on a confessional quality.

Lady Margaret's guarded, proud gaze put a question to him, about tolerance or appearances—he wasn't sure exactly what—so he replied with a recitation of facts.

"Lady Elizabeth was not at home," he said. "Her aunt by

marriage agreed to bide here tonight, and just because you anticipated your vows with the dashing major doesn't mean you are a
disgrace to your gender. Most couples do likewise. My parents
certainly did."

She shook the spill, dousing the flame. "They did? A *marquess's
heir* anticipated his vows?"

"With an earl's daughter. Simon was born six months after the
wedding. Papa and Mama joked about it frequently, always adding
that Simon was a great strapping baby."

How ironic that the great strapping baby, who'd become a robust
man, had been eventually felled by influenza, while the younger son
had spent years at war and come home without a visible scratch.

Her ladyship put the smoking spill back in the jar, an economy
Marcus would never have thought to practice. "But your sainted
brother was legitimate," she said, watching the smoke rise in the
gloom. "Charlotte is not."

She could have told Marcus that the Regent had been seen
running naked through Hyde Park, and Marcus would have been less
shocked.

"I beg your pardon?"

"I'm supposed to beg yours, also God's, Society's, my brother's...
I became engaged when Peter was home on winter leave. We anticipated our vows, as you put it. Peter went back to soldiering, and
some weeks later, I realized I was increasing. I wrote to him, I
begged him, I wrote again, and finally wrote to his commanding officer, who informed me by return post that a man could not be
granted leave he hadn't asked for. By that time, the situation was
impossible to hide."

She rearranged the tools in the hearth stand so they stood in order
of height. "I wrote in desperation to Peter's father, and he demanded
that Peter get back to England to marry me. My best guess is that Mr.
Entwhistle Senior was loath to incur the wrath of a titled family. He's
comfortably well-off, as many of the gentry are."

And where was Charlotte's comfortably well-off grandfather

when the girl had no proper governess? "Major Entwhistle returned to England," Marcus said, "but Charlotte arrived before he did."

Lady Margaret might profess to be bitter, but Marcus had never seen a sadder smile.

"Charlotte was six weeks old on my wedding day. We had her christened that afternoon. I expected that Peter would bide with us through the winter, but he was bound for Spain within a week. I kept busy that first Christmas by decorating Webberly Hall as if Father Christmas himself dwelled there."

Far too many men enlisted to escape the consequences of irresponsible procreation. In the army, the fellow had a wage, a uniform, food and drink for the most part, the hope of advancement and the occasional spoils of war.

"I am sorry," Marcus said, rising and crossing to the glass breakfront that held a trio of decanters. "The recruiters specifically pander to men longing to turn their backs on their own progeny. The sergeants paint a picture of adventure, camaraderie, and freedom, while casting fatherhood as a drudgery no fellow should have to endure. I find this aspect of military life distasteful." He'd received those politely desperate letters from ruined young women, and where he could, he'd directed that half the man's pay be sent to the child's mother.

"You are sorry. Most people who learn of my circumstances are dismayed. I was certainly dismayed. Charlotte does not yet know how her situation will be viewed by the larger world, but the day approaches when I cannot keep it from her."

Marcus poured two brandies and passed one to Lady Margaret. "What did Major Entwhistle say when you asked him why he didn't come home?"

She accepted the brandy without any ladylike demurrals regarding taking spirits.

"I needed two years to gather my courage before I put the question to him. His reply was nearly scornful: Didn't I know he had a war to win?" She took a whiff of her brandy. "A major in Wellington's army wasn't free to come and go, and what had I thought would happen when I decided to throw myself at my fiancé? He was a red-blooded male, after all. I was supposed to know how to prevent *these sorts of things*." She sipped her drink. "We were engaged. I had no idea how to throw myself at a man, nor any idea how to refuse Peter without angering him. I'd thought to prevent illegitimacy by speaking my vows. Silly me."

Her recitation provoked a welter of conflicting emotions. Resentment because Entwhistle's betrayal of honor was none of Marcus's business, shame because no officer should have behaved as Peter Entwhistle had, and admiration.

For Lady Margaret, for her fortitude.

"And now," Marcus said, "you will make my humble abode fit for Father Christmas himself, because that is how you take your revenge on a man who should never have been a father to anybody."

She saluted with her drink. "You understand. I also earn my living by decorating other people's houses. The holidays are my busiest time, but families new to London or the occasional nabob need assistance setting up their households. The work is honorable and not too scandalous."

Lady Margaret also apparently enjoyed her work, but not as she should. "Something I do not understand, Lady Margaret: Earlier today, in this very room, you kissed me. No mistletoe, no prior bond of friendship or social connection to justify such an overture. I am not generally regarded as kissable, and I daresay you do not bestow tokens of affection easily, so why kiss me?"

The question had troubled Marcus the livelong day, and still, he'd surprised himself by asking it.

She set her drink near the silver standish and tidied up the documents strewn all over his desk. "You said the one thing I very much needed to hear, and you meant it. I'm sorry if I overstepped."

She held her papers before her, a flimsy shield for her dignity.

"You surprised me," Marcus said. "Not an experience that often befalls me. You did not overstep."

"I'm... I'm glad, my lord. Thank you for the use of your office. I must see what has become of Charlotte."

"Until dinner, my lady." He bowed, she curtseyed, and Marcus took the seat behind his desk.

Somebody had left a damned pillow on his chair, which he didn't bother removing, because—upon reflection—his arse was tired. Her ladyship had kissed him as some signal of approval or gratitude, but what the devil had he said that she had so desperately needed to hear?

He pondered that question while sipping his brandy, and he neither read his pamphlets, nor drafted his letters, nor sorted his morning mail.

CHAPTER FOUR

Meg went into a frenzy of holiday decorating each year, in part because she needed the money. She earned more in the Yuletide season than in the remaining ten months of the year combined, though each year was a struggle to find new customers and to keep old customers happy.

She also worked like a demon over the holidays because she needed to stay busy. Peter had been the next thing to a handsome cad, and she'd fallen for him utterly. *Fallen* in the sense of having given him her heart and *fallen* in the sense of having been taken in by his flattery and flirtation.

Had she not conceived Charlotte, Peter would very likely have sent her a gently worded letter releasing her from the *unfair* expectations of an engagement to a man whose future was so uncertain. He'd doubtless written several such letters, one for each winter leave.

And the seasonal reminder of her own stupidity was intolerable. Peter's holiday gift to her had been an education in the follies of romance and in the dishonor a handsome smile could hide. Meg could accept her own role in inviting Peter to bestow that token, but had yet to reconcile herself to the harm Peter's self-interest had done to his only child.

Lord Marcus had accused Meg of being sad, and she'd corrected him—she was bitter—but his observation plagued her. Maybe she was a little sad, for Charlotte more than for herself, though what must Charlotte think of her mama, abandoning an injured child for an entire afternoon?

Meg paused outside the library door, dredged up a smile, and summoned the energy for a brisk entrance. She stopped short just inside the door.

"Charlotte Marie, what on earth are you doing?"

The reading chairs had been arranged as tent poles, a pair of afghans stretched across them. Charlotte's quilts were spread on the carpet beneath the afghans, and a pair of candelabra sat on the floor immediately outside her lair.

"I am a princess of the desert sands," Charlotte replied. "Aunt Penny was showing me how to do a card trick. It's not cheating if you're doing it to entertain people."

Lord Marcus had mentioned something about an aunt coming to serve as chaperone, but Meg had been so groggy from sleep, so embarrassed to be caught napping, and so *upset* to have wasted hours resting that she'd missed much of what he'd said.

A tiny older woman crawled from the blanket-tent and bounced to her feet, brushing at her skirts. She was birdlike, with snow-white hair and snapping blue eyes.

"Lady Margaret Weissmuller, you look like your mama. Ah, but you married that handsome Entwhistle boy, God rest his soul. I'm Penelope Hennepin. Everybody calls me Aunt Penny, or Aunt Penny-Henny, or Aunt Henny-Penny. You are raising a thoroughly delightful child."

The thoroughly delightful child was using an ornately carved cane to hobble back to the sofa. "Aunt lent me her walking stick. I can use it to subdue the vandal hordes when they come to steal my camels or plunder my store of figs."

"Now, my lady," Aunt said, taking up an afghan and giving it a shake, "you are already deciding I am a bad influence on the youth of England. While I do get on well with children, having none of my own and thus tending to spoil the offspring of others, I am not a bad influence per se. Charlotte was restless, and I haven't subdued any desert vandals in this age."

The old lady had the afghans tidily arranged on the back of the sofa and was replacing the candelabra on the desk before Meg thought to restore order to the chairs.

"I am pleased to meet you, Mrs. Hennepin, and I thank you for diverting Charlotte."

"I'm not a missus, young lady. I am the dreaded spinster aunt." She raised her hands like they were menacing claws. "I say outrageous things that everybody else only thinks, and I threaten to do even more outrageous things, mostly to see my family quake in dread, poor dears. They are easily set to quaking. I'm in truth quite harmless."

"I like you," Charlotte said. "I've never had a dreaded spinster auntie before."

Meg had the sense of having stepped into some fantastical version of Lord Marcus's library. The books were all in the same places, Charlotte was still wearing the bandage fashioned for her knee, but this small, elderly woman had imparted a wisp of whimsy to a very serious room.

Whimsy—or dementia.

"I thank you for coming to stay here with us tonight," Meg said, putting the last chair back at the reading table. "I set great store by the proprieties."

"I gave up that folly decades ago," Aunt Penny replied, moving one of the candelabra to the table beside Charlotte's sofa. "I set great store by decency and happiness. Shall I read to you, child?"

"Would you read Aesop for me?" Charlotte asked.

"Wouldn't you rather your own dear mama read to you?" Aunt Penny asked.

Charlotte stole a glance at Meg, and the uncertainty in her gaze ripped a new hole in Meg's heart. Charlotte longed for her mother to read to her—clearly—but she would never ask.

"I would like to read Aesop," Meg said, setting aside all the schedules, lists, and diagrams she'd meant to spend her afternoon on. "He's full of interesting advice, and who can't use a little wisdom from time to time?"

"I thought you had work to do, Mama."

"The work will keep."

Aunt Penny bustled off toward the door. "Well, that's settled. I will confer with the housekeeper to ensure everybody has a cozy, comfy room for the night, including my own dear self. Then I must see that Charlotte's evening meal is suitably tempting for a convalescent, and lastly, I will tease our Lord Marcus into dressing for dinner."

"You need not go to that trouble," Meg said, acutely embarrassed. "I haven't anything formal to wear."

"I've brought you a few of Eliza's gowns to try on. They will be a bit loose on you—Eliza does love her sweets—but I guessed at your coloring based on your mama's good looks, and with all becoming modesty, I must admit I was correct in my choices. I usually am, but one doesn't admit that lest the Almighty attempt a few jests at one's expense."

She slipped out the door, and a profound, somewhat dazed silence bloomed in her absence.

"I like having an aunt," Charlotte said.

"You have an aunt—Evelyn."

"I like Aunt Penny more."

So do I. Meg chose the story about the crow who raised the level of the water in the jar by diligently casting pebbles into the water—a tale of industry and persistence—and Charlotte sat quietly beside Meg on the sofa for the whole reading.

"If I were the crow," Charlotte said at the end of the story, "I might instead hop into the water jar. I would drink my fill, have a nice little swim, and then fly away, all clean and no longer thirsty."

"But what if," Meg countered, "in that water jar you hadn't the room to spread your wings? You would thrash and call for help and thrash some more. You might possibly drown before anybody came to your aid."

Charlotte turned the page. "I would thrash so hard I knocked the jar over, and then I could hop free."

Not a bad solution, for a crow. "You have a powerful imagination, Charlotte Entwhistle."

Charlotte's gaze remained on the book. "Is that bad?"

A singular failing in a female, to hear Lucien or any of his ilk tell it. "I could not do my job without a powerful imagination. I often walk into a cold, dreary house, one going blind with cobwebs and dust, one that hasn't seen a kissing bough hung in ages. I must envision the place as it could be, as it wants to be, not as its owners have allowed it to become."

"So my imagination is a good thing?"

"Does Daisy say otherwise?"

Charlotte closed the book, and for one precious instant, she rested her forehead against Meg's arm. "Daisy says I am fanciful. I don't think she cares for fanciful girls."

Why did I stop reading to my daughter? "Fanciful girls are much more interesting than the other kind. I suspect Aunt Penny was a very fanciful girl."

"You do?"

"We can ask her when she comes back. Will you help me dress for dinner when the time comes?"

"Yes, Mama. I will help you. I will help you put up your hair and practice your curtsey. We can pretend you are being presented at court again."

They had not played that game in ages. "Very well, but first you must let me do a bit of work on tomorrow's schedule. You can read one more story, but only one."

Which meant Charlotte would spend a good deal of time comparing the lengths of every tale in the book, counting pages or trying to do the math in her head.

"I will read about the boy who rescued the lioness."

"Androcles rescued a lion, Charlotte, not a lioness."

"I don't think so, Mama. Everybody knows that the lionesses are the ones who do all the hunting, while the lion sits around looking lordly and lazy. If there was a great roaring beast out hunting in the woods that day, it was a lady lion."

"A logical observation. I will leave you to your reading." Meg kissed the top of Charlotte's head and gathered up the papers she'd set aside. The time lost to napping could not be recovered, so no use lamenting the wasted hours.

Meg had less luck when it came to parting with her worries. If Charlotte went to live at Webberly Hall, she would be severely casti-gated for imaginative flights. She would learn to hold her tongue unless spoken to and to never take issue with Aesop's faulty charac-terization of lions and lionesses.

And yet, Meg was considering consigning her daughter to such an existence, because she wanted Charlotte to be *happy*.

"THIS HAS GONE ON LONG ENOUGH." Marcus tried to adopt his commanding-officer tone of voice, but he apparently wasn't fooling Lady Margaret. She remained at his desk, swaddled in shawls, the blotter strewn with papers.

"This will go on," she replied, "until I am confident tomorrow's efforts are efficiently organized. The initial phase of decoration is intrusive and loud. Customers become difficult unless I execute my tasks in the shortest possible time."

Marcus closed the office door, rather than let the meager warmth of the fire out into the corridor. He'd told the footman to leave two buckets of coal by the hearth, and both sat nearly full on the bricks.

"You will catch an ague," he said, putting his carrying candle on the desk and adding a generous scoop of coal to the flames. "Then I will catch all manner of blame from Aunt Penny and my sister. Charlotte will sentence me to three hundred lashes. That gown looks well on you."

The red velvet fit Lady Margaret, and she had the dark coloring to carry off such a rich hue. Aunt had purloined both the dress and a soft green shawl from Eliza's wardrobe, but Marcus could not recall the ensemble flattering his blond sister nearly as much.

"The dress is warm, as evening gowns go." She readjusted the green shawl to more effectively cover her shoulders. "I will go up to bed soon, my lord, I promise."

"You promised Aunt Penny the same thing more than an hour ago. What sort of lady breaks her word to a frail, elderly woman?"

He remained by the hearth, elbow propped on the mantel. The fireplace threw out the only heat to be had, and he liked being near enough to Lady Margaret to enjoy her flowery scent.

"Aunt Penny is diminutive," Lady Margaret replied. "She is far from frail. I want to be just like her, should I be allotted my three-score and ten."

"You want to enjoy disrupting the king's peace? To thrive on creating chaos and misrule?" Though, Marcus liked Aunt Penny. No guessing where one stood with her, no carefully assembling a litany of flattery, no boring eternities spent listening to the same stories over and over.

"You are scowling, my lord. I think Aunt Penny does what she can to ensure that the peace enjoyed by others is genuine, and she thrives on being herself."

"I am scowling because I have just realized the true nature of my dealings with my own sister. I treat her as if she's already elderly and difficult, and I do believe that's exactly how she wants to be treated, though she's no older than you."

Lady Margaret set her quill in the pen tray and tidied her documents. "My brother has the same effect on me. I'm always placating, tiptoeing, tacitly begging for forgiveness, approval being a lost cause. I'm lately wondering why this arrangement has gone on so long, though it comes down to money."

The late hour, the closed door, the firelight... They apparently inspired honesty.

"Your brother holds your purse strings?" That arrangement would be expected, unless Entwhistle's late father or a surviving Entwhistle brother performed that office.

"He does not, I having no purse strings worth holding. Should the day ever come when my means are gone, Lucien is all Charlotte has. I antagonize him at peril to her well-being."

No purse strings? No means at all? For an earl's daughter, such a situation was unheard of. "Surely you have a widow's mite, a jointure of some kind?"

She closed her eyes and leaned her head back to rest against the chair. That posture was nearly alluring, exposing the graceful curve of her throat, the hint of collarbones, the clean line of her chin.

Perhaps I had too much wine with dinner. Or not enough.

"I had a jointure. I was eighteen when I married Peter and much consumed with having become a mother. The settlements were a hasty affair, and I was not informed of the details. My father was still alive then, though fading, and I gather he did not feel it wise to press too hard for financial contributions when Mr. Entwhistle Senior was unhappy with his son. Papa doubtless trusted that my family would always be able to provide for me."

A dying man might strike that bargain, but Marcus could not respect him for it. "Your family refuses to provide for you?"

"I get on poorly with my sister-in-law. I doubt anybody would fare well with her, but her fortune revived the earldom's flagging health very nicely. When Charlotte was three, Evelyn and I had a very great row over one of the governesses, who was much given to beating small children. I left the family seat, confident I could manage on the monthly funds the solicitors sent me."

Beating... small... children. "Of course you left. She likely hired that governess expressly to drive you out."

Lady Margaret studied him. "Do you think so? Evelyn is quite religious. She has a Bible verse for every occasion—nearly all of them Old Testament—and *spare the rod* was ever on her lips."

"But was the rod applied to her children, too, or only to Charlotte?"

"To be fair, caning in the nursery was not limited to Charlotte, but Charlotte was the youngest by several years, and she caught the worst of it. My brother refused to intervene, and Charlotte was developing a nervous disposition. Evelyn claimed a three-year-old was having nightmares and accidents to curry my sympathy. I had to leave."

Marcus fetched a pillow and lowered himself to sit on the raised hearth behind the desk. Very unlordly of him, but the night had reached an unlordly hour, and his day had been long.

"For the countess to use the child to establish household despotism was a low, scurrilous tactic."

"Her tactic was effective. I flounced off in high dudgeon, consigning myself to the comfort of righteous penury. That worked for about six months, then the solicitors informed me I would soon receive the final payment from the funds due me as a function of my marriage."

Her ladyship spoke dispassionately, reciting a tale of long ago and far away, in a land where young widows learned hard lessons.

"You were receiving payments from the principal, rather than from interest?"

"So I was told. My lord, this is all very old news, and the hour does grow late. If you leave me to my labors, I will go up to bed within the hour."

Lady Margaret's eyes were shadowed, and not simply from bodily fatigue. This recitation, more betrayal from Entwhistle and from her own family, wearied her in spirit.

"Now you spout falsehoods, and you look quite convincing doing it, but I am on to your tricks, Lady Mistletoe. We never did decide where the infernal kissing bough should go."

"You need not have a kissing bough if you don't want one."

Marcus abruptly and quite passionately wanted at least three, all hanging in close proximity to wherever Lady Margaret tarried. The impulse took him halfway by surprise, but also halfway as confirmation of a looming suspicion.

He was attracted to his houseguest. Of all the peculiar turns to be served by a body that had mostly learned to leave him in peace.

"I will have my kissing boughs," he said, "so Aunt Penny can ambush the unsuspecting. She has a powerful sense of humor, which the footmen apparently share."

"I love that about her," Lady Margaret said. "I have not laughed in ages as I laughed at dinner."

Aunt Penny had told a story about Marcus's own father, one from Papa's misspent youth, before Mama had sorted him out.

"I enjoyed her stories too." Marcus had enjoyed seeing Lady Margaret relaxed, relishing a good meal, attired as an earl's daughter should be. He did not enjoy contemplating the realities she faced. "Would your brother truly leave his own niece on the parish if your ability to provide faltered?"

"That is the question, is it not? I don't think he would. Peter appointed me guardian of Charlotte's person in his will. She is a girl, and I believe he was making a final statement regarding whose 'fault' Charlotte's conception was. It's unusual, but a widow can have custody of her children."

The Duchess of Kent had legal custody of her daughter, Princess Vicky, as a result of her husband's documented final wishes. The child's royal uncles were most unhappy with that arrangement, but it was entirely legal.

"So you bear the burden of Charlotte's expenses." And thus, of dowering Charlotte when that daunting task arose. "I could have a word with your brother. A word involving my fists, pistols, or swords."

Marcus didn't approve of dueling in the usual course, but a duel to the first touch or first blood could force a man to address an oversight of honor.

Lady Margaret stroked his hair with ink-stained fingers, brushing an errant lock back from his brow. "You are such a sweet man. You cannot know what a lovely offer that is, but I am playing a chess game against my brother—or against his countess—and the cost of my defeat will land on Charlotte. I cannot afford to antagonize him. The best I can hope for is a draw."

The hour approached midnight, and Marcus was distracted by a surprisingly insistent desire, but Lady Margaret's situation sat ill with him. Some aspect of the battle with her brother wanted further study. Why would an earl reduce his own sister to penury? Why cling to an old scandal so ferociously? Why wouldn't a conscientious brother do all he could to bury the talk regarding Charlotte's illegitimacy? If the titleholder acknowledged the mother and child enthusiastically, polite society would at least tolerate them.

Marcus would consult Aunt Penny on the matter and have a word with Papa and Eliza. Lady Margaret's situation needed pondering.

And the lady herself needed her rest. "You are cautious where your family is concerned, a sentiment I share. One loves them, but one treads carefully. If you should develop a lung fever, you will be in no fit state to decorate anything but a sickroom, my lady, and your family will deal with me most un-carefully. Won't you please allow me to light you to your room?"

Because he sat on the hearth, and she'd turned the chair behind the desk toward the flames, they were nearly at eye level. Another question came to Marcus's mind: *Won't you please share a kiss with me?*

He sat back and consulted his pocket watch. "You will never last through tomorrow's great busyness if you go short of sleep again tonight. I can have a maid wake you early, but let's to bed, shall we?"

The question should have been a brisk conclusion, not an occasion for the lady to smile—to smile mischievously—at his wording.

"Your effusions of charm have convinced me, my lord, as has my aching back. If I remain here much longer, I will fall asleep over my papers anyway. An early waking would be appreciated. You are well advised to go out tomorrow immediately after breaking your fast. You will think a thousand devils have invaded your house at first light."

A few imps had apparently invaded Marcus's imagination, for Lady Margaret was looking more kissable by the moment. He rose and offered her his hand.

"The arms of Morpheus await, as do warmed sheets, snug quilts, and soft pillows. I will call upon family tomorrow, and your invading army can plunder the peace of my home unopposed. Expect Aunt Penny to appoint herself your second-in-command."

Lady Margaret took his hand—her fingers were like ice—and rose. "I have never had a second-in-command. We will either come to blows or conquer the known world together." She leaned closer, close enough to drop her forehead against his chest. "Thank you for your many kindnesses, my lord. For the first time in ages, as the holiday season approaches, I wish somebody very specific well-earned, sincere joy."

She straightened quickly, before Marcus could turn the moment into an embrace. Where the hell had his reflexes gone, the ones that had saved him so often in battle? He inquired politely about Charlotte's knee on the way up the steps, he asked what time her ladyship would like to be awakened—*roused* had almost come out of his mouth —and he made sure the candles in her sitting room were lit before offering her a good-night bow.

"And good night to you, too, my lord. I did not think it possible, but I am enjoying the hospitality you have extended, and I know Charlotte will treasure the time we've spent in your household."

Marcus set aside his candle and possibly the last of his wits too. "Is that an early farewell? If so, might I ask for a farewell kiss?"

He kept his hands to himself when he made that request, for this woman had been ill-used, and the consequences to her had been grave. Still, he did not withdraw the question. She was no defeated wretch to be cozened into reluctant folly. She was a very self-possessed female and the first lady to attract his masculine notice since he'd sold his commission several years ago.

"I ask for only a kiss," he clarified, "one freely shared. Or I can bid you good night and make no mention of this request ever again."

Oh splendid. She was smiling at him again as if he'd bungled a recitation of Wellington's titles. "You have stolen other kisses?"

"On rare occasion."

"You aren't very good at it, asking permission first, offering assurances of discretion and disclaimers of honorable conduct. If you were a thief, you'd summon the watch to observe your crime before you committed it."

"I am not a thief, and a shared kiss is the furthest thing from a crime. Sending a fellow off to mind his own business is certainly a lady's prerogative as well."

He wanted to kiss her—and more—but he also liked standing close to her and debating the philosophy of flirtation.

She gathered her shawls, and Marcus resigned himself to a night spent in self-recrimination—after he'd indulged in self-gratification. Instead, Lady Margaret opened her shawls like angel wings and stepped near enough to envelop him in their warmth.

"My holiday token," she said. "It's time I bestowed one out of joy, rather than duty. Past time."

And then she pressed upon him the sweetest, boldest, most luscious kiss imaginable.

MEG TRIED to hide in her rooms when the household began to stir in the morning. She wanted to enjoy a few minutes of peace and privacy over a cup of tea and a buttery croissant.

She also wanted to hide from Lord Marcus.

The man reading his newspaper at the breakfast table could not possibly measure up to the swain who'd kissed her good night. His military bearing had turned to a sheltering embrace, his hands had ever so gently urged her closer. That mouth of his, usually a grim, disapproving line frequently making crisp pronouncements and issuing terse commands, had turned tender and subtle.

His lordship was a terror, or perhaps Meg's limited amatory experience was the problem. She'd had *no idea* a man could send a woman's wits fleeing straight up the chimney with a good-night kiss. She'd told herself Peter's initial overtures had been masterful. In hindsight, Peter had been pushy and crude.

Lord Marcus had been—why not be honest?—wonderful. He'd parted from her on a polite bow, but he'd also kissed her lingeringly on the cheek before disappearing into the corridor. Meg had ducked into her bedroom and leaned against a bedpost, her insides a-flutter, her mind full of doves on the wing and merry choruses.

In the frigid light of dawn, the doves had departed for warmer climes, taking Meg's courage with them.

She was startled out of her ruminations by a sharp rap on her bedroom door. "Wake up, child. We've work to do and cinnamon buns to consume."

"Come in, Aunt Penny."

"You are awake and dressed. All to the good, or Marcus will escape before we can interrogate him. He mustn't be allowed to wander off before we've given him his orders."

Aunt was dressed all in green, a miniature version of Father Christmas, though to Meg's knowledge, that venerable figure had never worn a bright gold shawl and gold slippers. More fool he, because Aunt looked both festive and warm.

"I had a croissant," Meg said. "You may interrogate his lordship in private, while I look over my schedules one last time."

"One croissant? No wonder you are so wraithlike. You must fortify yourself for the ordeal ahead, my dear. I know of what I speak." She thumped her cane on the carpet, making the tea service on the hassock rattle.

"The ordeal of decorating the foyer? I assure you, ma'am, that as ordeals go, that one—"

Aunt thumped her cane again and started for the door. "Of course I don't mean a spot of decorating. You know what you're about when it comes to the boughs of holly and so forth. I mean the ordeal of putting up with Marcus early in the day. The poor boy left his sense of humor in Spain and his grasp of joy somewhere on the slopes of the Pyrenees."

No, he hadn't, though perhaps he'd tucked that sense of joy so far out of sight it might as well be misplaced. Meg followed Aunt from the sitting room into the corridor. "His lordship intends to visit family today. You need not give him orders."

"Of course he'll visit family. Heaven knows they can't be bothered to call upon him. I vow Maria was the pick of the litter, and she had the bad form to go and die on us. Cathcart is bereft, of course, but then, they were a love match."

"Cathcart, ma'am?"

Aunt was off and down the steps. "The present titleholder, Cathcart Helmsford Aurelius Boethius Bannerfield, whom I have known since he was still in dresses. He spends more time moping in his library than being a marquess. I've been tempted to take him in hand, even if he is getting a tad venerable. One doesn't want to intrude on grief."

Heaven help the marquess. "One needs friends most when one is grieving."

"You grieved for that ridiculous Entwhistle boy? I'm sorry to hear it. The story that went around was he had to be tied to the mast and brought back to England bodily to do his duty by you and the child. That is not the conduct of a man overcome with devotion. Don't waste your youthful good looks grieving for the likes of him."

That was certainly honest. "Not even a little?"

Aunt waved a hand adorned with white lace finger gloves. "Oh, one must observe the expected rituals. He was cut down in his prime, the flower of young manhood and all that, but he was a rotter. A disappointment to his papa, who no doubt sent him to the military where his swaggering about wouldn't cause a scandal. Somebody should have made sure he never stood within twenty feet of you."

She peered at Meg as if this observation merited a reply.

"That somebody would have been me, and I was apparently not up to the task."

They had reached the breakfast parlor, and Meg longed to step down the corridor and examine her reflection in the nearest mirror. She wore another borrowed dress, a lusciously warm raspberry velvet with a cream underskirt that rustled softly as she walked. A pair of black wool stockings—cashmere, perhaps?—had been included with the dress, and Meg was warm despite the chill permeating the house.

"You had been out exactly one Season when you met Entwhistle," Aunt said. "I recall the sensation you made, how everybody remarked on your resemblance to your mama, and how proud she would have been of you. She would still be proud of you, you know. Somebody needed to stand up to young Webberly. I know he's your brother, but men have it all their way all too often. It is our bounden duty to keep them humble despite their conceits."

After that extraordinary speech, Aunt pushed into the breakfast parlor, letting a warm whiff of cinnamon and butter into the corridor.

"Come along, Lady Margaret. His lordship will think he has only me to deal with, and he will shortly excuse himself. He won't beat such a rude retreat if you are here to keep him on his manners."

Oh gracious. Lord Marcus was in there, and Meg must face him.

She summoned a smile and discarded it. Not for him, the brisk, pleasant, false expressions she used on customers. This man had heard her troubles, offered to take up arms on her behalf, and kissed her good night—*after asking her permission.* That kiss probably meant nothing to him, but to Meg, the memory was precious.

"Good morning, my lord." She curtseyed.

He rose and bowed. "Ladies, good day. I trust you both slept well?"

Aunt took up a plate and lifted the lid of a warming tray on the sideboard. "Old people do not sleep well, I'll have you know. We doze, we drift, we toss and turn and wake up tired, which explains half of our surly mood. The other half is explained by the world we wake up to. Your cook knows precisely how to treat a strip of bacon, bless the woman."

Lord Marcus stayed on his feet. Meg remained standing near the door. Aunt helped herself to an enormous portion of bacon, and the moment became exactly what Meg had dreaded—awkward.

"But did *you* sleep well, Lady Margaret?"

What was he asking? "I did, my lord. I was dreaming before my head hit the pillow."

He fetched a plate from the warmer and gestured for her to join him at the sideboard. "One hopes your dreams were as pleasant as my own. Would you care for some eggs?"

Meg cared simply to stand near him, which was ridiculous. Had he, too, dreamed of that kiss? "Please, and don't be too sparing. Eggs and buttered toast have seen me through many a long day."

"Huh." Aunt took the place to the right of the head of the table. "That's not enough to keep a Christmas elf on his mettle. Offer the woman some meat, Marcus."

He offered Meg a smile, a slight curving of his mouth, accompanied by a subtle light dancing in his eyes. "You refuse Aunt's direction at your peril, Lady Margaret. The ham is quite good."

"He means," Aunt Penny said, pouring herself a cup of tea, "you should leave the bacon for me. I will assist you today in the decorating, and I need my full energies."

"One shudders to contemplate such an eventuality," Lord Marcus said, spearing two thick slices of ham onto Meg's plate, "if your present demeanor is an example of your diminished energies."

"And this," Aunt said, gesturing with her fork, "is the man as he rises after a full night of *pleasant dreams*. One shudders, and all that. Heavens above, I do adore bacon."

Meg took her plate from his lordship and indulged in the silliness of allowing her fingers to brush his. He seated her with all proper dignity, but as he bent to give the chair one last push, his lips ended up near Meg's ear.

"Minx." The word was barely whispered, but Meg *felt* the brush of warmth against her neck.

This would not do, it would not do at all, though Meg would leave Lord Marcus's household at the end of the day, so where was the harm in a little breakfast flirtation?

"Marcus, you will not allow Elizabeth to interrupt the proceedings here," Aunt said. "She will be overcome with curiosity, but then, the whole open house was her idea."

Meg took a bite of fluffy, perfectly salted eggs and had a nibble of the best ham she could recall tasting in ages. The day would be busy, but she'd at least face it on a full stomach.

"What open house?" his lordship asked, taking his seat at the head of the table. "I am decorating this abode in preparation for the arrival of my nieces. They deserve some holiday cheer, and it is my privilege to provide it."

He poured Meg a cup of fragrant black tea and put a honey jar and a pitcher of cream—not milk, *cream*—at her elbow.

She allowed herself to enjoy the precious sense of budding intimacy that these little courtesies created. Lord Marcus was to appearances being a proper host, but Meg had kissed him. She knew the warmth of his touch, the passion lurking immediately beneath his veneer of self-discipline and detachment.

Of all the holiday surprises... Meg was powerfully attracted to her host, though, of course, nothing could come of it. She was simply grateful that a time of year she had learned to dread had instead brought her unexpected pleasure.

"Perhaps my lady prefers sugar to honey?" his lordship asked.

"We have our own honey brought up from Sussex, though not everybody finds the flavor agreeable in tea."

"The honey is wonderful." Meg took up her knife and fork lest she descend into simpering glances and fatuous smiles.

"So you're to call on Eliza today?" Aunt Penny said, biting off the end of a piece of bacon. "Spike her guns all you please, but she will have her open house."

Lord Marcus finished his tea and poured himself another half a cup. "Is Eliza planning an open house? Mr. Hennepin will have something to say about that. Feeding a throng of hungry guests will cost a pretty penny, and if Eliza is making up the guest list, it will be a throng of biblical proportions."

Aunt reached for the teapot. "She is making up the guest list, but you will be hosting the event. She's probably waiting until the children are underfoot to spring it on you. Wants the place all decorated and the invitations sent out, I'm sure."

The good humor in his lordship's eyes was replaced by his usual wintry sternness. "Make no mistake, Aunt, I am not having my household turned upside down, my peace invaded by strangers, and my larders stripped for my sister's convenience. Her own domicile is perfectly commodious, and the children will require calm and quiet as they settle in."

Aunt set down the teapot, and Meg passed her the honey and cream.

"Marcus, my dear boy, you are reasonably intelligent, considering the limitations of your gender, but Eliza is determined to see you married off. The children are but a prop she feels will increase your appeal to her various friends and their daughters. She intends that you host a holiday open house in two weeks, and the purpose will be for her to choose the young lady to whom you will offer a holiday proposal." Aunt poured half the cream pitcher into her tea cup. "I do so enjoy a little pampering every now and then. I should come visit you more often."

Before Meg could choke on her buttered toast, Lord Marcus was on his feet. "Lady Margaret, the staff is prepared to obey your every wish and whim. Aunt Penny, you might have warned me sooner. I bid you both good day. I am off to threaten my sister with a permanent estrangement."

He left at a brisk march as Aunt Penny stirred her tea. "You see the thanks I get. If Marcus hadn't galloped off to parlay with his sister, I could have informed him that the only truly suitable name on Eliza's guest list belongs to Miss Davina Andrews-Clapshot. Easy on the eye, beauteous settlements, nobody's fool, and possessed of a very determined mother. Eat your ham, my lady. We have a busy day ahead, and you must look your best when Eliza comes to survey the battlefield."

Meg took a small bite of ham, though her pleasure in the meal had fled. She'd been getting ideas about Lord Marcus, foolish, hopeless ideas. His family was picking out a fiancée for him, and whoever that lucky woman was, she would not be a disgraced widow of limited means.

CHAPTER FIVE

"Eliza, you go too far. *Again*." Marcus stalked up to his sister, who was leafing through music as she sat on the piano bench. "You all but saw me compromised with the Clevinger heiress, you tried to talk me into a literary liaison with Lady Antonia Mainwaring. Now you manipulate a pair of grieving children for the sake of your schemes."

Her ladyship set a sheet of music on the piano's music rack and placed her hands on the keyboard as if Marcus hadn't spoken. She made a very pretty picture at the keyboard, and she knew it. Her playing was only passable, but her *performing* was first-rate.

Marcus closed the cover over the keys, forcing Eliza to snatch her hands away. "You think because I don't shout and hurl porcelain as you do that my temper remains in check. That I am merely annoyed, rather than furious. I am both, and more to the point, sister mine, I am disappointed in you."

Eliza let out a histrionic sigh. "You needn't shout. I am only trying to help."

He leaned closer. "I am not shouting. When need be, I can make myself heard over the din of five thousand men-at-arms engaged in mortal combat. The task before me is to make myself *understood* by one stubborn, selfish female."

Next came... Yes, there it was, the protruding lower lip, not to be confused with the quivering lip, a display reserved for moments of dire frustration.

"I aid you in a task you are unable to satisfactorily complete on your own," she said, "and you rail at me and hurl accusations. If anybody should be disappointed here, I should be."

How gently Eliza chided, how becomingly she blinked at him, the epitome of the damsel bewildered by male dunderheadedness. Lady Margaret had come face-to-face with much worse than male dunderheadedness, and *she* wasn't carrying on like an aging schoolgirl.

"Very likely, you are disappointed," Marcus said, "in your latest batch of hats or your dearest friend's inability to partner you profitably at whist. If we're to be very honest, you might be disappointed in Hennepin's behavior as a spouse. That is none of my affair, just as my choice of wife—or my choice whether to take a wife—is none of yours."

She scooted past him and rose, doubtless because the program had reached the pacing-and-muttering portion.

"I despair of you, Marcus, truly I do. You intimate that you might not marry, but we both know you must. Papa is nearly in a decline, while you refuse to take the one step that might revive his spirits. And yet, you call *me* selfish. Never has a sister been as vexed by her only sibling. Tell me about Lady Margaret."

That abrupt change of subject was supposed to deflect Marcus from the stated agenda of chastising his sister. Elizabeth tossed out such commands in conversations she couldn't otherwise control. *Fetch my shawl from the library, Marcus,* was the imperative of last resort, but Marcus wasn't indulging her tactics on this occasion.

"Elizabeth, I will some sad day become the head of the Banner-field family. We are a lamentably small tribe, and any offspring you have will need every ounce of my consequence, particularly if

Hennepin doesn't rein in your proclivity for shopping. I will recall then how frequently and vexatiously you interfered in my personal business. I will have a list at hand of every occasion on which you publicly embarrassed me or tried to manipulate me—a long list. You either cancel this damned open house, or I will tell Hennepin exactly how much I spent this year to cover your gambling debts."

The pacing stopped. "That is a low blow, Marcus. I put my trust in you, rely on your discretion as a gentleman and my only surviving brother, and you threaten me with exposure because I am trying to save Papa's life. He needs to know the succession is secure, needs to know that you will not fail in your duty to the title. I am subtly—only subtly—making that task easier for you, and you come here pitching a tantrum like some spoiled schoolboy. I am very tempted to wash my hands of you. I truly am."

Marcus bowed to her. "I commend your selfless devotion to creating drama and meddling in other people's lives, Eliza, but I am not hosting an open house so you can parade me before the match-makers yet again."

She fisted her hands against her skirts and raised her gaze heaven-ward, St. Joan contemplating her martyrdom.

"That is the very point, Marcus. I have tried and tried. You stood up with only the most staid of the wallflowers all last Season. For the little Season, you partnered only dowagers or widows at cards and drove out only with sisters in pairs or threes. You will soon be seen as a confirmed bachelor, and all of Society will blame me for your unmarried state."

He was supposed to relent soon, to give Eliza credit for having a scintilla of sense to her arguments. From there, he'd unbend enough to grant that a small portion of her motivation for disre-garding his stated wishes might be concern for Papa, or even—when the handkerchief of doom came out—concern for Marcus himself.

Alas for Elizabeth, Marcus had met a woman who was entitled to cry, rant, stomp, and throw vases. Lady Margaret had been served one bad turn after another, and her response was to put pride aside and deck the damned halls.

"You need a charitable project," Marcus said. "You need to come face-to-face with women who haven't one good pair of shoes, much less the dozens you hoard for no reason. Find some means of entertaining yourself that doesn't burden others, Eliza. You are bright, you have connections, you could make a difference. Instead, you choose to pester me with your matchmaking. Have done, or you will wish you had. Good day."

He left the room without offering her another bow, and that bothered him—a little. That he'd put her in her place and refused to let her little drama paint him into yet another corner felt wonderful.

"Marcus, wait." Elizabeth hurried up the corridor and latched on to his arm. "Don't let's quarrel, please."

Now she wanted to make peace? "We are not quarreling. You are canceling the open house you have attempted to foist onto my exchequer and my residence. Badly done, Eliza, and if Aunt Penny hadn't put me wise to your schemes, then I would be raising my voice."

Eliza glanced up and down the corridor, then stepped closer. "The invitations have gone out. I cannot cancel this affair, Marcus. I know it was bad of me, but I am worried for Papa."

She looked genuinely contrite, which was a complete sham.

"You can send out word the affair has been canceled, or better still, moved to your own residence. Hennepin can host it with you. He's your husband, after all." To his credit, Hennepin never had a word to say against his wife and regarded Eliza with a sort of exasperated affection.

"He's being difficult, Henny is." Elizabeth glanced around again. "He's cut me off, Marcus, until the first of the year. He gave me an annual budget, you see, and my head for numbers isn't the best. I had to ask for a bit more... in March." She smoothed her hand down Marcus's sleeve. "And June, and September. I am in disgrace as a wife and as a hostess. My friends invite me to their affairs, but I cannot afford to return their hospitality."

This tale might very well be a tissue of misrepresentations, or it might be all too true.

"Elizabeth, your grasp of mathematics is quite sound. You overspend because it annoys Hennepin, who has done nothing to deserve that aggravation."

"He's always busy. Always, Marcus."

Marcus had theories about why Hennepin was so busy, but he also aspired to live to see his thirty-fourth birthday, so he kept those theories to himself.

"I will speak with him."

Elizabeth straightened. "Don't you dare. He is my husband, and I will deal with him. I apologize about the open house, Marcus. I thought you'd be pleased. You have no hostess, and I don't like to think of you alone for the Yuletide season."

He almost believed her. "Have you truly sent out the invitations?"

Her lower lip quivered.

"Elizabeth?"

"No."

Marcus was unmoved by neither her contrite expression, nor by the worry she affected in her smile. Eliza deserved to suffer the consequences of her mendacity and manipulation.

And yet, *Lady Mistletoe's handiwork should be displayed.* All of Mayfair—*all of London*—should see what Lady Margaret Entwhistle could do with some time, ingenuity, and coin. She deserved to pick and choose among her customers, to charge whatever she pleased for her time and talents.

London's best tailors, cobblers, and modistes were thronged with custom. Its best holiday decorator should be too. Well-born women owned banks, steel mills, chain-making enterprises, shipping ventures... Why not a decorating service?

"Heed me, Eliza," Marcus said, shrugging into his coat. "I will open my home to visitors two weeks hence between the hours of three and six of the clock. The guests will find a buffet in the gallery, and the music will consist of a small holiday chorus in the library. Invite no more than one hundred people, at least half of them elderly, widowed, far from home, or new to London. I will ask Papa to come. You will handle the invitations."

Her brows drew down, but her infernal lip ceased quivering. "I will have to revise all of the invitations."

"Ask Hennepin to help you. Hang a perishing kissing bough in your private parlor. Order a bottle of good brandy, build up the fire, and tell the staff you don't wish to be disturbed for the duration of the evening. I'm sure Hennepin will come to your aid if you ask him directly and cease your damned scheming."

Marcus bowed over her hand and left her standing, her mouth slightly agape, in her own foyer.

MARGARET QUIT THE BREAKFAST PARLOR, starting her day with a full tummy and an aching heart. One kiss did not an infatuation create, but a kiss, a patient listening ear, an unhesitating willingness to take on orphaned nieces, a subtle sense of humor... They created a memorable impression.

Meg was not smitten with Lord Marcus, but she had noticed a man in a good way for the first time in ages. She told herself that was an unlooked-for boon, a small reason to take heart, and threw herself into decorating his lordship's foyer as it had never been decorated before.

"The young gents have the outdoor greenery about half put together," Daisy said. "The young ladies have a dozen oranges completed, and we're halfway done twining the ribbon on the bannisters."

They were on schedule, in other words, but that wasn't the point of Daisy's report. "Then it's time for our morning break," Meg said.

Daisy took up a bosun's whistle dangling from a string around her neck and gave a shrill, two-pitched tweet that cut through the tapping of hammers from outside and the chatter of the girls working at a makeshift table across the foyer.

Charlotte's face appeared over the bannister. "Is that all hands on deck?"

"Indeed it is," Margaret said. "Stop what you're doing and report for orders."

Aunt Penny appeared beside her. "We're not quite finished with our carrying candles."

Charlotte used Aunt's cane and the bannister to hobble down the steps. "Morning tea has arrived, Auntie. This is the best part of the job, besides afternoon tea."

Well, no. The best part of the job was seeing a drab, formal space surrender its cold grandeur to the warmth and color of Yuletide decorations. The even better part was what the work did for the children, who in the coldest, darkest time of year had some coin, some sustenance, and some camaraderie to see them through. Meg also took satisfaction from the clients' reactions when they beheld the transformation of their homes and realized how splendidly welcoming a domicile in holiday finery could be.

And for Lord Marcus, Meg wanted to make an especially magnificent impression, even if he would be using her Christmas decorations to gain the notice of his prospective marchioness.

A half-dozen boys varying in size from quite small to half grown trooped in from the front terrace. Their cheeks were rosy, their eyes bright, and they'd all started the day with at least a cinnamon bun and a cup of milk. Meg included these terms in her contract, finding the gain in productivity more than outweighed the diminished profit.

"Daisy tells me we are exactly on schedule," Meg said, holding up Papa's watch. "Well done! The morning tea break is ready, and Daisy will let us know when it's time to get back to work."

Daisy blew another series of tweets, and the children formed a line around another table that Lord Marcus's footmen had laid out. The queue arranged itself from smallest to tallest, with Charlotte waiting beside Meg and Aunt Penny joining them from the steps.

"In all my born years," Aunt said, "which will soon rival those of Methuselah, I have never seen such well-behaved boys."

"Mama explains it to them," Charlotte said. "We are guests in another's home when we decorate, so we must be on our best behavior."

The children took their plates and sat around the foyer in small groups as blessed quiet descended. Meg loved this part of the job, when the transition to Christmas was only started, the potential visible only to her.

"You must join us, Aunt Penny," Meg said. "You could tell the children stories that will keep them enthralled for hours."

"By enthralled, you mean they won't slide down the bannister."

"May we, Mama? Slide down the bannister?"

"Charlotte, you are to be a good influence on the elves."

Aunt eyed the great sweeping curve of the bannister. "If I were ten years younger…"

"If you landed in a heap," Meg retorted, "Lord Marcus would never forgive me." Lord Marcus, who might be engaged by Yuletide. For him to take a bride at the holidays would be an occasion of joy, of course. An extra reason for the family to come together and celebrate.

Charlotte had hobbled over to the table, and Aunt Penny was filling a plate for her when a knock sounded on the enormous front door. A footman hurried forward from the corridor and admitted two older women in plain cloaks and two small, pale girls.

The footman closed the door, regarding the larger of the women with veiled curiosity.

"I am Miss Trumble, Miss Gertrude Trumble, and I have completed my obligation to deliver Lord Marcus's nieces."

She said this as if she'd galloped through enemy territory, eluding capture and durance vile. The little girls stood looking at their damp, muddy boots.

"We were not expecting the young misses until tomorrow," the footman said, as if that lobbed some unexploded ordnance of fault back at the new arrivals.

Margaret made her way across the foyer, her footsteps echoing hollowly, for of course, every pair of eyes was on the little drama at the door.

"The children have to be chilled and hungry," Meg said, "as are, without doubt, Miss Trumble and her companion. We can offer you hot tea, sandwiches, and cakes, or I'm sure the kitchen will send up a tray if you'd like to await his lordship in a guest parlor."

Miss Trumble inhaled, which caused a generous bosom to heave upward. "I have done that which I was charged with doing. If I were to take tea, I'd do it in the servants' hall, as is proper. I refuse to tarry, however, and will send his lordship my direction that he might remit the agreed upon remuneration to me. Come along, Miss Dinwhiddie. We have fulfilled our duty."

The footman barely had time to open the door before Miss Trumble and Miss Dinwhiddie swept from the premises on a gust of cold air.

"Did we fail inspection?" Charlotte asked, a tea cake in her hand.

The little girls stood very close to each other. Meg could not tell if they were relieved to be abandoned by their minders or terrified.

"We in no way failed an inspection," Meg retorted. "But I suspect we have two more pairs of hands to aid us in our labors. I'm Lady Margaret." She knelt to unbutton the smaller girl's cloak. "Who are you?"

"That's Amanda," the larger girl said. "I'm Emily. Where is Uncle Marcus?" She posed her question with a hint of hope and a helping of dread. For a child to inquire of an adult's whereabouts was quite forward—also quite brave.

"Your uncle wasn't expecting you until tomorrow," Meg said, "which is why the holiday decorations aren't finished yet. He will be overjoyed to have you safely under his roof." She added a smile to that assurance and passed Amanda's cloak to the footman.

"I'm c-cold," Amanda said. "And h-hungry."

Aunt Penny sent Meg a look over the children's heads.

"Of course you are," Meg said, moving on to Emily's cloak. "You have come a great distance at a disobliging time of year. We will have you warm and fed in no time. Aunt Penny, Charlotte, perhaps you can keep the young ladies company in the nursery until a tray can be sent up."

The footman cleared his throat. "Beg pardon, my lady, but we haven't lit the fires in the nursery yet. The maids are still making the beds and whatnot."

Charlotte came over and bobbed a semblance of a curtsey. "I'm Charlotte. I hurt my knee, but Aunt Penny has lent me her magic sword of doom." She thumped her cane. "You can help us put the ribbons around the carrying candles once you've had something to eat."

"I'm c-cold," Amanda repeated with an ominous wailing note in her voice.

"Then you must have a proper cup of tea," Aunt said. "And James, perhaps you could purloin a few afghans from the library. A princess on the day of her coronation needs appropriate robes."

"A princess?" Emily asked.

"We princesses toil away in our tower," Charlotte said, gesturing to the top of the steps. "It's warmer up there, and we can see the whole of our courtyard. Princesses also dine on tea cakes to keep up their strength. Follow me."

Charlotte's inherent friendliness and talk of tea cakes were apparently enough to lure Emily and Amanda to the buffet.

"You have raised a kind girl, Lady Margaret," Aunt Penny said, "and a lively one."

"That is a compliment?" Meg asked as Charlotte passed each girl a plate.

"A very fine compliment. Those little girls have a tale to tell, and I don't believe it's a happy one."

"The ending will be happy," Meg said. "Lord Marcus will see to it." Lord Marcus and his Yuletide bride.

"Huh." Aunt left Meg's side and supervised the plundering of the tea cakes, a task to which she was admirably suited, in Meg's opinion, and soon the hammering had resumed, the footmen were removing the remains of the buffet—likely to be enjoyed in the kitchen—and Amanda, Emily, Charlotte, and Aunt Penny were at their eagle's nest/tower/magic carpet overlooking the foyer.

The day was going well, and if Meg let her gaze stray to the front door in hopes of seeing a tall, occasionally cranky lord who also kissed like every foolish woman's dream, well, nobody need know of that folly.

She was admiring the precisely patterned cloved orange completed by her smallest elf when the door opened to admit the object of her imaginings. Lord Marcus, greatcoat damp with snow, took one look around the foyer and delivered Meg a thunderous scowl.

"Lord Marcus, good day."

He shoved his coat at the footman. "At the risk of arguing with a lady..."

"They're here!" Charlotte caroled, coming back down the steps at a fast hobble. "Princess Amanda and Princess Emily have arrived to their castle!"

Lord Marcus's scowl resolved in an utterly blank expression. "Not so soon."

"Yes," Meg said, aiming a ferocious smile at him. "Your nieces are safely arrived and already helping with the decorations. Try to contain your joy."

To his credit, his mouth quirked. "And you have all in hand, of course."

"They are up there," Meg said, gesturing to the landing. "Make them welcome, or I will deal with you sternly."

"Yes, ma'am." He started for the steps and then paused, leaning near. "I know where I want my kissing boughs."

"You do?"

He came close enough to whisper in Meg's ear. "Everywhere. I want those damned things everywhere."

He trotted up the steps as Meg stood at the bottom, not knowing whether to laugh or toss her orange at him.

MARCUS'S first impression upon walking into his foyer was one of utter pandemonium, a pitched battle with chaos, and the forces of order about to sound retreat. He'd approached the house to the sound of hammers banging incessantly. Bits of greenery had littered his front walkway half covered in the falling snow. Small children were scampering up and down ladders, calling to one another in impenetrable cockney accents, and a wreath half as tall as Marcus had been propped near the front door.

Inside, matters went from bad to worse. Chattering replaced the hammer-chorus as only a half-dozen little girls could chatter. Bright red, green, and gold ribbons dangled from sconces and curled in snippets on the marble floor. The scent of fresh oranges blended with the piney fragrance of the greenery, and some child with more enthusiasm than talent was singing about Good King Winces-slob.

In the middle of this tribute to misrule stood Lady Margaret, calm and smiling, resplendent in her raspberry dress and green shawl. She confirmed the arrival of Amanda and Emily and offered a smile that promised doom to uncles who reacted with anything other than ebullient joy at such marvelous news.

Marcus climbed the stairs, feeling anything but rejoicing. The children were a day early, the weather was turning up nasty, his house was besieged by small people speaking in foreign tongues, and he wanted nothing so much as to be alone with Lady Margaret.

Duty first, of course. He consulted with her ladyship regarding the kissing boughs—plural, of course—and rounded the landing at a smart pace.

At the top of the steps, on the balcony-cum-balustraded-corridor, Aunt Penny occupied a quilt on the carpet, three small girls tailor-sitting at the remaining corners of the blanket. Pale beeswax carrying candles were scattered on the quilt, red and green ribbons tied about the brass carriers.

"Ladies, good morning."

All three girls looked up, Charlotte wreathed in smiles, Amanda and Emily with caution. Amanda looked back down at the ribbon now twining about her fingers.

Emily scrambled to her feet. "Good day, Uncle Marcus." She executed a curtsey as Amanda rose and smoothed down a hopelessly wrinkled pinafore.

"Good day, Uncle Marcus."

What to do? Bow? Hug them? Bow over their hands? The disorder Marcus had observed in his house abruptly took up residence in his heart. These small people were now his responsibility, and he hadn't any idea how to greet them.

Soft footsteps on the stairs behind him presaged Lady Margaret's arrival. "Foreign princesses have crossed the hostile plains in the dead of winter to seek refuge in your fortress, my lord. What say you to your royal guests?" She took Marcus's arm and smiled at the girls.

Amanda's return smile, so uncertain and hopeful, broke Marcus's heart. "I say," he began, as if he'd a clue how to go on, "welcome... Your Majesties."

Aunt Penny nodded, suggesting he'd made an adequate beginning.

"I say," he went on, "welcome to your new home. Every knight and damsel in the castle rejoices at your safe passage across enemy territory, and we hope you will be happy here."

Where were their governesses and nurses? Why weren't the girls tucked snugly into the nursery, for pity's sake?

"Th-thank you, Uncle Marcus," Amanda whispered. "We're not really princesses."

"You are my nieces, which I daresay is preferable to being princesses. Your grandfather is fifty-sixth in line for the throne, you know, and that makes you nearly royalty in truth."

Emily frowned at him, while Amanda fixed her gaze on Marcus's cravat. "If you say so, Uncle Marcus."

This was not going well at all, and Marcus had a sense that how the girls settled into their new lives would depend largely on their early impressions of him.

"Are we excused from the royal presence?" Lady Margaret asked.

Aunt Penny waved a hand, both green and red ribbons trailing from her wrist. "You may be excused. The princesses and I will take a proper picnic lunch in the library in two hours' time. You may join us then, if your other duties permit."

Lady Margaret tugged discreetly on Marcus's arm. "We would be honored," she said. "Until then."

Just as if she'd been presented at court, she backed slowly from the royal presences, dragging Marcus with her. He managed a slight bow before withdrawing, Lady Margaret at his side. When she'd towed him a good ten yards down the corridor and around a corner, she dissolved into laughter.

Marcus was displeased to find his abode in such a state of uproar.

He was concerned that his nieces had arrived early and were apparently less than confident regarding their welcome in his household.

He was angry with his sister and her silly schemes, and he was still—even more than ever—behind on his correspondence.

But the sound of Lady Margaret overcome with mirth put all those concerns to rout and, better still, gave Marcus hope that this year, Yuletide could truly be a happy season.

CHAPTER SIX

A marquess's heir doing his best to play *let's pretend* for the benefit of two small children had to be the most endearing thing Meg had come across in years.

"I made a complete hash of that," Lord Marcus muttered, pacing the width of the corridor. "I am the worst uncle ever to court banishment from my own kingdom. How could I have confused the children's arrival date? I must have a word with the governess."

"You can't," Meg said. "Miss Trumble and Miss Dinwhiddie have decamped in high dudgeon, and at least one of them had made a thorough sampling of the rum punch before she dropped the children on your doorstep. I suspect any confusion was on her end of the bargain."

"Rum punch?" Lord Marcus ran a hand through his hair. "*Rum punch* when she had small children in her care? I'd sack her for that alone. One cannot attend to such a weighty duty when half soused."

Bless this man. "Miss Trumble will forward her final demand for wages to you by post."

"Delightful. Now, I haven't a governess on staff. I haven't nursery maids. The children need familiar faces and consistent routines.

They have suffered much upheaval and considerable grief. I am all but a stranger to them, and—"

Meg touched her fingers to his lips as the strains of a soprano/alto version of *Good King Wenceslas* drifted up from the foyer. "You are working yourself into a state, my lord."

"I am not working myself into a state. I *am* in a state. The army of the North Pole has invaded my house, orphans have arrived on my doorstep ahead of schedule and without their paid staff, and my sister is determined to see me married off by the New Year. This is not how I envisioned the start to my holidays, Lady Margaret."

Married off by the New Year? Meg weathered that pronouncement, hoping it was hyperbole, though really his lordship should marry, and she should stop entertaining daft notions on the strength of a single kiss.

"The maids you do have on hand will keep an eye on the children until the agencies can send you candidates to interview."

His lordship took Meg's hand and led her down the corridor. "You do not mention Lady Elizabeth's attempts to besiege my bachelorhood. She intends this open house as another occasion to lob prospective marchionesses at my head."

Meg derived some comfort from Lord Marcus's lack of enthusiasm for his sister's scheme, but she had honestly hoped there would *be* no open house. Selfish of her.

Foolish too. "You have eluded the matchmakers thus far," she said. "Perhaps your luck will hold."

"Perhaps my luck is changing." He stopped beside a carved door and cocked his head. "The army of the North Pole can sing."

From outside the house, the boys had added the tenor and baritone parts to King Wenceslas's tale. They hadn't a bass to their names, though the arrangement was lovely nonetheless.

"They are rehearsing, my lord. They earn coin when they are in good voice, provided nobody expects them to look like angels. And they will retreat from your abode by this evening, leaving your foyer pristine and beautiful."

"But they will return," Lord Marcus retorted, "wreaking havoc on my library, my guest parlors. The sacrifices one makes for duty..."

He opened the door, and Meg beheld a gallery at least sixty feet long. The hearths at both ends of the room were unlit, the space frigid. Dark portraits graced the walls, each painting hung to fall between the weak shafts of light admitted by tall windows along the outside wall.

"You did not show me this room on our previous tour," she said. "Am I to decorate here as well?" The space had possibilities, but focusing on a decorating scheme was difficult when Meg knew that at his lordship's open house the gallery would be thronged with Society's most-eligible young women.

"I realize costs will be incurred as part of the undertaking," his lordship said, pushing a curtain aside, "but I was unsuccessful at dissuading my sister from her open-house scheme. The guests will number well over a hundred if Eliza runs true to form, which means every available public room must be put to good use."

Meg would have liked to have told his lordship that she was too busy to add his gallery to her list of responsibilities, but in truth she had yet to line up much work for the coming Yuletide season, and he did not quibble over coin. Duty, as his lordship had mentioned, required sacrifices.

"I'll put together an estimate when I go home this evening," Meg said, though for once the prospect of additional income didn't provide the lift to her spirits it ought to.

"Go home?" Lord Marcus peered out the window. "That is out of the question, my lady. The way this snow is coming down, nobody with any sense will be abroad if they can help it. Come see for yourself."

Meg joined him by the window, which overlooked a back terrace blanketed in white. More snow was falling at the steady, this-means-business rate of the season's first real winter storm.

"I should send the children home now," Meg said. "Some of them are quite small, and deep snow is dangerous when a child lacks decent boots."

"Will their parents worry for them?" Lord Marcus asked, dropping the curtain over the window.

"They haven't any parents. Some of them have older siblings, relatives who would let them shelter for a short time, but these children are largely homeless, my lord. I can't keep them here all afternoon, then send them out into deep snow."

"Then don't." Lord Marcus started for the door. "Keep them here, proceed with your decorating. We will contrive to shelter them from the elements until the weather is more obliging." He held the door for Meg, and the corridor felt like a tropical conservatory compared to the gallery. "Have we a bargain, Lady Margaret? You will add the gallery to your list of tasks, the children will complete the foyer today, and you and they will bide here for the present?"

He pulled the door closed, once again the military officer securing compliance with orders, executing his duties. Meg wanted to retreat to his office, curl up under his old morning jacket, and shed a few tears—the holidays were always such a trial, and she was still short of sleep—though time spent in nameless regrets would be time entirely wasted.

Instead she tarried with him in the corridor. "I am forced by circumstances to agree with your lordship's plan, but I like it not."

"Neither do I, when I know King Wenceslas boasts at least forty verses, but needs must when Christmas approaches. What have you in mind for my gallery?"

"I'll think of something," Meg said. "I always do. I'd best have a look at how the greenery is coming along on the front walk."

His lordship peered down at her, a damp lock of hair curling over his brow. "And what shall I do while I await our *proper picnic* in the library?"

She folded her arms, rather than smooth his hair back. "Inspect the handiwork of your princesses, my lord, and do try to look impressed."

Meg left him by the doors to the gallery, but before she donned her cloak to brave the elements and offer the boys encouragement, she did step into his lordship's office and allowed herself just a few moments of disappointment. Not tears, of course, or not many tears, but a little disappointment, and a wish that this Yuletide could somehow be more joyous and less dutiful than its predecessors.

"MARCUS HAS HIRED A PROFESSIONAL DECORATOR, though she's something of a mystery," Lady Eliza said, dipping her quill into the inkpot, letting the ink pool into a drop at the tip of her pen, then fall back into the bottle.

"The answer is no, my dear," Ralph Hennepin murmured, head bent over the invitation he was writing. "No professional decorations. You haven't the coin."

He said that as if reminding a small girl that she'd neglected to bring her parasol, so she must suffer the disobliging beams of the sun in her eyes.

"And where in my settlements," Eliza asked from her side of the desk, "does it say that the annual expense of kitting the house out for the holidays is to come out of my accounts? When the coach must be repainted, you pay for that, though it's also an annual expense."

The increasingly foul weather meant Ralph was trapped in the house for the day, and Eliza had seized the moment. The sooner her invitations went out, the more likely they were to be accepted. The holidays could be so busy for those who spent them in Town.

And yet, somehow, the holidays could be lonely too.

Ralph sent her a calculating glance. "I admit that I pay for the repainting of the coach. That is an entirely different matter. The coach is attached to the stables, and the stables are a masculine province."

Eliza put pen to paper, this invitation going to Lord Grimston. His lordship was unlikely to accept—enthusiasm for the holidays was not among his noted fortes—but Marcus had demanded that some invitations be sent to the less fashionable, the elderly, the widowed, and other unfortunates.

"My mare bides in your stables, husband. You made me pay for her new saddle."

He sprinkled sand over vellum and sat back. "That sidesaddle was made for your elegant backside, Eliza. Nobody else in the household has a prayer of using it. It's as personal to you as a ballgown or a pair of shoes."

He was looking directly at her. Eliza realized how rare that had become, but then, she rarely looked at him. They read their respective newspapers at breakfast, they arrived separately to social affairs, they retired to separate chambers in the evening.

Now that she was looking at Ralph, she realized he was more handsome than when she'd married him. Then, he'd been down from university for only a year or so. Now, he'd developed gravitas to go with his dark hair, piercing blue eyes, and trim figure.

"My saddle is my expense," Eliza said, "though the stables are your province. You dwell under this roof. You expect me to entertain all of your friends and enemies here, but the cost of those gatherings comes entirely from my accounts. Do you know, sir, the difference between the expense of hosting one of my at homes, versus the cost of one of your political dinners?"

He cocked his head at the angle that warned Eliza she was about to be charmed.

"How could I know such a detail, my dear, when both undertakings are entirely in your capable hands?"

She named him a figure that had his brows coming down as he set aside his pen.

"That much? A single dinner costs that much?"

"I hire extra footmen to ensure the food arrives to the table hot, and that means we keep extra livery on hand for those footmen. Cook needs more help in the kitchen for the evening itself and several days prior. The wine you fellows consume boggles the mind, and you lot stay up so late debating that we can run through a week's candles in a night. Beeswax, of course, lest it be said that Ralph Hennepin is pinching pennies. I am very aware of your consequence, Ralph, and I try my best to protect it."

"But, Eliza," he said gently, "you gamble. I know you have gone to Marcus for assistance more than once. He never says anything, but your creditors stopped approaching me, and he's the logical source of relief. One doesn't care to be indebted to one's brother-in-law."

"Everybody gambles, and Marcus would be horrified if I asked anybody else for money. He likes to be of use and considers scolding me periodically to be his duty. I merely give him the pretext for the exercise that delights him most in the whole world."

That was a bouncer, and Ralph's smile said he knew it as such. "Does the Regent allow his loyal subjects an opportunity to show their regard when he expects us to pay his enormous bills?"

"Marcus is not the Regent. He worries for Papa, and chiding me gives him a target for his anxieties. The day grows chilly. Shall I pour us some brandy?" In theory, ladies did not take strong spirits. In private, theories were of little merit.

"Please," Ralph said. "Snow is lovely, but chilly and hardly convenient."

Eliza brought him his drink. "Was that a comment directed at me?"

Ralph took the brandy, set it aside, and much to Eliza's surprise, tugged her down onto his lap. "My wife is lovely, make no mistake about that, but she's a puzzle as well."

Eliza hadn't sat in her husband's lap for ages, not since they'd courted, probably. She surrendered to the urge to curl against Ralph's chest.

"You are warm," she murmured, "and you puzzle me as well."

Ralph had such a marvelous way with a caress. His hands drifted across her back in sweet, slow strokes, and Eliza closed her eyes, the better to listen to his heartbeat.

"I puzzle you? Eliza, I am the most forthright of fellows. I go about my business, I dote on the children, I meet your father or brother for dinner at the club at least once a month. I ride out on decent mornings and stand up with those of your friends whom you deem it appropriate for me to partner. How can I be anything like a puzzle?"

Life went along, relatively smoothly, like a stream flowing over and around rocks and fallen logs. Then something happened—a washed-out bridge, a storm, a farmer with a new irrigation scheme— and a change of course became possible.

Eliza had that sense about this rare midday privacy with her husband. She could pat his lapel, stand up, and go back to rewriting invitations, or she could talk to Ralph as they'd once talked to each other about everything.

"In your recitation of duties and appointments, Ralph, you do not mention this wife who puzzles you so." She burrowed closer, hiding her face against his throat. "I miss you."

His hand on her back stilled. "I beg your pardon?"

"I miss you. Once upon a time, you danced with me before you stood up with anybody else. I always had your opening set. Once upon a time, you'd bring your breakfast plate down to my end of the table and share the paper with me. Once upon a time... I'm not too old to have more children, Ralph. Not nearly."

He still came to her bed, but nothing like enough to suit Eliza.

"One doesn't want to impose on the woman he has pledged to protect from all harms," he said slowly.

Eliza kissed his cheek. "Does one want to neglect that woman? To fill his days with business and his evenings with dinner at the club or political discussions? Is it so awful to spend time with me, Ralph?"

He gathered her into an embrace, and Eliza braced herself for a lecture about sentiments mellowing and marriage being a cordial alliance rather than a romantic folly.

Ralph sighed, probably rehearsing his explications, and Eliza abruptly wanted to cry. Marriage was not supposed to be lonely, for

God's sake. Marriage wasn't supposed to be a constant battle to win a spouse's notice.

"I have concluded," Ralph said quietly, "that I bore you. You are so vivacious and friendly. I am a dull old stick who can only talk politics and the latest gossip on 'Change. I try not to avoidably annoy you with my presence."

Ralph was an honest man. Eliza treasured that about him. But was there a limit to his honesty?

"I have concluded," Eliza said, "that you are keeping a pretty, clever, wicked mistress, and you find me tedious and tiresome. You would rather stand up with anybody but your own wife. I don't even like to play cards, Ralph. The chairs are seldom comfortable, and finding a partner worthy of the name is nearly impossible."

A gust of bitter wind rattled the windows and even moved the heavy velvet curtains a few inches. The fire danced in the grate, and the candles flickered.

"Eliza, are you saying you gamble to get my attention?"

"Do you carp at me for exceeding my budget just to remind me that I have a husband?"

His hold on her became more snug. "My dearest darling, I do believe we have been at cross purposes. I miss you too."

Thank God. Thank God, thank God, and thank Marcus for suggesting that Eliza seek her husband's help with the invitations.

"I am actually quite talented at whist," Eliza said, "and I don't really want a holiday decorator telling me what to do with our house. As to that, I'd rather nobody else hired Lady Mistletoe's Holiday Helpers."

"You will explain your reasoning to a poor, befuddled husband, please."

"You are not befuddled. Witness your ability to spot worthy investments. I don't want anybody else hiring Lady Mistletoe, because Marcus's decorations—and his open house—must be the talk of Mayfair. Lady Mistletoe has a reputation for doing exquisite work, and I will ensure Marcus's buffet is equally impressive. He will set the standard for holiday entertaining, see if he doesn't."

Ralph rose with Eliza in his arms and shifted to the sofa facing the fire. "You are scheming, my dear. Marcus will not thank you for meddling."

"I am not meddling, I am helping. Marcus has nobody else to aid him in his search for a wife. If the ladies aren't dazzled by his understated wit or rare smiles, they can at least be impressed with his holiday decorations."

"You are daft," Ralph said, nuzzling Eliza's throat. "Marcus is a dear fellow, but he has no charm, less wit, and his smile is more fleeting than summer lightning. I love how you smell right here," he said, pressing a cool nose to Eliza's throat. "Gives me ideas."

"We didn't lock the door, dearest."

"The staff would never intrude, and you used to like it when we didn't lock the door."

He kissed her right below her ear, and Eliza shivered, not with cold. "Do that again."

"Leave Marcus in peace, Eliza. Peace on earth and all that. He's gracious enough to host this open house, and you should be content with that."

Eliza was growing anything but content. As Ralph untied the ribbon of her décolletage, she made a mental note to tell Lady Stephanie Hambleton how expensive Lady Mistletoe's services were —*unbelievably exorbitant* would do. Her ladyship's penchant for exaggeration and gossip would do the rest, and Marcus—who had a lump of coal where his heart should be—would come across like Father Christmas determined to secure himself a bride by the New Year.

"Did you mean what you said about more children, Eliza?"

All thoughts of Marcus and holiday brides flew from her head. "Another child would be the most precious, wonderful, and dear Christmas present you could give me, Ralph. I mean that with my whole heart."

"Then I will devote my whole heart to ensuring your holiday wish is granted."

THE CAMPAIGN TO see Amanda and Emily settled into Marcus's house traversed an unexpected route, led by Charlotte and Lady Margaret, supported by Aunt Penny, and further advanced by a horde of ill-spoken urchins.

As evening approached, the children had taken over the library, where Marcus's footmen had passed out blankets, sandwiches, and other provisions suitable for Lady Mistletoe's minions. After darkness had fallen, and Aunt Penny had chivied Charlotte, Amanda, and Emily up to a well-heated nursery, Marcus found Lady Margaret at the library desk, trying to work by the light of a single candelabrum.

"They've sung themselves to sleep," Marcus said, stepping gingerly around a heap of blankets from which a mop of blond hair peeked. "I have never heard so much seasonal music, nor seen so much gingerbread disappear so quickly."

Lady Margaret sat back and rubbed her eyes. "They are good workers, and I am lucky to have them. They will need a substantial breakfast, and I would appreciate it if—assuming the weather obliges —you could send them on their way with a hot potato or at least some bread and butter when they leave."

Marcus peered at her ladyship's sketches. "You are working on plans for the gallery. Might the children start on that task rather than go trudging off through the snow first thing in the day?"

He could feed them breakfast and lunch that way and dispatch a few footmen to see that the youngest reached whatever destinations they needed to reach. Then too, London merchants would clear the walkways by midday, and the going would be easier for the children.

"We could make a start," Lady Margaret said. "I will need another hour or two finishing the plans, and you will have to approve them first thing in the morning. Has it stopped snowing?"

"Let's have a look, shall we? We can leave your elves to their deserved slumbers, and you can work in my office."

Where Marcus would light every blessed candle in the room for her, rather than see her toil in near darkness for the benefit of a dozen scamps and rapscallions.

"Go along, your ladyship," said a sleepy female voice. "I'll keep an eye on things here."

Lady Margaret rose and gathered up her papers. "Thank you, Daisy. I'll be across the corridor."

Marcus picked up the candelabrum and escorted her ladyship to the office.

"You must be ready to make an extended visit to your father's house," Lady Margaret said. "I have brought more upheaval to your doorstep than even I had foreseen." She sank into the chair behind his desk with a weary sigh.

Marcus passed her a pillow. "That chair belonged to my father. The seat could use restuffing."

When she'd situated the pillow to her satisfaction, he draped his old morning coat over her shoulders and went about lighting more candles.

"You need not cosset me," Lady Margaret said. "I am quite used to fending for myself."

He lit the candles on the mantel and set the candelabrum on the desk. "That is not exactly true, is it? You fend for your daughter, for a dozen cast-off children, and probably for the various seamstresses and merchants who supply your wares. I suspect that the very last person you fend for is yourself."

She sent him a peevish look. "Is that the pot calling the kettle black? You worry over your papa, you are guardian to your brother's daughters, you accommodate your sister's social schemes and even allow me to invade your home with cloved oranges and satin ribbons, but your own wishes and wants go unacknowledged."

He could not read her mood, but he knew very well how he'd like to end this interesting, challenging day.

"Not unacknowledged, but very often set aside for the sake of duty. I do have a wish I'd like to indulge, though, if your ladyship is willing."

Another look, more puzzled than peevish. "You have been beyond hospitable and accommodating, my lord. If your wish is within my power to grant, I am happy to do so."

Marcus twitched at the old coat, drawing it more closely about her shoulders. "You don't sound happy. You sound out of patience, ready to plant somebody a facer."

She wrinkled her nose, making her look very much like Charlotte. "I am out of charity with my brother. He has been much on my mind lately. I have conducted myself not as most widows do, with a view to my own discreet pleasures, but as if I were still unmarried and subject to Society's censure. Society has all but forgotten me, so whose favor am I trying to win with my saintly behavior? I have already stepped over the threshold of strict propriety by engaging in trade, or something close to it. I have no wealth, no youth, no influence, nothing Society values, and yet the good opinion of strangers has bounded my every thought and word."

"And this brings your brother to mind?"

"Lucien is hopelessly proper, and I will never please him. Not ever. A mistake made in good faith years ago has condemned me in his eyes for all time."

Marcus knew her brother only in passing, and the earl did seem rather stuffy. "Have you forgiven yourself for this supposed lapse?"

Lady Margaret's smile was a blend of a cat in the cream pot and a queen holding court. "I *have* forgiven myself, at long last, and no thanks to my dear brother. I also know what holiday boon I'd ask from you, my lord."

"Not another rehearsal of King Wenceslas's saintly tale, please, my lady. I am the servant of duty at all times, but another rendering of that song will propel me to the outer reaches of either martyrdom or imbecility."

Her ladyship rose, Marcus's coat draped over her shoulders. "I would like another kiss, my lord. A passionate, lovely, wonderful kiss, freely given, freely shared. Not duty. The furthest thing from duty. I know your sister seeks to find you a bride, and I wish you the joy of that undertaking, but first, I'd like a little discreet joy for myself—if you are willing."

If he was willing? *Willing?* Of course he was willing, though something in her ladyship's admission wanted more discussion.

Later. Later, they could discuss everything from kissing boughs to meddling family to the royal succession.

"The wish I was hoping you'd grant, my lady, is another kiss." He drew her forward by grasping the lapels of his old coat. "A kiss freely shared between adults of like minds and willing bodies."

She went up on her toes and pressed her mouth to his. "Passionate bodies, please. I'd like a passionate kiss, as passionate as our first kiss."

Oh, Marcus could do much better than the little moment they'd shared the previous night. Much. He got a firm hold of her and sat her on the edge of the desk, then stepped between her knees.

"Hold on to me," he whispered. "Please, hold on to me tightly."

He kissed her with all the longing and wildness he never acknowledged, all the determination and joy he could muster. She kissed him back, answering him taste for taste and sigh for sigh, her hands plundering his person and his wits. Marcus felt as if he were London on Christmas morning, the church bells pealing wildly as blinding sunshine poured down on pristine snow, every street corner filled with song.

"I have changed my mind," Lady Margaret panted, her forehead resting against his chest. "My wishes are no longer limited to your kisses."

Desire rendered Marcus stupid, but he eventually parsed her words into something like sense. "What would you have of me, your ladyship?"

She twined her arms about his neck and put her lips near his ear. "Everything. Tonight, I would have everything of you."

She wrapped her legs around Marcus's hips and drew him nearer, then tucked herself so close to him his arousal had to be obvious to her.

"Everything, Margaret?"

"All forty verses," she said, "and then a complete rendition of *In Dulci Jubilo* too."

In sweet rejoicing... "I know that tune," Marcus said, stepping away to lock the door. "It has ever been one of my favorites."

"Then perhaps we'll sing it more than once."

He vowed then and there to make sure she had cause for sweet rejoicing at least three times before they left the office.

MEG HAD INSISTED that Lord Marcus bring nothing of duty to this stolen moment. For herself, she'd bring nothing of shame. She had conducted herself more properly as a widow than she had as a girl or a wife, and years of lonely propriety weren't enough to appease Lucien and others like him. She had done her best as a mother, done her best for her clients, and for once—for one precious hour—she would have who and what she pleased.

Thanks be to whatever kind powers looked after tired widows, Marcus Bannerfield was of the same mind as she was. He locked the door with a quiet, decisive *snick* and shrugged out of his coat.

"The house is abed," he said. "We will not be disturbed. Will you join me on the couch?"

"Yes." Though now that the adventure had begun, Meg had no idea how to proceed. The couch was well cushioned, but what did one do with one's clothing? She had knotted off her stays in front, but she had been married long enough to know disrobing wasn't critical to the endeavor.

Marcus settled in the middle of the sofa and patted the place beside him. "Sweet rejoicing requires a certain proximity, Margaret."

She approached, then hesitated as Marcus began unbuttoning his falls. "How does one—how do we... go about this?"

"Enthusiastically, I hope." He took her wrist in a warm grip. "However we please. You can straddle my lap, we can find a handy place against the wall. The desk is about the right height, or we can use the couch to make the beastie with two backs."

She had no earthly idea what he was talking about, though straddling his lap—upon reflection—had possibilities.

"You will think me woefully unworldly."

"I think your late husband woefully inconsiderate and more than a bit dull. Kiss me, Margaret."

Peter *had* been dull—honesty was not the same thing as speaking ill of the dead—*and* woefully inconsiderate. As inconsiderate as he'd been handsome. Exceedingly inconsiderate.

Meg bent down and kissed her lover on the mouth. Marcus was not strikingly handsome, but he was attractive. What a pity she'd not grasped the distinction years ago.

He brushed his thumb over the inside of her wrist. "Are you wearing drawers, Lady Margaret?"

She was abruptly wearing a heated blush. "I am. In bitter weather, drawers are sensible."

"I can assure you, this office is about to grow quite warm, my lady."

What had that to do with—? *Oh.* Meg turned her back, fussed with her skirts, and stepped out of her drawers. She folded them and laid them on the desk, feeling ridiculous for doing so. What sort of merry widow folded her drawers before disporting with a willing bachelor?

When she turned back to the couch, Marcus tossed her his cravat.

He'd undone his falls, unbuttoned his shirt, and removed his neckcloth. The picture he made by candlelight was decadent, naughty, and male in a way that made Meg long for a bed—and for more candles.

"Come here, Margaret, and rejoice sweetly with me." He held out his hand, and Meg managed to straddle his lap without too much awkwardness.

"Closer," he whispered, kissing the corner of her mouth.

By patient, stealthy degrees, Marcus kissed and caressed her until she was kissing him back, and little problems like what to do about clothing faded beneath a rising tide of pleasure. Marcus Bannerfield knew what to do with his hands, with his mouth, with soft words.

Meg shifted closer and came up against incontrovertible evidence of masculine desire.

"Don't be shy," Marcus whispered. "I want you, and I hope you want me too."

Shyness beat a hasty retreat as desire advanced. Meg took her courage in one hand and Marcus in the other and sank down upon him in one slow, sweet slide. The moment was like homecoming and wonder and wishes coming true, all at once.

The physical sensations were exquisite, the emotions more complicated. This joining had a little bit of anger in it, a fist raised to all who would condemn a woman for putting her trust in the wrong man, while society regarded the man as a hero unfairly distracted from his battles.

But the anger was faded and worn, while the gratitude—for *this* man, for this moment—was sincere. Affection was part of lovemaking, as was trust, generosity, courage... Meg had forgotten that, and the reminders Marcus shared with her were lovely.

A delicate brush of his fingers along her cheek, kisses pressed to her brow, a quiet pause in the dance toward mutual gratification. Each pleasure and consideration brought both physical closeness and a closeness of the heart that Meg had been yearning for without knowing it.

"A moment," Marcus breathed, his hands on Meg's hips. "Please... just... give me a moment."

Meg took that still moment for herself, to revel in the warmth of Marcus's hands, the perfection of their joined bodies, the quiet and peace all around them, and the combination of circumstances that had brought them to this shared intimacy.

Tomorrow, she would return to her chilly little rooms and her chilly little worries. She would face again the question Lucien had posed and choose between hard options. Tonight, she would marvel at the pleasure and joy to be had despite all the troubles and disappointments.

"I want to move," she said, giving an experimental little flex of her hips.

"Slowly, please."

She went slowly, then not slowly at all, and she might have heard Marcus laughing softly, but she couldn't be sure because her ears were roaring and her body was a conflagration of raptures and longing. He held her through it all—all three times—until she was boneless, replete, and half asleep on his shoulder.

"Again?" he asked, moving lazily beneath her.

"I cannot."

His fingers glided around the undersides of her breasts, which some helpful fellow had freed from her stays. "That's what you said last time."

"Wretch." But what a luscious, considerate wretch Marcus was. Regret threatened to steal the joy from the moment, because he was not *her* wretch.

"Are you sure?" he asked.

Meg forced the gears of her mind to turn and realized what he was asking. "You have not found your pleasure yet."

"I will withdraw first."

She nibbled on the muscle wrapping his shoulder. "In public you exude all manner of propriety, but lock the door and you become lusty and plainspoken."

"The same might be said of you, Margaret, though I hope we both go on fooling the world."

Meg did not want to part from him, did not want to leave his embrace or embark on the fooling-the-world part, but she would fall asleep if she did not rise. With Marcus's assistance, she gained her feet, feeling tipsy with lassitude and tenderness.

She leaned against the desk as Marcus fished a handkerchief from his pocket and brought himself to completion in a few lazy, wanton strokes. The whole time, he looked into her eyes, never once breaking her gaze. In some way, that experience was as intimate as what had gone before and nearly as erotic.

I have learned more about true intimacy in the past hour than I learned in years of marriage. The realization was a little sad, but not wholly so. Meg was in Lord Marcus Bannerfield's debt, for making her feel desired and cherished, for showing her what marital intimacy could have been.

The courage to seize this opportunity, to embrace this risk, had been all hers, though, and she took satisfaction from that. A lot of satisfaction.

Marcus stood to tuck in his shirt-tails and button his falls, then he assisted Meg with her stays. While she got her drawers sorted out, he fashioned a knot for his cravat, until they were once again properly attired.

"I feel as if I have restored order on the outside," Meg said, holding his coat for him, "but as if I will be forever changed on the inside."

He left his coat unbuttoned and wrapped her in his arms. "You honor me with such honesty, Margaret."

His embrace was secure and dear, an unlooked-for pleasure in the coldest season of the year. The office was quiet, the fire having burned down to embers. The wind had dropped as well, and Meg left her lover's embrace to go to the window.

"The snow has stopped." Moonlight shone on a wonderland of pale shadows and white drifts. "I will make my way home tomorrow."

Marcus's arms encircled her. "I don't want you to go."

"Thank you for that." Meg did not remind him that she'd be back to finish his decorations, and did not offer to stay. A stolen pleasure could forever be only that, and she would always treasure this one, but she wasn't foolish enough to wish it could be more.

"YOU WILL NOT RECOGNIZE my house, Papa," Marcus said, giving his eggnog a stir. "*I don't recognize the house.*" A sedate, even drab dwelling had become a place of light, grace, and sweet scents. Lady Margaret had worked a special brand of holiday magic, though as far as Marcus was concerned, she'd taken the real sparkle with her when she'd departed four days ago.

"The girls have turned it all topsy-turvy, I take it?" The marquess had a robe over his knees, despite the fact that the fire in his family parlor was—on Marcus's orders—kept roaring, as were the fires elsewhere in the house. What mattered the cost of coal when an old man's joints ached?

"Emily and Amanda are settling in comfortably, and the staff does seem livelier for having children on hand." This was not entirely true. Amanda and Emily were making the adjustment to a new home, but they asked repeatedly about when Charlotte Entwhistle could come to play with them. Then too, the staff loved the decorations.

"Noisy business, children," the marquess said, twitching at his lap blanket. "Eliza could make more fuss than you and Simon together."

"You miss him," Marcus said, because this was the first mention Papa had made of his departed firstborn since Simon's funeral.

"Simon was always quite busy, always preoccupied with the estate, the children, his darling wife. I actually didn't see that much of your brother unless you were home on leave. Then he troubled himself to look in on me more often, but that's as it should be. Children grow up and take on the world, in their turn, and old people applaud from their armchairs."

The eggnog was good—rich and spicy—but the eggnog recipe Lady Margaret had given Marcus's cook was better.

"Will you bestir yourself to come to my open house?"

Papa made a face. "Eliza and her socializing. I expected Ralph to do a better job of taking his wife in hand. What is the point of an open house at the holidays, I ask you? Half of Town has gone to the country, the other half has plenty of opportunity to rub shoulders during the little Season or at the clubs. The weather turns up most foul, and we demand more socializing of each other. Your mother loved the holidays, but I..."

"You miss her too." Why hadn't Marcus realized that this time of year would be especially hard on a man carrying multiple griefs?

"I miss her every day, my boy." A slight smile appeared. "And many nights."

I want Lady Margaret to miss me like that, as I already miss her. Lady Margaret apparently wanted something else entirely.

"Papa, what do you know of a Major Peter Entwhistle, son of Elijah Entwhistle?"

"Of the Hampshire Entwhistles? Entwhistle Acres?"

"The same." Marcus had used military connections to find out that much.

"Elijah is a decent sort. He's done quite well with wool in recent years. Spent time with the Company in India and did very well for himself there too. He also did a stint in the Commons, and our paths occasionally crossed when the farm bills or tariffs were under discussion."

A decent sort. Did Elijah Entwhistle know that his granddaughter needed new boots? Aunt Penny had passed that fact along in the middle of a pointed lecture about men who lacked the sense God gave a head-injured goat.

"And what of Lucien, Earl of Webberly?"

"I don't know him well. I have no reason to like or dislike him, but he did have the great misfortune to marry one of Piety Parmenter's puritans."

"I beg your pardon?"

"War is a terrible thing, but at least your years away spared you the more ridiculous gossip. Lady Ursula Upcraft, daughter of the Earl of Monteith, married John Parmenter, a younger son of the Viscount Halloway. Lady Ursula is obnoxiously Christian, if I might say that without offending the Deity. Always blessing everybody and exhorting one and all to pray about everything. Goes into near hysterics on the topic of foundlings and fallen women."

Papa gazed at the fire as if looking into the past. "One could not offer a common complaint to the woman—about gout, bad weather, Mad George—without her returning a sermon on suffering drawing us closer to the Almighty. Meanwhile, she was hell to work for. When Parmenter inherited the title, she got appointed to half the charitable societies in London, but never seemed to be able to locate her purse when those charities were taking donations. Parmenter— Halloway, rather—died about ten years ago, having drawn closer not to the Lord, but to the brandy bottle, poor fellow."

"And the Earl of Webberly married into this family?"

"Halloway had a head for business. He left his three daughters, dubbed Parmenter's puritans, very well dowered. Exceedingly well dowered. Nobody could blame Webberly for marrying one of them, but I doubt the man's existence has been pleasant. In my day, a bloviating hypocrite like Lady Halloway would have been scorned for the devil's imp that she is. Such is the power of her money these days that she regularly entertains bishops. Her daughters apparently aspire to wield the same sort of power upon their mama's passing and are busily out-praying each other as loudly and humbly as may be."

The tale Papa told was far from lively, but the telling of it had put some color in his cheeks and some life in his voice.

"And what of the Webberly daughter? Lady Margaret?" Marcus was careful to pose the question casually.

"She married Entwhistle's wastrel son, who got a bastard on her, then married her very nearly at the end of his father's fowling piece. Your mother said she seemed a sweet girl, but she'd be widowed by now. She's doubtless living quietly on remittance in some cottage of her brother's."

No, she is not. "She did my holiday decorations. You must come to my open house to have a look."

Papa left off studying the fire to turn a keen gaze on Marcus. "She *did your decorations*? Whatever does that mean?"

"You are worse than Aunt Penny. I mean exactly what I said: My home has been exquisitely decorated for the holidays by Lady Margaret Entwhistle, who charges a fee for providing that service. Her taste is impeccable and her work nothing short of beautiful." Not as beautiful as Lady Margaret overcome by passion, but beautiful nonetheless.

"You hired a decorator. I suppose Eliza had a hand in this nonsense?"

"She wanted the house to present well for holiday entertaining." That Eliza had dissembled regarding her motivations was not relevant to the present topic.

One corner of Papa's mouth kicked up. "She wanted you to pay for the entertainments and these lavish decorations, wanted your staff run off its feet. Eliza is very much her mother's daughter, though she lacks her mama's subtlety. I don't suppose Penny Hennepin will attend this gathering?"

"Aunt Penny has informed me, with no less than three thumps of her cane, that she would not miss that open house for all the rum punch in London."

"That is not a cane she carries, my boy, that is a royal scepter-cum-cudgel-to-the-conscience. One crosses dear Penelope at one's peril. Has spirit, she does."

And she apparently had Papa's respect, the first woman to claim that honor other than Mama.

"Perhaps you'd be willing to escort Aunt Penny to my open house? Eliza and Hennepin will doubtless arrive early to inspect my preparations."

Papa's smile faded, and the animation left his gaze. "I really have no use for the social whirl anymore, Marcus. That's for you young people."

In the days since Marcus had last seen Margaret, he'd found himself frequently consulting her in memory. What would she say to such a declaration of defeat?

"Then you abandon your granddaughters at a time when they need allies badly. Everything Amanda and Emily face these days is new and strange. Their nursery staff from Sussex has abandoned them, they have no friends in the area, most of their treasured possessions remain back at Innisborough Hall. They are grieving as we are, Papa, with only my clumsy efforts to comfort them."

And Aunt Penny's. She'd called twice in the past week, bringing books and privately threatening Marcus to find the girls a puppy.

"I'm sure you'll manage well enough. Keep them warm and fed, praise any schoolroom effort made in good faith, chide them away from selfish thinking. They'll come right."

"They have asked after you, asked if you are very busy in the Lords, and if you have to meet with the king."

Papa folded the blanket over his knees and set it aside. "A telling shot, Marcus. Worthy of your mother."

"Will you come?"

"Will the Entwhistle woman be there?"

In the Bannerfield family, clever intuition had always been attributed to Mama, but occasionally, Papa tipped his hand. He paid attention to his family, or he had before Mama's death.

"I fear Lady Margaret will not make an appearance. She regards the circumstances of her daughter's birth as a blight on the family honor and does not socialize. I have the sense she conducts this decorating business because her brother refuses to support her."

Papa pushed out of his chair with surprising vigor. "That is the most imbecilic thing I have heard short of inviting the Corsican to take up residence in Paris. Half the heirs in the peerage arrive in the nursery less than nine months after their parents' wedding, our Simon being a case in point. In my day, we knew enough to overlook such minor lapses. Of all the ridiculous vanities... but my day is past."

Mama's portrait hung above the mantel. The marchioness

seemed to be smiling at Marcus, or perhaps offering him encouragement. "Is that what Penelope Hennepin would say, Papa? That her
day is past, so she'll sit about in a Bath chair, slurping porridge, and
letting young people blunder on without any guidance from wiser
heads?"

Papa said nothing for a moment, then turned a glare on Marcus.
"Penelope and your dear mama would say, as *I* say, that you are a
rude and disrespectful puppy who'd best recall his manners."

Ah, there was the marquess who'd offered thundering speeches
in the Lords, captured the heart of the fairest belle, and raised his
sons to be honorable gentlemen.

"I am a puppy in love, Papa. Lady Margaret swept into my house,
hung cloved oranges in every window, draped my prized busts of
Aristotle and Plato with greenery, and made off with my heart. I went
to war and never saw such plundering of a man's sanity as she
effected on my wits."

Marcus hadn't meant to say any of that. He was the heir now, the
prop and stay upon whom his father and sister could always lean, the
guardian of orphaned nieces and keeper of the family exchequer.

He was not a puppy of any variety.

Papa's glare remained fixed, then a short, loud sound came from
him. "About damned time somebody made off with your wits, lad.
Bannerfields are late to lose their hearts, but when we fall, we fall
hard and well. I gather her ladyship is leading you a dance?"

"Must you sound so approving?"

"Yes." Papa settled back into his chair and helped himself to
Marcus's eggnog. "Your mother tied me in knots and had a merry
time doing it. That lamentable behavior persisted after we spoke our
vows, but I learned to tie a few knots myself."

"Lady Margaret treasures her independence, Papa. She has had
every opportunity to pay several calls on me as the decorating has
progressed in the past few days, and she has instead sent minions and
junior officers. The results are lovely, but I don't care for pretty decorations half so much as I long to see her ladyship."

How callow that sounded, how... human.

"Perhaps it's time you paid a call on her, Marcus. A lady likes to be courted."

Pay a call on her where? Marcus's coachman had reported that her ladyship and the young miss had got out at a street corner in a neighborhood of shops. Their rooms could be anywhere, and Lady Mistletoe's correspondence referenced only a posting inn in that same neighborhood.

"I don't know how to find her, Papa, but when the decorations come down, I can ask her second-in-command." Though, would a mere request compel Miss Daisy to convey Margaret's whereabouts? Marcus could not pin his hopes on that possibility.

"On second thought," Papa said, "I believe I will attend this little gathering. Warn my grandchildren to be on their best behavior."

Marcus offered his father his hand. "I will do no such thing. I'm off to call on Aunt Penny. If for any reason, I should fail to return from that mission, you will host my open house, sir."

Papa's handshake was firm, and his eye held a twinkle. "Give Miss Penelope my regards. Good luck, son."

Marcus departed, keeping his reply to himself: *I will apparently need it.*

CHAPTER SEVEN

"But, Mama, why can't I send Emily and Amanda a note? Families correspond at the holidays. Aunt Evelyn wrote to us, and you said I must send greetings to my cousins." Charlotte paused in her sketching to send Meg a predictable pleading look.

Charlotte's knee had healed. Meg's nerves were deteriorating apace. "Amanda and Emily are not family. I commend your generosity of spirit, Charlotte, but we must not assume undue familiarity."

Charlotte set aside her sketch and went to the window. "The snow has melted. We could pay a call on them."

"Children do not make social calls in polite neighborhoods." Oh, how that waspish note in Meg's voice horrified her. "I'm sorry, Charlotte. I don't mean to be a bear, but there are rules about such things, and those rules are sometimes difficult to observe."

Charlotte wandered over to Meg's desk. "You are sending out a lot of letters, but you aren't receiving any, except from Aunt Evelyn."

The countess had written to inquire whether Charlotte would be joining her aunt and uncle when they repaired to Webberly Hall in a week's time. Evelyn hadn't included good wishes for the holidays, hadn't inquired about Meg's well-being, hadn't invited Meg to spend *her* holidays at the family seat.

"I have every confidence that this afternoon's post will bring more requests for estimates," Meg said. "The weather has doubtless distracted people from their decorating." The weather had been sunny enough to melt the snow into a dirty slush that froze at sundown. Ice slicked with melting snow made the streets treacherous, though Meg would have gladly braved a blizzard to answer a summons from a customer.

She had half expected, half dreaded a summons from Lord Marcus Bannerfield, but none had arrived. Daisy reported that his lordship's home was in great good looks, Meg's decorating schemes having brought out all the house's best features and—as was usually the case when a job turned out well—putting the staff in a fine humor.

"Can we go to Lord Marcus's open house?" Charlotte asked, twiddling Meg's pen. "Amanda and Emily will be there."

"May we," Meg said, "but no, we may not. We haven't been invited." Thank heavens. As much as Meg longed to see Marcus again, to hear his voice, to... spend time with him, she knew that wish was ill-fated. He must take a wife, despite his protestations, and she must provide for her daughter, or reconcile herself to allowing Lucien to do that.

"That's the mail!" Charlotte bellowed as a tap sounded on the door. She flung open the door to find the grocer's boy, red-cheeked and out of breath, on the other side.

"Fetch George a biscuit, Charlotte," Meg said, going to the door. "George, what do you have for us today?"

"Just this, my lady." He passed over two sealed pieces of paper. "Papa said to tell you we'll be getting in more greenery on Friday."

"Thank you, George. I'll tell the children." Lady Mistletoe's Holiday Helpers would fashion that greenery into wreaths, swags, kissing boughs, and other more profitable products. Their pay would be modest, but they would spend the day in the warmth of the grocer's stable and take home blemished produce and an apple or an orange, if they worked quickly.

George went on his way, his cheeks bulging with the last of the biscuits Lord Marcus's cook had sent home with Meg. The ham was nearly gone, and the tea wouldn't last another week.

"Do we have projects, Mama?" Charlotte asked, brushing crumbs from her pinafore.

Meg slit open the first epistle and found a stilted rejection of her services. The second was more direct. A loyal customer in years past had simply scrawled *not this year* across Meg's polite inquiry. Almost all of her regular customers were declining to hire her this year, with the exception of a few widows and cits who did not circulate much in Society.

Lord Marcus's project had inspired in Meg such hope—maybe the better neighborhoods and wealthier homes had noticed her work, maybe her business was poised to grow. In the past few days, that hope had been dashed into small pieces.

Meg returned to the lumpy chair behind her desk. "Charlotte, how would you feel about spending some time at Webberly Hall?"

Charlotte bounced onto the sofa and took up her pencil and sketch pad. "I would not like that at all, Mama. The Hall is cold, everybody pulls my hair there, and we are always praying until our knees scream. Let's not go to the Hall."

Another rap on the door had Charlotte bounding off the couch. "It's George again!" she bellowed, quite unnecessarily.

"I found two more for you," George said, passing over sealed letters. "Sorry about that." He tarried in the doorway, letting out the heat and doubtless hoping to earn another biscuit.

"You ate the last biscuit, George, or I'd offer you another."

He tugged his forelock, grinned, and went whistling down the steps, while Meg slit open another letter.

"Is it a project, Mama?"

"No." Another *not this year*. Lord Marcus had paid Meg in full, and that sum would last a little while, but then what? If holiday decorating had gone out of fashion, or some other service was having more success with Meg's customers, Meg and those who depended on her were out of business.

"And the children will need what money I have," she murmured.

"Beg pardon, Mama?"

"Just talking to myself," Meg said. She took the last letter to her desk, for the seal was crested, and she'd seen the same handwriting on documents at Lord Marcus's desk. An invitation lay within, for Lady Margaret, Miss Charlotte, *and friends* to attend an open house hosted by Lord Marcus Bannerfield and family. The favor of a reply was requested.

Across the bottom, in a tidy hand, somebody had added, *Please come. I miss you. M.*

I miss you too. I will always miss you. Meg considered the invitation for a long while as the fire burned down in the grate and Charlotte sat sketching on the sofa.

When the task could be put off no longer, Meg penned short, unremarkable regrets. Nothing could come of a liaison between a disgraced widow and an eligible bachelor, nothing but further tarnish on Meg's reputation. Lucien would demand guardianship of Charlotte in that case, and Meg would have to acquiesce.

She sealed her reply and tossed the invitation on the coals in the hearth.

"Is that another estimate, Mama?"

"No," Meg said, watching the heat curl the edge of the invitation. At the last moment, she tried to snatch the paper free of the flames, but she'd waited too late, and the only tangible link she had to the man who'd stolen her heart burned to ashes.

"THIS IS MARVELOUS," Eliza cooed, bussing Marcus's cheek.

"Even better than I had planned. Where did you find that children's chorus?"

The children were out of sight, on the foyer's mezzanine, under the watchful direction of Miss Daisy. Marcus had negotiated with her directly, but no amount of coin or cajoling could pry Lady Margaret's direction from her.

"Lady Mistletoe supplied the chorus," Marcus said, raising his voice as if to be heard over the buzz of goggling, gossiping guests and the cheerful din from the mezzanine. "Just as she provided the decorations, provided the recipes for the punch, and chose the musical selections." Daisy had selected the songs, based on her ladyship's typical choices.

"More guests," Eliza said, taking Marcus by the arm. "Do try to smile, your lordship."

"Your husband is smiling," Marcus retorted. Hennepin had appointed himself Lord of the Punchbowl, and every time Marcus glanced that direction, Ralph was toasting Eliza from across the room.

"I am smiling too," Eliza said. "We received almost no regrets."

So where is Lady Margaret? Marcus was surprised to find no less luminary than the Earl of Webberly handing his hat to Nicholas, while Lady Webberly passed her cloak to a maid.

"My lord, my lady, welcome and Happy Christmas." Marcus bowed over the countess's hand. "I believe you know my sister." The introductions proceeded along the usual lines, then Eliza drew the countess away, insisting that her ladyship would adore the decorations in the gallery.

"Perhaps you would like to see what Lady Margaret has done with the gallery as well, my lord," Marcus said.

Webberly's smile was strained. "Not too loudly, please. Margaret's little projects are something of an embarrassment."

"Little projects?" Marcus made himself take a visual inventory of the foyer, which had never looked as festive, nor smelled as luscious. Cinnamon, clove, citrus, and nutmeg perfumed the air, from cloved oranges, sachets, and discreetly placed scent pots. The bannisters were wrapped in spirals of red, green, and gold ribbon, and the statues and portraits wore garlands of holly. On the sideboard and in each of the foyer's deep windows stood a small evergreen adorned in the German tradition with red bows and delicate beeswax candles.

Four different kissing boughs hung from the central chandelier and had already occasioned much merriment. The parlors had been kitted out in the same finery, and the gallery was a work of art.

"My sister is stubborn," Lord Webberly muttered. "Pride is a sin, and in this case, the fall has already occurred. That is rather a lot of mistletoe."

His expression suggested any mistletoe was too much. "You disapprove of tradition?" Marcus asked.

"I disapprove of licentious behavior, my lord. My countess and I look the other way regarding a bit of frivolity in the servants' hall, but our own seasonal joy is solemn and sincere in nature."

What a dreary old stick, though Marcus doubted Webberly was much past thirty years of age. "And what of your sister? Do you include her in your seasonal joy?"

Webberly looked pained as a blushing young lady planted a kiss on the cheek of a smiling swain.

"Why the interest in my sister, my lord?" He moved to the edge of the foyer. "Margaret lives a life of quiet obscurity, for the most part. If she has provided decorating services to your satisfaction, then no more need be said on the matter."

"Ah, so your sincere seasonal joy doesn't include gathering with family *or* respecting tradition. I am remiss as a host to keep you standing here admiring my decorations. Surely a cup of Lady Margaret's punch can find its way past your prejudices?"

"Good God, you mean to tell me she's handing out recipes for punch now?"

Marcus led his guest down the corridor, the sconces on each side positioned within fragrant wreaths. Kissing boughs hung at regular intervals, and the usual lace table runners had been replaced with red and green quilted fabrics. Guests stood about with plates and cups of punch, and the music from the foyer added to the holiday air.

Marcus stopped outside the gallery doors. "Lady Margaret hands out recipes for punch, for gingerbread, for Christmas pudding. She fashioned the little sprigs of holly you see on the footmen's livery. She rehearses the choir, she makes the kissing boughs. She personally selects the spices that make up those luscious sachets, and she employs the least among us—orphans, climbing boys, foundlings—to carry out her work. In my opinion, Webberly, Lady Margaret Entwhistle has a far more sincere grasp of what the holidays should be about than your sniffy, condescending lordship can even fathom."

Webberly drew himself up like a strutting pigeon. "I would see satisfaction for those insults, Bannerfield, but you are apparently not yet acquainted with the details of Lady Margaret's introduction to motherhood. She has brought shame upon her family, and all her little mercantile ventures, however prettily they dazzle you and the rest of Society, cannot atone for the fact that my niece can never claim legitimacy."

The children had launched into a hushed version of *Jubilate Deo*, so Marcus hardly had to raise his voice to be heard over them.

"*You pathetic, posturing, pompous, prosing hypocrite.* Your own parents anticipated their vows, but I am willing to bet my Town coach you never once castigated them for that lapse. You never looked down on your dear mama, never considered her behavior a blight on the family escutcheon. You reserve your contempt for your own sister—who tells me you yourself introduced her to Entwhistle— and yet you have the effrontery to call yourself a Christian."

In the silence that followed, Webberly's hauteur faltered, then dissolved into panic. The two footmen positioned on either side of the gallery doors exchanged an equally fraught gaze and then, for reasons Marcus would never understand, swung open the double doors and stood at attention.

Gracious everlasting angels, the entire room was facing the doorway, not a single person making a sound. Expressions ranged from shocked, to blank, to gleeful, to worried.

"I beg you," Webberly muttered, "not another word."

Aunt Penny had passed along her recollections regarding Webberly's parents. Marcus now knew her speculations in other regards were accurate as well.

"You either lavishly admire your sister's work," Marcus replied quietly, "and sing her praises until we're tired of hearing them, or I will mention that you and your countess *also* anticipated your vows." A fact Aunt Penny had confirmed with reassuring certainty. "Explain to your lady wife that her days of making Margaret's life difficult are over as well, and find the courage to apologize to your sister for having abandoned all honor where she is concerned."

Webberly nodded once, took a slow breath, then sauntered into the gallery. He stopped two yards inside the doors, his gaze tipped up.

"Margaret did this?" The amazement was genuine, as Marcus's had been. "Margaret and those... *those urchins?*"

"Every bit of it," Marcus said, taking in again the heady scent of greenery crisscrossing overhead and the myriad candles in their brass-backed holders. A red runner ran down the center of the room, and red and gold ribbons laced the pine boughs looping from the ceiling. Margaret had also draped greenery at the windows, suspended bunches of mistletoe among the swagging, and hung delicate golden bells on ribbons from the pine roping as well.

The effect was magical, turning a staid, chilly gallery into a medieval banquet hall full of merriment, beauty, light, and warmth.

Aunt Penny caught Marcus's eye. Papa stood beside her, his expression alert and watchful.

Do something, they seemed to be saying. *Do something right, whether duty demands it or not.* Marcus took a glass from the nearest footman's tray and held the drink aloft.

"To good friends, to family, and to Lady Margaret Entwhistle's phenomenal talent!"

Aunt Penny beamed at him, Papa clapped heartily, and Eliza and Ralph took up the applause. Webberly was forced to join in, and he did so, gaze turned upward, as if nobody had ever shown the poor man how to properly decorate for the holiday season.

And yet, for Marcus, the holidays would not truly begin until he'd offered a token to the woman who'd filled his home with warmth, laughter, and kindness. He worked his way through the smiling throng of neighbors and friends until he found Eliza under a kissing bough with her husband.

"Hennepin, is this done?" Marcus asked. "To kiss your spouse under the mistletoe?"

"It's done," Eliza replied, "and done quite well. Your open house will be the talk of the holidays, Marcus. Lady Margaret will have more custom than she knows what to do with."

Hennepin looked like he was about to say something, but Eliza kissed her husband *again*.

"You mentioned that we hadn't received many regrets," Marcus said. "Where are they?"

"In your office, left-hand drawer of your desk. I'd knock—loudly—before you go in there."

"It's my own damned office, Eliza. Why should I knock?"

"Because," Eliza said, leaning close enough to pat Marcus's lapel, "I saw Miss Davina Andrews-Clapshot ducking in there, and five minutes later, she was joined by a certain young gentleman whose papa is a duke."

"And you will take credit for bringing them together."

"As I should."

"You should also make my excuses to the guests if I have to step out," Marcus said. "Be particularly kind to Webberly. He's had a shock."

Hennepin laced an arm around Eliza's waist. "About damned time somebody hauled him and his holier-than-the-archbishop countess up short. Well done, my lord."

Eliza cuddled closer to her husband, proving that Lady

Margaret's punch must truly have magical qualities. "Where are you off to, Marcus?"

"I must step out to offer a holiday gift to a deserving party." He bowed before Eliza could ask yet another question, but the only thing he heard as he stepped away was his sister giggling, for the first time in years.

A TAP on Meg's door of late brought a sense of sinking hope, but it was too late in the day for George to be delivering yet another disappointing missive.

"I'll get it," Charlotte bellowed, and Meg's spirits sank yet another foot. At Webberly Hall, Charlotte would have to learn to never raise her voice. She would learn that servants opened doors, and little girls walked through those doors in ladylike silence. She would learn never to dash about, never to hum to herself as she sketched.

And because of that, because of all of that and so much more, Meg could not allow Charlotte to face a return to the family seat alone.

"Emily!" Charlotte squealed. "Manda! You came! I wished and wished and wished. I drew you a picture of the foyer, and I added angels and everything. Greetings, your lordship." She bobbed a curtsey more enthusiastic than refined, and Meg's heart did a somersault.

"Lord Marcus, welcome. This is quite an honor."

"Quite a shock, you mean. Might we come in?" He led the girls into Meg's modest parlor before Meg could make up some tale about needing to go out on urgent business.

"Daisy finally took pity on me," he said. "She allowed as how you lived above the bookbinder's in Kringle Lane. You will give the girl a raise, please."

Meg's parlor, small by any standards, was dwarfed by Lord

Marcus's height, particularly when he wore a top hat. His fine three-caped coat made her all the more aware of her worn carpet, shabby pillows, and threadbare curtains.

"May I take your hat, your lordship?"

He passed it to her and ran his hand through his hair. "I have come here for a purpose."

That sounded like the Lord Marcus who'd wanted an estimate the same day Meg had toured his home, the Lord Marcus who believed wholly in duty and did not suffer fools.

The little girls ducked into Charlotte's room, and Meg wished she hadn't been free with the biscuits where young George was concerned.

"I can put the kettle on," she said, setting his lordship's hat on the deal table by the door, "but isn't your open house today?" The children had been rehearsing their carols all week long, even as they'd fashioned their boughs and wreaths for the green grocer.

"My open house is today, but Eliza and her husband have all in hand. I'm afraid I was rather rude to your brother."

"You weren't." Meg had spent most of the day drafting an epistle to Lucien, accepting his offer to provide a home for Charlotte, but if and only if Meg was welcome to dwell with her daughter. Charlotte had a mother who loved her, and separating the girl from that mother —her only surviving parent—would be an unnecessary cruelty.

"I rather was," Lord Marcus said, unbuttoning his coat one-handed. "The blighter had it coming. Your sister-in-law was spared my wrath because I was more interested in finding my way to your side."

Meg took his coat and hung it on a peg beside the door. "You've found me." And oh, the joy and pain of seeing him again, of hearing his voice, of realizing that her desire for this man eclipsed a mere holiday frolic, a stolen moment.

She was in love with Marcus Bannerfield, more fool her. Not infatuated, not impressed with his physique, but in love with the whole person. Impatience, honor, humor, family loyalty... *kisses.*

"If the decorations are too much," Meg said, "I can have the children take them down before Christmas. They need the work, in fact, and I—"

"Take them down?" Lord Marcus advanced on her. "Take down those beautiful decorations before Christmas has arrived? Have you been sampling the punch, Margaret?"

He smelled like Christmas, all piney and spicy. Meg backed up a step lest she *sniff* him. "I have not taken leave of my senses, but I will soon leave London. I am prepared to throw myself on my brother's mercy, for all of my customers, or almost all of them, are apparently no longer interested in my services."

She sidled away, putting the desk between her and her guest. From Charlotte's room came the sound of laughter, then an attempt on Charlotte's part to sing a French carol, though her version of the lyrics was hopeless.

"You will soon be flooded with requests for your services," Marcus said, closing the distance Meg had tried to establish. "Inundated. Deluged, which is why I must put my question before you now, before you are too busy to bother with a grouchy fellow who hasn't much holiday spirit."

What was he going on about? "You have abundant holiday spirit, my lord. You decorated your home for your nieces, you would not allow me or the children to brave the storm, you hired Daisy and her choir for your open house, you went shopping for gifts all on your own, and you indulged your sister's need to entertain while sparing her the expense of hosting the event. You are generous, kind, honorable, loyal to your family, and in every way a fine fellow to have about as the holidays approach."

He'd maneuvered around the desk without Meg catching him at it. "And what about under the kissing bough, Margaret? Do I acquit myself adequately there? I hope so. I have brought you a holiday token, but you must not feel compelled to accept it." He took her hand and pressed a kiss to her knuckles.

"My lord, your duty requires no displays of honor where I am concerned," Meg said. "I am an adult, I make my own decisions, and what happened in your—"

A knock sounded on the door, and Charlotte thundered from her room. "I'll get it!"

"What a fine set of lungs our Charlotte has," Marcus murmured.

Our Charlotte, who now sported an afghan about her shoulders like a long cape, swung the door open. "Grandpapa? Mama, it's Grandpapa Entwhistle."

What on earth? "Mr. Entwhistle," Meg said, shaking her hand free of Marcus's grasp. "Good day. This is a lovely surprise. What brings you to London?"

Mr. Entwhistle stomped into the parlor, but then, he stomped everywhere. He was more weathered than the last time Meg had seen him, and the resemblance to Peter was still marked, but Mr. Entwhistle also had a ready smile and kind eyes.

"You bring me to London, as does this young lady here. She cannot possibly be my Charlotte, because Charlotte is a wee tot."

"I am Charlotte. What's in the sack?"

"Charlotte Marie Entwhistle, for shame."

Mr. Entwhistle set his sack on the desk. "A lively curiosity in a child should always be encouraged. I assume you're Innisborough's son?"

Marcus bowed. "I have that honor. Marcus Bannerfield, at your service."

"Got your letter," Mr. Entwhistle said, tugging off his gloves and jamming them into a coat pocket. "Decided to deliver this year's Christmas pudding in person. I've been remiss, Lady Meg. The land is a jealous mistress, but that's no excuse. His lordships says you and Charlotte could use some family about at Yuletide. I might be old, but I'm still capable of climbing into a coach from time to time."

"You brought Christmas pudding?" Charlotte asked. "Emily and Amanda, Grandpapa brought Christmas pudding!"

"I'm sure her ladyship is very happy to receive you," Marcus said, "but I was trying to put a question of some import to her."

Charlotte twirled to a halt. "What sort of question?"

"A personal question," Marcus replied as Emily and Amanda scampered out of Charlotte's bedroom. "An important personal question."

Mr. Entwhistle tossed his coat over the back of the sofa. "Like that, is it? Well, Lady Meg can use some Yuletide joy, heaven knows. Charlotte, who are your friends?"

Meg dearly, dearly wanted to know what question could have brought Marcus out into the winter weather, away from his guests, with both of his nieces in tow.

"I'm listening," she said, leaning closer to him. "If you still want to put that question to me."

"I most assuredly do, but perhaps another time, when we have more privacy and—"

A tap on the door interrupted him, and all three girls yelled, "I'll get it!"

"Aunt Penny!" Charlotte caroled, while Amanda and Emily called, "Grandpapa!"

Marcus seized Meg's hand again. "Do not abandon me amid this horde, Margaret. Aunt has been at the rum punch, unless I'm very much mistaken, and she doubtless inveigled Papa into having a nip as well."

Aunt Penny jabbed her walking stick in Marcus's direction. "My hearing is excellent, young man, and I'd be a fool to pass up Lady Margaret's punch. Have you asked her to marry you yet?"

Meg barely kept from covering her ears—or Aunt Penny's mouth.

Marcus muttered something that sounded like, "Papa, how could you?"

Papa—none other than Lord Innisborough—took Aunt Penny's coat and hung it on the last available peg.

"Eliza said you were off to find Lady Margaret and Miss Charlotte," the marquess said, "and nothing would do but Penelope must follow you. Miss Hennepin is a determined woman, and as a gentleman, I was compelled to abet—to provide her my escort."

Aunt peered around at Meg's parlor. "Why isn't there a kissing bough in here, young lady? The Christmas elf herself has no wreaths, no sachets, no holly... not a single sprig of mistletoe? Marcus, you had best be about your business. The situation grows dire."

Marcus withdrew a sprig of pale greenery from his coat pocket. "I am prepared as always to do my duty. Lady Margaret Entwhistle, before Father Christmas himself interrupts me, would you please, in the generosity of spirit which has characterized you at every—"

"I'll get it!" Aunt Penny bellowed, opening the door.

"She truly does have the hearing of a cat," Marcus muttered.

Lucien, Earl of Webberly, stood in the doorway. "I hope I'm not interrupting."

"You most assuredly are," Aunt Penny replied, opening the door wider. "So are we. Marcus has turned quite slow in his dotage, or perhaps he had a nip too many of the punch."

"I did not over-imbibe," Marcus said, very firmly.

"Are you proposing to my mama?" Charlotte asked. "You should go down on one knee, like a knight."

"You should, Uncle," Amanda said.

"And then we can have some Christmas pudding that the nice man brought," Emily added. "Once you are done proposing, that is."

"I would cheerfully take a knee," Marcus said, "but you lot leave a fellow no room to properly propose."

"Propose," Meg whispered. "You are truly here to propose? Marcus?"

He went *down on bended knee*, and all the whispering, giggling, shuffling, and talking stopped. "Margaret, my dearest lady, would you do me the very great honor, the inexpressibly precious honor, of accepting as your Christmas token, my heart, to guard and cherish for all the rest of our time on earth? Would you share with me the hard days and the holidays? Will you decorate our home with love and laughter and save all your finest kisses for a man who longs to—"

"Lad," the marquess said, "I think she takes your point."

"Let him say his piece," Mr. Entwhistle chided. "I haven't heard such flummery since I was standing for a seat in the Commons."

"Can we have the pudding now?" Charlotte asked.

"No," Aunt Penny replied. "Lady Margaret has to put us all out of our misery. Say yes, Lady Meg, so we can get back to the open house before all the gingerbread is gone."

Meg's parlor had never been so full, and neither had her heart. Across the room, Lucien was watching with a sort of wistful longing in his eyes.

"Say yes, Margaret. You deserve to be happy, you and Charlotte. Lord Marcus is mad for you, or possibly simply mad, but if you can be happy with him, say yes. If you and his lordship, and Charlotte too, would honor the countess and me with your company at dinner before we leave for the country, I would be obliged."

The humble note in Lucien's voice, the contrite look in his gaze, should have been proof to Meg that miracles could occur, but she was too busy relishing the miracle of Marcus Bannerfield proposing marriage to her and sounding utterly serious about it.

Marcus took Meg's hand and pressed the wilted sprig of mistletoe against her palm. "Please say yes, Margaret. A home decorated for Christmas is lovely, but I want Christmas in my heart, every day, with you."

What else was there to say to such a declaration? Meg took the mistletoe, held it high over Marcus's head, and kissed his cheek. "Yes. I say yes, and Happy Christmas, and yes!"

General mayhem ensued, with much cheering and laughter and Christmas pudding eaten from shared plates. Meg put the sprig of mistletoe on a windowsill where it would be safe from pirates, princesses, and Aunt Penny, and Marcus suggested that the company repair to his house, where abundant food and drink were still being served.

In four separate coaches—Lucien offered to take the children— the party processed back to Mayfair, everybody, even the coachmen and grooms, joining for a few verses of *Hark! The Herald Angels*

Sing. Daisy's choir was launching into its final number as Meg and her Christmas elves—her other Christmas elves—joined the open house, and the Marquess of Innisborough, interrupted twice by Aunt Penny, announced the happy couple's engagement.

Marcus and Margaret—who soon came to be known as Lord and Lady Mistletoe—welcomed their firstborn son to the family eight and a half months later and christened him Stephen Wenceslas Bannerfield.

TO MY DEAR READERS

To my dear readers,

Is there any happily ever after quite like a holiday happily ever after? I had such fun with this little novella, and I hope you enjoyed it too. Finishing a story always raises a question, though: What to read next? If you're in the mood for a light bite, I recently published another novella duet, **Love and Other Perils**, with author Emily Larkin (excerpt below). I'm also soon to publish my next **Rogues to Riches** story, *Forever and a Duke* (*Nov. 26, 2019*). I've included an excerpt for that story below as well.

If you'd like to stay up to date with new releases, pre-orders, or discounts, the easiest way to do that is to follow me on **Bookbub.** Bookbub will never bother you unless they have useful information to share. You can also keep an eye on the **Deals** page of my website, where I discount a different book each month or so. My **newsletter** is another way to keep in touch, though you might be subjected to the occasional kitten pic. I will never, not ever, share your personal information for any reason, and you can easily unsubscribe from the newsletter at any time.

As the holiday season approaches, know that I wish each of my readers peace on earth, a joyous heart, dear companions, and plenty of good books to read—and a little warm gingerbread too!

Happy reading,
Grace Burrowes

EXCERPT — CATNIP AND KISSES

From **Catnip and Kisses** by Grace Burrowes, in ***Love and Other Perils…***

Lady Antonia Mainwaring is volunteering at a London subscription library, which puts her ladyship in company with a very different sort of person than she's used to. When a patron comports himself in a less than gentlemanly fashion, she's not entirely sure how to respond. Fortunately for her, Max Haddonfield just happens along…

Mr. Paxton slapped the book down on Antonia's desk loudly enough to wake the cat, who was curled in a basket beside the fireplace.

"I specifically told Mr. Kessler to locate a *first* edition of Richardson's treatise," Mr. Paxton snapped. "This is not a *first* edition."

Across the reading room, the Barclay sisters peered at Antonia over their sermons. They'd intervene if she indicated a need for assistance, so she ignored them and met Mr. Paxton's glare with a calm eye.

"This is a fourth edition, sir, though your request was made only the day before yesterday. We'll be happy to notify you if and when a first edition arrives. You are welcome to borrow this copy until then."

Antonia remained seated, while Mr. Paxton drew himself up, a hot air balloon of male self-importance preparing to lift into a flight of indignation. The bell on the front door tinkled and Lucifer left his basket. He greeted each patron as conscientiously as a butler would, then went back to his basket, almost as if he were expecting one caller in particular.

"What sort of librarian," Mr. Paxton began, "cannot tell a first edition from subsequent printings? What sort of institution employs staff who cannot fulfill a simple loan request? Was I not clear that I wanted a *first edition?*"

He braced his hands on the desk and leaned closer. "Did I not complete your form to Mr. Kessler's satisfaction? Did he perhaps allow Mr. Lincoln Candleford to have the first edition before I was permitted to see it? I know the library on Constable Lane has one, but it's lent out, and they won't tell me who has it."

Mr. Paxton needed a closer acquaintance with several sheaves of fresh parsley. His breath reeked of the tobacco habit, which did not blend well with the excessive rose pomade in his hair.

"Libraries value the privacy of their patrons," Antonia replied. "If Constable Lane had a first edition available to lend, I'm sure they'd have sent it around. Did you seek to research a particular topic covered by Mr. Richardson's treatise?"

Mr. Paxton's gaze crawled over Antonia's feminine endowments. He might have been any one of a hundred half-drunk, blond, blue-eyed fortune hunters forgetting himself in a Mayfair ballroom, and in that setting, Antonia would have known what to do about him.

The cut direct, a raised eyebrow, a knowing glance to the chaperones waiting to pounce on a man's reputation from among the potted ferns. He'd find himself in want of invitations for the remainder of the Season, which was a fortune hunter's version of doom.

"Young woman, are you listening to me? Is your female brain overtaxed by a patron's request when that request is plainly and succinctly put before you? Must I complain to Kessler about his paltry collection *and* his dimwitted staff?"

Antonia rose, standing eye to eye with Mr. Paxton, the desk between them. "Your request has been submitted to our sister institutions. Is your male brain too limited to grasp that Mr. Richardson's treatise was published in 1788, and first editions have had nigh three decades to become lost, damaged, or destroyed? Locating one might take more than two days, though I suggest you retrieve your manners in the next thirty seconds."

His gaze roamed over her in a manner so far beyond insulting that had Antonia been at one of polite society's social functions, she would have slapped him.

He obviously knew she couldn't. Not here, where she was a volunteer on probation until a paying post became available. Not now, with only a pair of old women to gainsay Paxton's version of events. At the library, Antonia was simply "young woman," not an earl's daughter with a private fortune. For the first time since embarking on this literary adventure, Antonia understood why her cousins had tried to dissuade her from it.

She wasn't afraid, exactly, but she was uneasy.

"You were a governess, weren't you?" Paxton said. "A long meg like you was passed over by the bachelors. You probably lost your position because you got above yourself. You think a little French and a smattering of Italian make you an *intellectual*. What you need is—"

The smell of freshly baked bread gave Antonia an instant's warning that her conversation had acquired another witness.

"What *you* need," Mr. Haddonfield said, positioning himself at her elbow, "is to leave. Now."

Paxton put a hand on his hip. "Who might you be and what gives you the right to intrude here?"

"Max Haddonfield, at your service. Your rudeness invites any gentleman in the vicinity to intercede. Apologize to the lady for behaving like a petulant brat and find another library to patronize."

"Please do leave, Mr. Paxton," Antonia said. "You've disturbed the other patrons, and contrary to your imaginings, librarians are not magicians. Finding a thirty-year-old first edition will take some time."

"Go," Mr. Haddonfield said, making a shooing motion.

"And are you a librarian, sir, to be so dismissive toward a man of my academic credentials?" Paxton sniffed, picking up the book.

Mr. Haddonfield plucked the book from Paxton's grasp. "I'm a chemist." He smiled at Paxton as if being a chemist was better than having put Wellington on his first pony. "Haven't blown anything up in more than two weeks. I grow short-tempered when I can't blow something up."

Paxton took two steps back. "Kessler will hear about this."

Mr. Haddonfield crossed his arms, which made his coat stretch over broad shoulders and muscular biceps. "He certainly will. Your rudeness toward both the staff and the other patrons will doubtless result in revocation of your lending privileges."

"Other patrons? I assume you refer to yourself?"

Mr. Haddonfield twirled his finger. Paxton glanced over his shoulder, to where the Barclay sisters were no longer even pretending to read. Miss Dottie waggled her fingers. Miss Betty smiled over a bound volume of the Reverend Fordyce's wisdom.

"Other patrons," Mr. Haddonfield said. "Away with you. Be gone." He clapped his hands rapidly at Mr. Paxton, like a housekeeper impatient with a sluggardly maid.

Paxton leapt back, jerked his coat down, and marched for the door. The silence in his wake was broken by bells on a passing gig, a merry sound.

"Do you really blow things up?" Antonia asked.

"Yes, but usually only on purpose."

Order your copy of **Love and Other Perils** and read on for an excerpt from **Forever and a Duke** (Nov 2019).

EXCERPT—FOREVER AND A DUKE

From ***Forever and a Duke,*** book three in the **Rogues to Riches** series...

Wrexham, Duke of Elsmore, has a problem—somebody very clever is stealing from his ducal coffers. He takes the extraordinary step of appealing to Eleanora Hatfield, a ferociously talented bank auditor, to help him quietly resolve his difficulties. Much to Rex's consternation, the woman he's hired to catch a thief is making off with his heart...

Mrs. Hatfield unbuttoned her cloak, and without thinking, Rex drew it from her shoulders, gave it a shake, and hung it on the drying pegs above her hearth. A small silver teapot sat in the middle of the mantel, a sketch on either side in plain wooden frames. He wanted to study those drawings—wanted to snoop about her entire abode—but not when Eleanora could see him doing it.

He braced himself for a scold as he passed her a shawl that had been draped over the back of a reading chair. "Shall I light the fire?" he asked, for want of anything else to say.

By the limited illumination of a few candles, the relentlessly businesslike Mrs. Hatfield looked weary. "I'll be going out again, just across the street, and I don't light the hearth until I'm in for the night. Thank you for your escort, Your Grace."

Eleanora Hatfield, like much of London, had no cooking facilities in her domicile. Of course, she'd go out to fetch a hot meal, and of course she'd shoo him away before she did.

Rex wasn't feeling shoo-able, for once. "I'm still dressed for the weather," he said. "I'll get us some food, while you consider a strategy for organizing our efforts over the next two weeks."

He bowed and left before she could argue. By the time he returned, she'd curled up in a chair, her shawl about her shoulders, her hearth crackling. She'd also fallen asleep.

Rex dealt with the cat first, unwrapping a morsel of fish and leaving it on its paper in a corner. For himself and his hostess, salty fried potatoes came next and slices of hot roasted beef followed. The scents were humble and tantalizing, and apparently enough to tempt Mrs. Hatfield from her slumbers.

"You bought beef and potatoes."

She looked at him as if he'd served her one of those fancy dinners Mama made such a fuss over. Six removes, three feuding chefs, footmen run ragged, the sommelier pinching the maids, and all the guests more interested in flirtation than food.

"Voltaire has started on the fish course," Rex said. The cat was, in fact, growling as she ate, and sounding quite ferocious about her meal.

"Her manners were formed in a hard school," Mrs. Hatfield said, sitting up. "Where are my—?"

Rex passed her the spectacles, though he preferred her without them.

"Have you cutlery," he asked, "or do we shun etiquette for the sake of survival?"

"In the sideboard." She took a plate from him. "I can put the kettle on if that—you brought wine."

"A humble claret, but humility is a virtue, I'm told."

The shared meal reminded Rex of something that ought to also be part of a peer's curriculum: Some people had the luxury of chatting and laughing as abundant food was put before them. Other people had such infrequent acquaintance with adequate nutrition, that the notion of focusing on anything other than appreciation for food was a sort of blasphemy.

Eleanora Hatfield ate with that degree of concentration. She did not hurry, she did not compromise her manners, but she focused on her meal with the same single-mindedness she turned on Rex's ledgers.

"You have known poverty," he said, buttering the last slice of bread and passing it to her. "Not merely hard times or lean years. You have known the bleakest of realities."

She took the bread, tore it in two, and passed half back to him. "There's no shame in poverty."

"I doubt there's much joy in it, either."

"We managed, and I am impoverished no longer." She launched into a lecture about concentric rings of responsibility, redundant documentation, and heaven knew what else. Rex poured her more wine, put an attentive expression on his face—he excelled at appearing attentive—and let his curiosity roam over the mystery of Eleanora Hatfield.

She'd known hardship, and she'd probably known embezzlers. She'd decided to wrap herself in the fiction of widowhood or wifehood, but not the reality, and she was truly passionate about setting Rex's books to rights.

The longer she talked about the many ways his estates could have been pillaged—while he'd waltzed, played piquet, and debated the Corn Laws—the more he appreciated her fierceness and the more he wondered how she'd come by it.

"When should I call upon you tomorrow?" he asked, rising and gathering up the orts and leavings of their meal.

"At the end of the day," she said, standing to take the greasy paper from him. "I'll use this for kindling, and I leave any empty bottles in the alley for the street children to sell. In cold weather, their lives grow more perilous than usual."

She drew her shawl up and looked away, as if those last words should have been kept behind her teeth.

Rex shrugged into his great coat, wrapped a cashmere scarf about his neck, and pulled on gloves lined with rabbit fur. Autumn had not only turned up nasty, winter was in the offing.

"I want you to consider something," he said. "Something in addition to the various ways my trusty staff is bilking me of a fortune."

"Not all of your staff, we haven't established that."

Not yet, though anybody seeking to steal from the Elsmore fortune was doomed to eventual discovery, now that Eleanora Hatfield was on the scent.

"Please consider a theoretical question: If instead of allowing my coffers to be pillaged by the enterprising thieves in my employ, I had donated that money to charity, where would you have had me put those funds?"

He had her attention now, and having Eleanora Hatfield's attention was not a casual state of affairs.

"You are asking about thousands of pounds, Your Grace."

"No, actually, I am asking for your trust. You will soon know all of my secrets, Eleanora. You will know where I have been lax, where I have been less than conscientious about my duties. You will know who has betrayed me. Not even my priest knows me that well, not even my siblings. I am asking much of you, and in return, all I can offer is an assurance that your secrets would be safe with me."

Her gaze was momentarily dumbstruck, then puzzled, then troubled. "Thank you, Your Grace, but in my line of work, I can afford to trust no one."

Interesting choice of verb—*afford*. "You like it that way."

"I need it that way."

How honest, and how lonely. Elsmore brushed her hair back over her ear, and when she did not protest that presumption he bent nearer. She stood still, eyes downcast, though he well knew she was capable of pinning his ears back.

"Eleanora?"

She closed her eyes, and he realized that was as much permission as he would get from her. He kissed her cheek and let himself out into the chilly corridor, pausing only long enough to make sure she locked the door after him.

As if her mind had imparted its restlessness to his own, Rex walked the distance to his home, turning over questions and ignoring the persistent freezing drizzle. Two streets from his doorway, he took off his gloves and scarf and left them in an alley.

Why had he kissed Eleanora Hatfield? Even a chaste gesture such as he'd bestowed on the lady was an intimacy, and with the least intimacy-prone female he knew. Why cross that line? Why blur those boundaries? His musings yielded no satisfactory answers, but then, a man who failed to notice his trusted staff dipping into his coffers, a man who overlooked drinking from the wrong tea cup, was probably overdue for an audit of his own sentiments and motivations.

Order your copy of **Forever and a Duke**!

Next up: **The Viscount's Winter Wish by Christi Caldwell!**

THE VISCOUNT'S WINTER WISH

BY CHRISTI CALDWELL

COPYRIGHT

The Viscount's Winter Wish
Copyright © 2019 by Christi Caldwell
Kindle Edition

For more information about the author:

www.christicaldwellauthor.com
christicaldwellauthor@gmail.com
Twitter: @ChristiCaldwell
Or on Facebook at: Christi Caldwell Author

OTHER TITLES BY CHRISTI CALDWELL

Heart of a Duke

In Need of a Duke—Prequel Novella

For Love of the Duke

More than a Duke

The Love of a Rogue

Loved by a Duke

To Love a Lord

The Heart of a Scoundrel

To Wed His Christmas Lady

To Trust a Rogue

The Lure of a Rake

To Woo a Widow

To Redeem a Rake

One Winter with a Baron

To Enchant a Wicked Duke

Beguiled by a Baron

To Tempt a Scoundrel

The Heart of a Scandal

In Need of a Knight—Prequel Novella

Schooling the Duke

A Lady's Guide to a Gentleman's Heart

A Matchmaker for a Marquess

His Duchess for a Day

Lords of Honor

Seduced by a Lady's Heart

Captivated by a Lady's Charm

Rescued by a Lady's Love

Tempted by a Lady's Smile

Courting Poppy Tidemore

Scandalous Seasons

Forever Betrothed, Never the Bride

Never Courted, Suddenly Wed

Always Proper, Suddenly Scandalous

Always a Rogue, Forever Her Love

A Marquess for Christmas

Once a Wallflower, at Last His Love

Sinful Brides

The Rogue's Wager

The Scoundrel's Honor

The Lady's Guard

The Heiress's Deception

The Wicked Wallflowers

The Hellion

The Vixen

The Governess

The Bluestocking

The Spitfire

The Theodosia Sword

Only For His Lady

Only For Her Honor

Only For Their Love

Danby

A Season of Hope

Winning a Lady's Heart

The Brethren

The Spy Who Seduced Her

The Lady Who Loved Him

The Rogue Who Rescued Her

The Minx Who Met Her Match

Brethren of the Lords

My Lady of Deception

Her Duke of Secrets

Regency Duets

Rogues Rush In: Tessa Dare and Christi Caldwell

Yuletide Wishes: Grace Burrowes and Christi Caldwell

Memoir: Non-Fiction

Uninterrupted Joy

PROLOGUE

Winter 1822

Not much had changed in the Read household.

That was, in the three years Miss Merry Amaryllis Read, daughter of the Earl and Countess of Maldavers' steward and housekeeper and soon-to-be new housekeeper for Lord and Lady Maldavers, had been sent off to receive proper training for her future role.

At that very moment, Merry's two younger siblings were seated in the main gathering room of their peak cottage as she prepared her tea, she listened on while they engaged in the activity they were most noted for—one-bettering.

Somewhere around her tenth and eleventh year, she'd grown tired of the boy-girl twins' bickering. Somewhere around her thirteenth year, Merry had become quite adept at blocking it all out.

"...oh, and of a sudden, you, with every hour of every day spent training to one day be steward, also find yourself in possession of the latest London scandals?" Matilda, her younger sister, challenged.

This time, there was something altogether different about the stories and challenges flying back and forth.

This time involved the unlikeliest of subjects: Lord Lucas Grimslee, the earl's stuffiest, stodgiest, most-well-behaved son… which, given that all the Holman boys—now men—were notoriously proper, was saying a good deal indeed.

"You think you're the one in accurate possession of the gentleman's goings-on?"

"Hardly, I'm just in possession of more information." Matilda launched into an impressive list of all the ways by which she'd become an aficionado of the subject at hand.

Her twenty-four-year-old sister leaned forward in her carved-walnut armchair and spoke in a loud whisper. "*I* heard he broke out into song in the middle of a Covent Garden performance he was attending."

"What?" Merry blurted. Apparently, she *had been* adept at ignoring their sparring.

Matilda whipped her attention over to Merry. By the pleased little smile that split her face, Merry's reaction had been reward enough. "Indeed. He was… singing in the middle of the performance."

"Luke Holman… *singing?*" She knew it was an echo of what her sister had said, but it was just too far-fetched. The gentleman, who couldn't manage more than a polite—albeit curt—greeting whenever she was near, had sung aloud… in public?

Matilda nodded. "From what I read, it was quite an exuberant performance, at that."

"And here I'd believed he'd not even hum a happy tune in the privacy of his own company," Merry said without malice and earned another round of giggles from her sister.

"It has been wildly shocking. All of it."

"That was surely the first time in the whole of a lifetime that anyone has ever charged the Holman family with being even remotely out of step," Merry noted, eyeing the confectionary treats her mother had prepared before plucking another gingerbread.

"Yes, but much has changed since you've been gone," Diccan intoned.

"Everything," Matilda added with a nod, for good measure.

"First"—Diccan stuck a finger up—"Lord Lathan Holman, a perfectly respectable clerk at the Home Office, was accused of high treason."

When Merry only took another bite of her treat and didn't indulge her brother with any questions, Diccan frowned. "Surely, you must wonder *what* he did."

After Merry finished chewing and then swallowing her bite, she carefully dabbed at the corners of her mouth with a napkin. "No," she said simply.

Diccan bristled. "And whyever not?"

"Because it is impossible." Not many years younger than she, the youngest Holman brother had been bookish, without even a hair out of order in his life. "Not a single Holman would ever do something as shameful as to betray King and Crown." In an effortful display of nonchalance, Merry rearranged the tray of goodies her mother had set out. "And what of Lord Ewan?" He had been the only Holman child to play with her as though she were equal in birthright.

Her brother eyed her peculiarly. "What of him?"

Snatching up the nearest pastry, she set it on her plate. "Has Lord Ewan become as pompous as the rest?" If he had, it was going to be utter misery serving in that household.

"Hardly."

She released the breath she'd not realized she was holding.

"Either way, returning to the more interesting Holmans. Mr. Lathan Holman was cleared," Matilda confirmed. "Though some say strings were pulled and that the Crown will ultimately have their vengeance." She made a garish slashing motion across her throat and hung her head sideways.

"Matilda," she chided.

Their brother grunted. "All nobles are invariably cleared of wrongdoing," he pointed out, not inaccurately. "Even the guilty ones like Mr. Lathan Holman."

Their mother, the former housekeeper who'd been employed by the Holmans, ducked out from the kitchens. "Hush," she whispered.

Alas, the former head of the female staff, who'd terrified the maids with her no-nonsense attitude, had never managed that feat with her own children.

Diccan scoffed. "They are hardly going to hear us from our cottage."

"*Their* cottage," their mother aptly pointed out. Wiping her hands with the cloth she held, she waved it at her only son. "Furthermore, it doesn't do to talk unkindly about the one who employs you." Their mother looked pointedly at Matilda. "And you." Her gaze landed on Merry, the sole member of the Read family who was not yet employed by the Earl and Countess of Maldavers. "And, well... all of you need to be quiet."

The trio of Read siblings went silent.

With a satisfied nod, their mother hurried back into the kitchens.

The moment she'd gone, they dissolved into silent laughter. Merry's form shook with such mirth that she keeled over into her sister's side. How good this felt. How very wonderful it was simply being home.

"I hear you." Their mother's warning came muffled by the kitchen doors.

"Of course she does," Diccan muttered.

He continued on with his gossip about Lord Luke as though there'd been no interruption. Planting his hands on his legs, he leaned forward. "Now, returning to the Holman scandals."

Merry's heart kicked up. Lord Ewan. The one gentleman who'd not yet been spoken of. The kindest, most affable of... well, all the Holmans, really.

"Lord Luke"—she stifled a disappointed sigh as Diccan returned to the heir—"I heard he was seen entering the Duke and Duchess of Bainbridge's."

"I'd hardly consider that scandalous," Matilda shot back.

"I must agree with Mattie," Merry said to her sister's older-by-seven-minutes twin. Stirring cream into her teacup, Merry paused to take a sip. "In fact, I'd quite expect that visiting a powerful peer and his wife is precisely the manner of thing Lord Luke would do." Luke, who she'd once predicted had entered the world somber and composed. Whereas Ewan had played children's games with Merry, Lord Luke had never joined in. Instead, the bookish Lord Luke had peered down at them with a scowl to match those of his equally stern tutors.

With a triumphant flounce of her blond curls, Matilda stole a biscuit from the tray and held it aloft like a confectionary trophy she'd awarded herself.

"I agree it doesn't seem outrageous for the gentleman to pay a visit to another lord," Diccan conceded. He looped his thumbs into the waistband of his trousers. "And it wouldn't be. That is, if he'd been invited."

Merry flared her eyes. Surely her brother wasn't saying...

Matilda scrambled to the edge of her seat. "What did he do?" she demanded, her question conceding defeat to her twin.

With a sly half grin, Diccan added, "Apparently, a very inebriated Lord Luke entered his neighbor's townhouse." He continued over his sisters' matching gasps. "He stumbled into their foyer and relieved himself in a plant stand that he'd mistaken for a chamber pot."

A laugh exploded from Merry at the sheer outrageousness that image painted, even as it could not be true that Lord Luke would do anything so outrageous. She laughed until tears leaked from her eyes.

"It is true," Diccan insisted defensively, through his sisters' noisy amusement.

She laughed all the harder, until her sides ached from the force of her own amusement.

When their laughter had ebbed, Matilda curled onto her side and rested her cheek atop Merry's lap, as she'd done so many times as a girl.

Merry stroked her sister's curls.

"I've missed this," Matilda said softly.

"I have, too," Merry murmured. It had been three years since she'd left, and for all the tears she'd cried continually during her first three months gone, in time, she'd found joy in her studies and work. Only to find now just how very much she'd missed all of these moments.

A firm knock landed on the door, splitting the quiet.

They all three went motionless.

Their mother came flying out of the kitchens, her rounded cheeks pale but for the splotches of red from the heat of the fires she worked over.

"Whoever is that?" Matilda whispered when the echo from the hard rap's wake had abated.

Frowning, Merry stole a glance at the clock.

Nine o'clock. Early on, she and her siblings had learned that only crises at the main household merited after-hours intrusions.

There came another heavy pounding.

Merry was across the room in several quick strides. She yanked the door open, letting in a blast of cold winter air and one unexpected noblewoman.

Oh, bloody hell.

The countess swept inside and gave a flick of her hand.

An unfamiliar-to-Merry-footman hovering on the stone porch hurriedly drew the door shut.

That click managed to spring the occupants of the cottage into motion. All the Reads scrambled to their feet and proceeded to drop belated curtsies or bows.

Lady Maldavers thumped her cane once. "I'll not waste time with it," the countess said in her slightly nasal, perfectly enunciated Queen's English. "I'm here on a matter of importance."

Merry and her siblings looked to one another and then their mother. As the former housekeeper rushed forward, her children began to wordlessly back from the room. "Yes, my lady. I'll fetch my husband immediately." Given the lady of the household hadn't ever set foot inside the cottage, and her ladyship, not her husband, was seeing to business, the situation must be dire.

"Not him." The countess stretched her other arm out and pointed at Merry. "You."

Or it seemed that that perfectly manicured digit fell in Merry's direction. Except... that hardly made sense. She was neither employed by the woman, nor, having arrived only that morn, had Merry seen the lady of the household. Even more to point, the countess had never sought Merry out—ever.

A log shifted in the hearth, the snap and hiss of the fire the only sound to meet the countess' pronouncement.

"Yes, you," the countess said impatiently. She thumped her cane twice, and Merry's siblings instantly fell into a neat line and filed into the kitchens. Her mother, ever the consummate housekeeper, was the last to take her leave. She followed after the pair and then closed the door in her wake, leaving Merry and the countess alone.

At one time, Merry had been a girl at sea around her parents' employer. Regal, austere, unsmiling, they'd been a cold family whom she'd spent far more time pitying than envying. For her time away, however, Merry had left the protected, countrified world of Leeds for the Continent. She'd explored some of the most magnificent artwork and households. She'd moved among the aristocracy. Therefore, she didn't have *quite* the same terror she'd once had around the countess.

Folding her hands primly before her, Merry stood in the middle of the room, her back straight. "Should I have refreshments called for, my lady?"

"This isn't a social call." The other woman laid her ornate ivory cane against the back of the armchair Merry had previously occupied and tugged off her gloves. "I shall get to it, Miss Read. As we're both aware, after the holiday season, you'll be taking on the role of house-keeper in place of your mother."

"I—"

"However, until then, I'd ask you to help ready the household for our guests."

Merry started. She'd have wagered—and lost—her family's cottage in Leeds that the Holman household had already been transformed. "My lady, I'm honored."

Lady Maldavers waved her hand dismissively. "It's less a matter of preference and more a matter of necessity. We've company scheduled to arrive."

They always did. Lord and Lady Maldavers were an expert host and hostess, never long without other leading societal guests for company.

Of all the tasks Merry had been charged with—polishing the silver, inventorying the linens—the only one she'd ever truly looked forward to with any real joy was that of preparing for Christmastide. "I can begin immediately," she promised, thrilling at the prospect of decorating the sprawling manor.

The older woman gathered her cane and gave it another thump. "Is this your conversation or mine to lead, Miss Read?"

"Forgive me." Born to two servants, Merry had known since birth that servitude was the future that awaited her. Even knowing that as she did, she chafed at that treatment. She wanted more.

"Our company was due to arrive here. However, we've decided to move the gathering to London."

That cut through her musings. "To London?" She'd been summoned back to England not to take on the role of housekeeper at the Mayfair residence, but for the role her mother was soon to retire from.

"It is essential our very important guests see that our affairs in London are as well taken care of as they are in Leeds."

In other words, the scandal that followed her eldest son merited a display of the Holmans acting in their perfectly proper way.

Lord Luke's antics also merited her leaving at the heart of the holiday season and saying her goodbyes to family she'd not seen for three years. And yet, neither could she decline, particularly given the countess was in no way presenting it as anything other than the demand it was. Merry compressed her lips and silently cursed Lord

Luke for choosing this time of all times to act anything other than a gentleman.

Tucking her cane under her arm, the countess pulled her gloves on. "Given the significance of the role I've assigned, in a household that you'll not otherwise be required to oversee, you'll be generously compensated. Shall we say two hundred pounds, Miss Read?"

Merry's lips parted, but she could not get a proper word out. Two hundred pounds? That was an amount that would have taken her father six years in his role as steward to earn.

"His lordship and I are set to depart within the hour. Given your only recent arrival, I've ordered your carriage to depart on the morrow afternoon." With that decree, the countess sailed over to the door.

She tapped the bottom of her cane against the panel that was nicked and marked with initials and images that Merry and her siblings had left over the years.

Merry rushed over to open the door and then sank into a deep curtsy. "My ladyship," she murmured.

Without so much as a parting greeting, the countess started down the walkway.

The nearly three-quarters-full moon hung like an orb upon the night sky, bathing the snow-covered path in white so bright it was nearly blinding.

The countess paused in the middle of the snow-covered path. A servant rushed forward to meet her, but she waved the strapping footman off. "Lord and Lady St. Albans," she said as she turned back to face Merry.

Merry brought her eyebrows together. "My lady?"

"Your siblings had the wrong of it. My son did not stumble into the Duke and Duchess of Bainbridge's, but rather, the Marquess and Marchioness of St. Albans'."

Oh, bloody hell. Even with the frigid sting of the winter air, Merry felt her entire body go hot. The countess gave her a knowing look.

With that, the regal woman marched off like the queen striding down a red carpet at court. Merry stood there with the door agape, letting all the precious heat slip out, all in the name of deference— until the countess boarded the carriage at the end of the drive. The pink conveyance lurched into motion, and the austere woman was gone.

When Merry closed the door, she turned and found her siblings and mother staring back.

"You're leaving," Matilda bemoaned.

"It will only be for a short while," she promised. "I'll be home before the holiday festivities even commence."

Instead of rejoining her earlier pleasures with her siblings, Merry reluctantly quit the main gathering room in exchange for the rooms she'd shared with her sister through the years.

A room she'd spend just one night in before being scuttled off to London to play at the role of decorator for the ungrateful, if generous, Lord and Lady Maldavers.

There was some consolation in knowing that while she worked, she'd be invisible to the lofty Holmans and therefore able to spread holiday cheer throughout their no-doubt cheerless household.

Merry smiled.

CHAPTER ONE

Two days later
London, England

Ding-ding-ding.

Lucas Holman, the Viscount Grimslee was dying.

Ding.

There was nothing else for the dull pain threatening to split his skull in two every time that high-pitched chime echoed around his darkened chambers.

Ding.

Despite his prior opinion on the matter, it appeared there was a God, after all, because the infernal chiming stopped.

With a forcible effort, Luke struggled to open his eyes. A welcome inky blackness hung over the room. It was still too much. Sliding his eyes closed, he searched a hand around.

Luke's fingers connected with the slit in the curtains hanging over his four-poster bed, and with infinitely slow movements, he parted the heavy fabric.

Even that minutest *swoosh* of the velvet landed like a blow to his head.

Oh, God. His stomach roiled. Death would be preferable to this.

When he trusted he could move without casting up the contents of his stomach, he rolled over and dragged himself to the edge of the mattress. At some point, the fire had died in his hearth, and a chill spread through the room. Even with that, sweat beaded on his brow at the efforts he expended, and he welcomed the cold.

He hovered there, facedown, and promptly fell asleep. His slumber proved all too short.

Ding-ding.

Luke groaned. This was his penance, then.

Ding.

Nay, punishment, for the night spent drinking at his clubs.

Ding-ding.

Somewhere after the fifth peal of the clock, he stopped trying to keep track of that hellish chiming. "I'm going to hack you up and burn you for kindling," he said, his words muffled by a mouthful of blanket.

Once more, there was a beautiful surcease in that ringing.

So, it was somewhere between five and twelve o'clock. Though whether it was day or night—or even, for that matter, what day it was —was all still a great mystery. Not that it mattered, either way. With the *ton* having retreated to their country properties for the Christmas-tide season—his parents fortunately among those numbers—Luke had no responsibilities.

None.

There were no gentlemen with whom to discuss the state of England.

No brothers to see, though they hadn't been seen since his youngest brother had been accused and, with the help of their other brother, cleared of treason.

And there was no wife. Or betrothed.

There was no Josephine.

His chest spasmed at the reminder that was always near just how badly he'd bumbled, well, *everything.*

He who, until five months ago, had never so much as had a cravat askew.

For thirty years, he'd made his role as heir to the earldom—and all the estates, wealth, and responsibilities that went with it—his only priority. From the moment he'd left the nursery for the schoolroom, the importance of the Holman name and legacy had been well ingrained into him. And never had he deviated from those commitments. With his head for business, the responsibilities of seeing to the familial finances had fallen to him. A mantle he'd taken on as happily as he had any other before... and after it. Between those efforts and maintaining proper relationships with ranking members of the peerage, there'd been no time for pleasure... until he'd met Miss Josephine Pratt.

She'd been unconventional, spirited, with a head for books, and he'd been alternately horrified and entranced by her. And then had come his brother's scandal with the Home Office, and it had commanded all of Luke's energies.

Nay, that wasn't altogether true. *You broke it off with her because you thought it was best to sever all ties with her... for the both of them...*

If he could have mustered the energy for a sufficient chuckle without throwing up in his bed, he would have set that cynical mirth free. Instead, Luke managed to lift his right hand in a mock toast to the empty room. "And all in the name of honor," he whispered into his sheets.

There was a light scratch at the door, because even knocks in the Holman household were delivered with utmost decorum.

Ignoring that irritating rap, Luke stretched both palms out and drew the curtains tightly closed.

They'd go away, because the servants were as loyal as the London day was wet and knew, unless instructions were given, they weren't to bother a Holman with visitors who'd arrived without an appointment.

Or, they had known.

Scratch-scratch-scratch.

"My lord?" His valet's slightly strident voice stretched through the heavy oak panel.

"Go away, Louie. I'm not to be disturbed," he called and then promptly groaned at the misery he'd unleashed anew in his head. Swallowing another emission, he caught his head in his hands.

"Yes, yes. I'm aware of your preferences—"

"If you were aware of them, you'd not be jabbering on the other side of that door."

"However, I thought I might urge you to rise for the day, because—"

"I cannot think of one damned reason why I should rise this day or any day," he bellowed.

Silence from the hall and a ringing in his ears were the only answers. That ringing sent another wave of nausea roiling in his gut.

Good, you deserve it, you miserable bugger. Yelling at servants. This was who he'd become, then.

The doors exploded open with a force that sent bile into Luke's throat. "I can give you *at the very least* three reasons why you should rise this day."

That booming and all-too-familiar voice confirmed one truth—the good Lord hated him, after all.

The Earl of Maldavers shoved the door shut with a thunderous boom that merely confirmed that, in addition to God, his own father despised him, too. And why wouldn't he? Luke was a miserable, starchy chap.

"Father," he returned. The greeting, muffled by his blankets, was a rote form of politeness that had come from years of being the dutiful son. Reluctantly, he reached for the curtains.

He needn't have bothered with those exertions.

His father ripped the fabric out of Luke's hands and threw them wide, then stormed across the room.

"Don't," Luke croaked.

That plea didn't so much as put a halt in the earl's forward strides. He yanked open the drapes. Sunlight poured through, made all the more blindingly bright by the recent snowfall.

It was too much.

Retching, Luke fished around for the chamber pot and emptied the contents of his stomach into the nauseatingly cheerful porcelain piece.

"There, that is a good deal better, my boy."

His father dangled a kerchief over the other side of the pot.

Wiping at his mouth, Luke collapsed onto his back. "Boy." He dropped a hand across his eyes. It'd been twenty-eight years since he'd earned that moniker from his father. "I'd hardly call myself a boy," he said with all the dryness he could muster.

"Well, given the way you've been conducting yourself these past weeks, I'd hardly call you a man, Lucas Holman." His father snorted. "And certainly *not* a gentleman." If displeasure had a sound, it would be that of his father's cool, aristocratic tones all stretched out like the blanket of snow that had lined the London cobblestones last evening.

"Ah, because being a gentleman matters above all," Luke said coolly.

"Yes. Yes, it does," the earl said with a finality that declared any debate or discussion at an end.

Not long ago, fool that he was, Luke himself had been of a like opinion.

His father dragged over a chair. Flipping up his coattails, he settled himself onto the upholstered edge.

Devil be damned. It was to be a lecture, then.

Luke would have groaned if it wouldn't have split his head in two all over again.

It'd been so very long since Luke had received a lecture, he'd very nearly missed the telltale signs—the my-boying, the deliberate seat upon a chair. Though, in fairness, the *grand presence* of the earl should have been all the indication Luke had required. Particularly given that his father should at this very moment be buried away in merry festivities for the holiday season.

Tick-tock-tick-tock-tick-tock.

His father took Luke's chin in hand and studied him as if he were some scientific experiment to be figured out.

Luke squirmed as, just like that, he'd become the boy of seven who'd made a pirate's map out of page twelve of his father's winter crofts ledger.

He stole a look at the eight-day, provincial French grandfather clock. Tuesday, it was. "Don't you have houseguests to entertain?"

"We did. We do. We will."

Well, that was confounding and ominous, all at the same time. No more ominous, however, than that deliberate way his father tapped his chin.

"Well, it can't be all three," Luke said when no further words were forthcoming.

At that insolent retort, the earl's red brows went shooting up.

But then, why wouldn't his father be filled with anything other than absolute shock at having his words countered or gainsaid? As a rule, none had dared to do it. At least not as long as Luke had toddled upon this earth.

At last, his father let his hands fall to the casings of his puce satin trousers. "Actually, my boy, it can very easily be all three. You see, we did have a house full of company set to arrive on Monday when, imagine my horror, I received a note regarding my son's antics throughout London."

"I never took our servants for traitors."

All the color bled from his father's cheeks.

Traitors. "Forgive me, I forgot the mention of traitors is still a delicate topic in this household," Luke said with a cool smile.

Alas, his father didn't rise to the bait.

"Gossip columns."

Luke furrowed his brow.

"Your name has been circulating. More specifically, your antics."

"I'd hardly consider enjoying fine French brandy antics."

"It is when you're falling facedown on Bond Street," his father rejoined without missing a beat.

"I was never facedown on Bond Street." It had been somewhere around Curzon.

"Either way, people are gossiping, and your mother and I won't let it stand."

Ah, the poor earl and countess hadn't learned from their other son's public shame that when it came to fodder for the *ton*, they didn't have the power that they did in every other aspect of their life. Luke closed his eyes and was very nearly drifting off.

His father tapped his face with his palm, bringing his eyes open.

"What in hell?"

His father dropped his voice to a whisper. "Allow me to help you, my boy. This isn't where you sleep, but rather, where you ask our intentions."

Warning bells went off...

Or mayhap that knocking at the back of his head was more a product of the bottle of brandy he'd downed.

"This is the 'we do' and 'we will' part," his father went on, a glee in his tones that added to Luke's rapidly spiraling unease.

"I don't follow," he said hoarsely.

"Given you smell like you bathed in brandy, I don't expect you're up to your usual tact." Coming out of his chair for a second time, the earl marched over to the window. "You stink, Lucas Lannister Reeve Holman." The words came muffled and slightly off-key from the way he pinched the bridge of his nose. His father unfastened the lock and brought the window up, letting in a sharp blast of cold. "There, that is better," the earl said, as triumphant as if he'd dealt himself the winning hand in a game of hazard. "Now, where was I?"

"Leaving?"

His father took up the seat he'd abandoned next to Luke's bed. "Trust me, I'd rather that more than you, my boy. The last place I care to spend my winters is in London."

Oh, hell and damnation. His stomach sank for altogether different reasons than his overindulgence. "You needn't."

"I needn't," his father agreed. "Until I received word of you. Just as all of the *ton* has heard tales of your scandalous escapades. Nay, I'm stuck here." His eyes narrowed. "With a house full of company."

With a house full of...

"Company," the earl finished, confirming Luke had spoken aloud. "But..."

"No buts. We've guests arriving for the holidays, and when they do you will be presentable, the household decorated, and all rumors about your escapades will be laid to rest." The earl leaned closer, the chair creaking and groaning under that movement as he dropped his palms onto his knees. "Am I clear, my boy?"

"Abundantly," he said through tight lips.

His father flashed a wide smile that curved up his rounded cheeks. "Splendid, my boy. Splendid." With that, the earl stood and took his leave.

The moment his father had closed the door behind him, Luke closed his eyes. In four days, the house would be crawling with guests. Nauseating, holiday revelers, at that.

This was the punishment his family was determined to inflict upon Luke for his bad behavior.

He'd been wrong, then, after all. *This* was to be his hell.

CHAPTER TWO

Merry Read had lived upon the Earl of Maldavers' properties for nearly twenty years of her life. She'd run through his gardens. She'd pilfered treats from his kitchens. She'd hidden within his French-inlaid armoires.

But never had she set foot inside his Mayfair townhouse.

Of course, she'd enjoyed those former luxuries only because, as the housekeeper's daughter, Merry had been invisible to the lord and lady of the household.

After all, the servants' children were invariably shadowy little figures who drifted about, but were never truly noted.

Now, as the butler escorted her through a maze of halls and corridors as winding as the ones in Leeds, Merry took in the austere, regal elegance that oozed from Lord and Lady Maldavers' residence.

Ornate gold frames hung upon the walls. They filled every space, the articles nearly touching.

Sconces lined the opposite side of the hall. From the gilded waterfall lamps, crystals hung like icicles atop the eaves at wintertime.

In fact, based upon her walk alone, she'd deduced that anything not constructed of gold was crystal, and everything else was a blindingly bright blend of the two.

Any other person wandering these corridors would be hard-pressed to be anything but impressed by the wealthy garnishing on display.

That was, anybody but Merry.

She tried to repress a horrified wince—and failed.

The place exuded wealth, but also coldness. In short, the Holmans' townhouse personified the family itself quite perfectly.

"Here we are, miss." The butler brought them to a stop before an open doorway. "The Yellow Drawing Room." Stepping forward, his back ramrod straight, the young man announced her... to an empty room. "Miss Read." His voice boomed off the high ceilings.

Merry swept her gaze throughout the room. The Yellow Drawing Room was hardly an apt name for the space. Gold. Every swath of fabric to the trim of the Aubusson carpeting contained gold or gilded accents.

"Well, well, step forward, Miss Read." The countess' voice echoed from the far left corner of the drawing room.

Merry found the older woman with her gaze. Seated at a round table, the countess remained engrossed in her task, not even bothering to lift her head in greeting. "You've hardly any time before the guests arrive, and therefore, you can hardly afford to stand there tarrying."

Taking that as an invitation to join Lady Maldavers, Merry marched across the room, but not before she caught a commiserative glance from the butler as he took his leave, closing the doors behind him.

The click of Lady Maldavers' pen filled the cavernous space.

As Merry stopped at the opposite side of the center pedestal table in mahogany, she craned her neck a fraction in a bid to see what so occupied the older woman's attention.

She squinted. Alas, it looked like it could be Blackbeard's map.

At last, Lady Maldavers set her pen down and looked up, a pair of spectacles perched at the far end of her hawklike nose. "I trust you're quite speechless at the beauty of 1896 Pembroke Place," she said, as if they'd been conversing the whole time on that very subject.

"It is impressive in its grandeur," Merry murmured, unwilling to offer her true grim opinions.

Frowning, the countess removed her spectacles. "Sit," she ordered, gesturing with those gold frames to the Louis XVI painted marquise chair.

Merry hadn't even fully seated herself on the mustard velvet upholstery before the other woman began speaking. "The household must be completely transformed. There can be no doubting that the adjusted plans had anything to do with... " Wonder of wonders, color splotched the other woman's cheeks. "With... with..."

"Your desire to return to London for a lovely holiday season," Merry neatly supplied.

The countess found her footing once more. "Precisely. As such, it is my expectation that the foyer, halls, and great ballroom are all fully decked for the Yuletide season." She pushed that large paper that had previously commanded her attention over to Merry.

Why... it hadn't just *looked* like a map. It *was* a map. Merry lifted a questioning gaze. "My—"

"It is a map, Miss Read. I trust you know something of maps?"

There would be a second wonder of wonders, because in that instance, the countess' eyes twinkled. That glimmer was gone as quickly as it had come.

Surely a flicker of the light. For the other woman could not and would not know the fun Merry had enjoyed making maps as a girl. She'd spent countless days designing countless maps for scavenger hunts she'd played with Ewan. His older and younger brothers had both been too serious to ever take part. "Yes, my lady," she finally said. "Maps are not foreign to me."

"This," the other woman went on as if Merry hadn't spoken, but then, an answer would never have been required from the countess, "is the layout of the townhouse." She turned the page around so

Merry could see. "Bedrooms here." She jabbed a finger at the area in question. "Guest suites"—she moved a long finger across the page —"here. And priority should be given to these following areas. The foyer." She jabbed her finger at the crude map as she spoke. "The music rooms. The ballroom. The dining rooms. In that order, Miss Read."

As the rapid-fire instructions flew, Merry struggled to commit the details to memory.

"There is, of course, no limit to what you may spend. You are free to decorate as you see fit. I'd only ask that it be tasteful and cheerful for the holiday season."

Merry stole a sideways peek at the garish rooms. Given their vastly different views on design aesthetic, the countess' ask seemed like a hard one indeed. "There is the matter of boughs and greenery and the yule log." Those trappings came far easier in the country.

Lady Maldavers pointed to another area on the map. "We have gardens with everything you might require, Miss Read." The countess proceeded to gather her things. "I suggest you begin by assessing the rooms you'll be working with, and then you may inventory the gardens in order to ascertain you've everything you require."

"Of course, my lady." Of course they would have everything she'd need. How very plebian for Merry to even think anything to the contrary. In possession of a title that went back to William the Conqueror, the Holmans held a level of wealth that people like Merry and her family could never dare wrap their minds around. It had been just one reason why she'd never been so foolish as to entertain the possibility that there could be more between her and the middle Holman brother. She'd not been so naïve as to think their futures could intertwine.

The countess set her spectacles atop her neatly stacked folders. "In the unlikely chance you can't find something you need, you may simply pass word to Blake, the butler, who will pass word to the maids and footmen, and they'll procure it for you in an instant." With that, Lady Maldavers started to sweep off. She paused in a whir of skirts. "Ah, there is one more thing."

"Yes, my lady?"

"Lord Grimslee."

Stiffening, Merry looked about for the gentleman and found just she and the countess remained the sole occupants of the room. "What of the viscount, my lady?"

"Lord Grimslee will be helping you."

Merry had oft suspected that when the countess had welcomed her firstborn into the world, she'd likely greeted him by his title.

The countess had turned to go when the implications of the matriarch's previous statement knocked Merry back on her heels. "I... what was that, my lady?"

The countess paused and faced Merry once more. "Is there a problem, Miss Read?" she asked in no-nonsense tones that brooked zero tolerance for so much as a question.

At any other moment, Merry would have cared about her place versus the countess' in this household. This, however, was decidedly *not* one of those moments. She plastered a smile upon her lips. "It is just... I take it I heard you *wrong*. For a moment, I *thought* you said—"

"Lord Grimslee will be assisting you."

"Your son?" Merry sought clarification, because... well, it really merited that elucidation.

Lady Maldavers sent a snowy-white eyebrow up in a terrifying arch. "I daresay there isn't another Lord Grimslee?"

No one—and certainly not Merry—would ever dare construe that droll retort as warm ribbing. Merry turned a palm up. "It is just... I'd be more efficient if I were to see to this alone."

"Ah, but you'll be as efficient as I tell you to be, Miss Read." Once more, the countess made to leave.

Merry quickly placed herself in Lady Maldavers' path. Her mother would have been horrified by her insolence, but there was no way Merry would be saddled with an underfoot gentleman, particularly one wholly uninterested in mirth and merry cheer at the holidays—or for as long as she'd known him, really. "I'm so very grateful for that offer. However, I trust Lord Grimslee has far greater responsibilities to see to."

The countess muttered something that sounded a good deal like *One would think*. Which was as preposterous an idea as the lady doing something as improper as muttering, and yet there it was.

Merry strained her ears. "What was that, my lady?"

"It wasn't an offer," the countess said coolly, perfectly composed once more. "As you well know, I do not make 'offers.' I place demands."

She tried again. "My lady—"

"I've already advised Lord Grimslee of your arrival. He is, as we speak, awaiting your presence in the front hall. He will show you a proper tour of the household." With a finality to those directions, the countess was gone.

Merry glanced down at the map in her hands. Frowning, she tipped it upside down and then right side up before abandoning those efforts. There were far more pressing matters to focus on—primarily the assistant she'd found herself saddled with.

Lucas Holman, the Viscount Grimslee, a gentleman she'd known since she'd been a babe. The earliest memory of her interactions with him went to the day she'd been fishing and had caught him lurking in the trees, all but crashing through the brush and leaving a calling card in the form of broken sticks and dried leaves. She'd called for him to join her.

"Do you intend to hide there all day, staring, or will you join me, Luke?"

There was a long pause.

Merry rolled her eyes. Did he truly believe she didn't know he was there?

"I wasn't staring. I have far more important things to do than hide or stare."

Only, he'd lingered for a long moment, and she'd been so very convinced he intended to join her. In the end, he'd stomped off and rejoined his tutor for some natural science lesson. It had been foolish to expect or believe he'd ever engage in any frivolous activity, such as fishing, for the sheer enjoyment of it.

"And now I'll be decorating the household with him?" Merry said quietly to herself.

She shuddered.

She'd been unable to reason with the mother, but mayhap she'd have luck with the son. After all, she'd known Lord Grimslee since they were children. As such, she'd wager her soul on Sunday that he had even less interest in assisting her than she had in having him underfoot while she transformed the earl and countess' Mayfair residence.

With that plan formed in her mind, she set out in search of the viscount. Yes, he might not have been the friendliest of males to her growing up, but he had been nothing if not reasonable. He could be reasoned with. Merry made her way back down the same windy trail she'd taken, finding herself lost at only two turns, before she reached the corridor that spilled out into the massive foyer. And stopped at the sight before her.

Lord Grimslee. Never had the *grim* in his name suited him more.

This was the man she'd be taking her help from?

It had been bad enough when she'd imagined receiving help from the stuffy, proper, more than slightly condescending in his stare Lord Grimslee.

But this?

To be saddled with a slumbering, disheveled Lord Grimslee stinking of spirits?

As if adding a punctuation mark to her rapidly spiraling horror, the prone figure on the too-small-for-him wooden entryway bench emitted a shuddery snore.

Merry narrowed her eyes.

Well, be he a viscount or future earl or the damned King of England himself, she'd not spent all those years studying in Europe to return to play nursemaid to a spoiled, indulgent man-babe.

Marching over to the tall and narrow foyer table, with the expected gold inlay, Merry grabbed the tolling bell there. She caught the clapper to keep it from chiming just yet, and then standing over Lord Grimslee's makeshift bed, she swung it hard.

With a gasping snort, the gentleman toppled off of the bench and landed hard on the floor.

Tightening her mouth, Merry leaned over her thirty-four-year-old charge. "Good morning, Lord Grimslee."

CHAPTER THREE

Luke had believed his body couldn't ache any more than it had when he'd first opened his eyes that morning.

Only to find, sprawled upon the marble foyer of his Mayfair residence, just how wrong he'd been. From his hip on up to his neck and on to his skull, he ached from where he'd struck the floor.

Which begged the bloody question: Why in blazes was he in the foyer... on the floor?

He struggled to slog through a still foggy brain to make sense out of it all.

Ding-ding-ding.

Oh, good God. More of that ringing. Not the one to have greeted him that morn in his bed, but an altogether new and different chime, louder and more grievous.

Groaning, he closed his eyes. "Stop with that infernal ringing." What might have otherwise been an impressive order was ruined by his gravelly tones, coarse from pain and lack of sleep.

A shadow fell over him. "Oh, my apologies for disturbing you."

"You hardly sound apologetic," he muttered. In fact, that distantly familiar, husky coloratura sounded anything *but*.

"Oh, that would be because I'm not really sorry," the woman said dryly.

Who in hell was his latest tormenter? He forced his eyes open.

And found a stern, decidedly angry young woman frowning down at him. He blinked slowly.

Surely his eyes deceived him.

His steward's eldest child, the once-precocious girl who'd sought out and found more trouble than he or all the Holman brothers combined. But it couldn't be. She'd been gone now... he searched his mind. Three... mayhap four years. And mayhap he was having the most peculiar dream about the young woman. Her hair was drawn back in a serviceable plait, and a handful of curls danced about her shoulders that had that same nearly coal-black hue as Merry Read had possessed. "Miss Read?"

"The very same," she said tightly, confirming she was, one, in fact, very real, and two, about as pleased with him as his father had been that morn. Alas, what other reaction should be expected of anyone who'd found a person sprawled upon the floor? His steward's eldest child folded her arms at her chest. "Though I must say I hardly recognize you, my lord."

For the first time, he felt a sentiment that had become so foreign, he'd doubted himself even capable of it.

Shame.

It clawed at his gut and made a mockery of the illusion that there was no opinion he cared for any longer. In fact, he cared a good deal more than he would have liked. A product, no doubt, of the longevity of his relationship with the woman before him... or, in this case, over him.

At the awkward lengthening of silence, he cleared his throat. "I was resting," he said in perfectly crisp tones.

Merry snorted. "In the foyer?" She leaned down, that slight movement sending the bell in her hand to jingling. "Might I suggest your chambers next time, my lord?"

Heat slapped at his cheeks, and with all the aplomb a man could muster while sprawled on his arse, Luke pushed himself up onto his elbows. "I didn't say I was sleeping," he reminded her.

"No." She paused. "Your snoring, however, did say as much."

His mouth moved, but he couldn't get a single word out. Nor did that struggle have anything to do with his night of excess. Never in the whole of his life had any man or woman dared to challenge him.

"Be that as it may," she went on with a mastery of conversation that even his expert hostess of a mother would be hard-pressed to emulate, "as you're well aware, I am here at your mother's behest."

Luke struggled to his feet. "Aren't we all," he muttered.

The lady drifted so close, her skirts stirred against his legs. "What was that, my lord?"

"Nothing at all." Despite her belief, Merry Read couldn't be further from the mark. He'd not been aware of either her presence in his household or any plans his mother had for him... or them? Or any of it. It was an admission, however, he'd not make. As it was, it was hard enough saving face from down on the cold, hard floor. "The countess may have mentioned something of it," he lied.

Merry opened her mouth to say something, but her gaze lingered on his gaping jacket.

"I trust you are somehow displeased with your assignment?" With as much as a gentleman in dishabille could manage, he buttoned his jacket, or he tried to see to the damned eyeholes. Alas, his senses and motions were dulled by a night of excess, and the task was not made any easier with Merry Read's eyes on his every movement.

She snorted. "Whatever gave you that opinion, my lord? You see, it is not that I'm..."

Only half listening, Luke struggled with a button. "Bloody hell," he mumbled through the young woman's ramblings. "Bloody buttons."

"Oh, just stop," Merry clipped out. "Here now. Let me see to that." Knocking his hands out of the way, she undid his previous work... his previous uneven work. "And furthermore, it's hardly the buttons' fault," she said coolly. "Now, as I was saying..."

Luke knew he should be wholly attending her, but he remained fixed upon the top of her bent head, entranced by the sheer intimacy of her movements. Any other lady would have averted her eyes. Nay, any other woman would have rushed off in the opposite direction. Merry Read, however, had never been like any other woman of his acquaintance. She'd been bold, unapologetic, and spirited, and growing up all the way unto adulthood, he'd not known whether to be horrified or captivated by her.

"...I am unable to see how you might..."

As she buttoned his jacket, her callused fingers brushed the flat planes of his stomach, and the muscles there rippled under the inadvertent caress as his white lawn shirt proved little barrier to her touch. Heat. Pure, unadulterated heat washed through him.

Merry made quick work of what had been an otherwise impossible-for-him task and proved remarkably unaffected through it. "There," she said with a little nod before taking a step away from him. She stared expectantly at him.

And he, who'd never lost track of any discourse or discussion, found his mind blank, and because of it, a proper response was absent. "Uh..."

Merry narrowed her eyes, and thick black lashes swept down like a blanket upon her cream-white skin. "You weren't listening."

"I was." How easy it had become for the lies to simply roll from his tongue.

"Then what did I say?" she shot back.

However, he was rubbish at the skillful ability to prevaricate. By the sparkle in Merry's chocolate-brown eyes, she knew it, too.

"You were expressing displeasure with your current assignment," he ventured.

The young woman's crimson rosebud lips formed a perfect moue of surprise. So, he was on the mark, then. "Though I did not say as much, I appreciate that you detected those undertones."

Feeling pleased with himself for the first time since he'd chosen honor over happiness, Luke smoothed his lapels. "You're welcome."

"I wasn't, at any point, thanking you," Merry said, her expression deadpan. Sticking a foot out, she drummed that serviceable boot on the floor. "I would, however, like to ask what you intend to do about my concerns."

Oh, blast and damn. This was where he really would benefit from those skills of prevarication. "Why don't you tell me how you would like me to handle your situation, Merry?" The use of her name slipped out easily, a product of the lifetime they'd known each other.

Nearly five inches shorter than his own six-foot frame, the young woman went up on tiptoes to peer at his face.

Luke resisted the uncomfortable urge to shift under that scrutiny. Being the recipient of disapproval and insolence was as foreign to him as the Latin language had been when his tutor had first set out those books.

Merry sank back on her heels. "You have no idea what I'm talking about."

Damn, she'd always been more clever than half. "I do know whatever it is has you displeased." He flashed a sheepish smile.

Her heart-shaped features remained set in an unimpressed mask. "I'm here to decorate for the holidays," she began slowly, as if schooling a lackwit.

"Which, given your love of the Christmastide season, I should expect would be something you enjoy." He'd said too much. It was a rare and uncomfortable slip.

Her eyes formed perfect circles in her face as—for the first time since she'd rung that bell, knocked him on his arse, and then seen to dressing him—she was the one knocked off-kilter. "You... knew that?" she asked softly.

Knowing was a vast shade different than *remembering*. The former implied he'd been oblivious to Merry Read, the other that he'd been a solitary, lonely boy more aware of the joys his steward's daughter had found around a house that had been only a sterile kingdom he'd one day inherit.

He gave an uncomfortable clearing of his throat. "How could I forget you and my brother trolling the halls, singing Christmas carols outside my rooms as I studied?"

A wistful smile hovered on her lips. "You remember that?"

"It had been intentional, then," he said as that mystery from his youth was at long last answered, and here at the unlikeliest of times by the unlikeliest of participants in that revelry.

Her eyes sparkled. Around the chambers of his mind, the blend of her and Ewan's exuberant laughter pealed in an echo of that long-ago day, and he was struck by the memory of his own wistfulness in that moment before he'd had his knuckles rapped and his Latin lesson resumed. "I remember it quite well," he murmured.

"It was never about teasing or tormenting you, Luke," she said in a low voice. "It was only to get you to join us in the fun."

Which he never had. His facial muscles strained under the effort it took to keep the mask in place. "I had my studies and—"

"Your responsibilities as the heir to one of England's oldest, most-respected titles," she intoned in a scarily perfect rendering of the words he'd uttered and the tones he'd uttered them in long ago.

He started. She should remember that long-ago day when he'd uttered those very words?

"Yes." Merry took a step closer. "I remember *that*," she said, following with an unnerving accuracy the path his thoughts had traversed. "As such, I'm well aware that you have far more pressing obligations to command your attention than assisting me in my endeavors this holiday season."

The young woman had hit the nail on the head with that assumption. There were any number of commitments expected of him. There was just one difference—he didn't give ten damns about any one of them. Not any longer. "If I've understood you this morn, Merry, you do not wish for my help. Am I correct in this?"

The minx had the good grace to blush. And here he'd believed the headstrong free spirit incapable of that expression. "You are."

There it was. At last, she'd bluntly spoken what she truly wished and felt—she didn't want him near her or her assignment this holiday season. Given that, he'd expect she'd at least dip a curtsy and be on her way, off to the task that his mother had ordered her here to fulfill. When she made no move to go, Luke winged a brow up. "Is there anything else, Merry?" he asked dryly.

The color deepened in her cheeks. Merry further straightened her narrow and already erect shoulders. "No. No," she said. "That is all, my lord."

It did not escape his notice that she'd my-lorded him. How could he explain the regret that sluiced inside at that formality she'd thrown back up into place? Because he was first, foremost, and only ever the future earl.

Except, as she turned to go, there was no deferential curtsy. Instead, Merry gave a snap of her skirts and marched off.

He stared after her retreating frame until she disappeared down the length of the hall. His mother had sought to saddle him with a nursemaid to keep him out of trouble. That alone should be reason enough to thwart her plans.

I'm well aware that you have far more pressing obligations to command your attention than assisting me in my endeavors this holiday season.

She wanted nothing to do with him or his help. And gentleman that he had been raised to be, the situation merited he honor the young woman's wishes.

Alas, he was no longer the gentleman she or anyone—himself included—recognized.

Luke grinned, and whistling *Hark! The Herald Angels Sing*, he sought out his offices and set to work plotting.

CHAPTER FOUR

Four o'clock in the morning was Merry's work time of choice.

It was early enough that most lords and ladies hadn't yet arisen, so there wasn't the worry of being underfoot or, more important, having an employer underfoot, overseeing all, and dictating what they felt a room called for.

That morn, she arose and set out to inventory the greenery available to her in the countess' limitless gardens.

Her head down, Merry evaluated the list she'd assembled last evening.

Ivy.
Mistletoe.
Sprigs of garland.

The list was incomplete. Since she'd begun going through her morning ablutions, she'd visited and revisited her notes. Alas, since she'd arrived yesterday morn, she'd been distracted. Hopelessly distracted.

And for the unlikeliest reason. Or, to be more precise, the unlikeliest person.

Lord Luke.

But the gentleman in the foyer had been Luke as she'd never seen him or known him. In fact, she'd never believed he could be... well, the person he'd been yesterday.

With scruff on his cheeks and his jacket discarded, he'd had the look of a rogue or scoundrel.

He'd also possessed a biting dryness she didn't remember. No, he'd only ever been polite and respectful and proper.

When she'd casually set to work buttoning his jacket, he'd simply been the stodgy Lord Grimslee whom she'd pitied as a boy for his seriousness. But this Lord Grimslee had a flat belly carved of muscle. His was the physique not of the padded peers, but of the artists she'd worked alongside in France.

From the corner of her eye, she peeked at the row of familial likenesses on the wall, and there staring down at her was Lord Ewan. In the portrait, he wore the familiar smile of his youth.

She'd so admired Lord Ewan and had been looking forward to her reunion with him... and yet, she'd not given him a single thought since she'd stumbled upon his stodgier, stuffier brother.

Or rather, the stodgier and stuffier brother he'd been. The gentleman in the foyer had borne no hint of the always scowling boy of her reminiscences.

"Stop it," she muttered. She'd far more pressing matters to attend than the physique of Luke, the future Earl of Maldavers.

The pencil in her fingertips quivered.

Or the devilish half grin on his firm lips.

As if to mock those musings, she looked up once more at Lord Luke's visage. It was a more recent rendering. Attired in dark sapphire with a snowy cravat, the austere figure bore no likeness to the man she'd come upon yesterday. This was Lord Luke as he'd been. This was Lord Luke as he'd always *be*, even with the aberration of yesterday.

That sobering reminder proved enough to bring her back to the task at hand.

Quickening her pace, Merry reread her partially completed list.

Cypress Branches
Nandina

Though it was unlikely the countess would have that elegant shrub, only new to Europe.

Spindle tree leaves

She was missing something. What was she missing?

Merry stopped abruptly. Of course! "Hol—"

"Well, hullo to you, too, Miss Read."

With a shriek, she collided with a hard wall.

Or rather, a hard wall that was Luke's muscular chest.

She shot her arms out to stop herself from landing on her buttocks right there in the middle of the countess' corridor.

Luke, however, already had her by the shoulders, steadying her. All the while, the folder that had been knocked from her hands sent papers sprinkling down like a heavy snowfall. "I daresay you'd be the first to be knocked head over heels by me." He grinned.

It was the wicked, devil's grin he'd briefly worn yesterday. And there was only one certainty—one would be wise to not dance with the devil at the Yuletide season. And if he wore that smile, ever, no lady's heart would be safe.

As if to punctuate that very real danger, her heart thumped erratically. "Forgive me. I was not looking where I was going." Dropping to a knee, she scrambled to gather up her pages.

Luke joined her on the floor, and shock brought her head shooting up.

"What are you doing?"

"I think it should be fairly obvious." He didn't pause in his efforts. "Nay, it should be *completely* obvious."

And yet, it *was* obvious and, at the same time, *not*.

Because servants had long been invisible to Lord Luke. *Merry* had long been invisible to him.

Not that he paid her any attention now. Now, he moved quickly about the corridor, rescuing her notes and maps. It didn't fit with who he was or, for that matter, any of the lords or ladies whose households she'd worked in.

"You don't help servants," she blurted.

He froze, her pages held in an uneven pile within his grip.

An immediate wave of guilt followed for having called him out for past behaviors, particularly when he assisted her in this moment.

But when he looked up, he wore that scoundrel's smile. "I'm not the same man I was." He winked and resumed cleaning up her mess.

Merry sank back on her haunches. Rogue's grins? Winking? *Winking?* Nay, Luke certainly wasn't the respectable and serious man she recalled. At every turn, she found herself vastly preferring this unbuttoned-down version of his previous stodgy self.

"Here we are," he said and jumped up. With one hand, he proffered the slightly sloppy stack, and the other he held out to help her to feet.

Without hesitating, Merry placed her palm in his. He folded his larger hand over hers in a hold that was tender but strong. As he drew Merry to her feet, a delicious tingling where he touched her traveled to her wrist and up the inside of her forearm.

Merry yanked her hand free and made a show of organizing her papers.

What madness was this response to Lucas Holman, the Viscount Grimslee, of all people?

There was only one certainty—he needed to be on his way. She didn't need a thoughtful-to-his-servants scoundrel with a quixotic touch anywhere near. "I thank you for your help," she said, her voice coming out more than slightly unsteady to her ears. And to cement the reminder of the station divide between them that he'd always kept perfectly erect, Merry dropped a curtsy.

His brows came together. "Did you just curtsy to me?"

She might as well have tugged a glove free, slapped him across the face, and called him out for all the outrage there. Her lips pulled at the corners. "If you could not tell, then I daresay that is hardly a testimonial to my skill."

"I've known you since you were in the nursery."

"I didn't have a nursery," she pointed out. She'd had a cottage, and the only visits she'd had to the manor house had been to join Ewan in play.

Luke frowned. "Since you were a babe, then," he corrected, still as hopelessly lost when it came to recognizing humor, even droll attempts at it.

She sighed. "Of course I curtsied to you, my—"

"Stop," he bit out.

Her lips moved, but no words came out.

"The days of that are at an end."

"To servants curtsying?" she asked with feigned somberness. "And here I thought that was a custom as popular as tea and rain in England."

"I referred to *your* curtsying." His frown deepened. "I *know* you."

I know you.

Those three words knocked her temporarily off-balance. His was an odd statement, given that she'd believed herself invisible to him. Merry made her eyes go wide. "And you don't know all your servants?"

Color rushed his cheeks. "I do. What I was referring to was the length of our—" He abruptly cut off his words. "You're teasing me," he mumbled under his breath. Luke adjusted an already immaculate cravat.

Merry leaned in and whispered, "Just a bit." How very... endearing this less-sure, more-open version of the viscount. For a very brief moment, she regretted that she'd declined to let him assist her in the organization of the countess' impromptu holiday affair.

That staggering realization brought Merry swiftly back to her task at hand. "If you'll excuse me, I have the greenery to see to."

"Of course," he said.

Continuing on her way, Merry consulted the countess' crude map as she went... before she registered the figure moving in harmony with her steps. Merry stopped, and Luke matched suit. "What are you doing?"

He folded his arms at his chest. "Awaiting your instructions, Merry."

It hit her. "You... still think to join me."

He scoffed. "Hardly." Luke grinned. "I *intend* to."

She cocked her head. Somewhere in the house came the chime of a clock marking the quarter hour, and still she remained rooted to the thin red carpet lining the countess' hall.

Merry didn't know when it happened.

Having been gone traveling, she didn't know how long it had been, but sometime in her absence, Lucas Holman, the Viscount Grimslee, had gone mad.

There was no other accounting for all the changes that had befallen him.

Not for the first time, she wondered at what had happened to bring about the transformation. Questions swirled, questions that she shouldn't be having about the earl's eldest son and heir.

Merry tried once more. "As I indicated yesterday, I don't require help organizing the festivities," she said gently, while infusing a firmness to her tone that she'd used on the servants who'd worked under her in her time in Europe. "And you agreed."

She made to go.

Luke slid himself into her path. "I'm going to force myself upon you, Merry, so I suggest you accustom yourself to the idea."

Merry strangled on a sound that was somewhere between a gasp and a laugh.

Luke's eyebrows climbed to his hairline. "Not that way!" He shot a hand out so quickly, he caught her in the nose.

She cradled the injured cartilage.

"Good God," he croaked. "I'm..."

"Not so very good at this?" she asked into her hand. Merry continued to venture completions to that unfinished statement. "Sorry? Usually not known for assaulting or threatening assault?"

"All of the above apply." Luke tugged at his cravat until the previously immaculate knot hung in hopeless disrepair.

They remained locked in a silent battle. She, tensed. He, with his features relaxed in casual amusement.

The blighter. He was so very determined to join her, and by the firm set to his shoulders, he'd no intention of leaving.

But why?

Why was he so very adamant about joining her? Why, when she had no desire for his *help*?

Because there had to be some reason.

Which brought with it only more and more questions. Questions she was determined to get to the bottom of so she could end this unwilling fascination with him.

"Very well," she allowed. "I'll accept your help." For now. But there were two certainties: She'd have her answers, and after she had them, well, he'd last not at all in his role.

And then she could resume organizing the holiday gathering.

"Fetch your cloak."

"My—?"

She gave him a look that silenced the remainder of his question. "Meet me in the foyer in twenty minutes, my lord."

With that, Merry mentally adjusted her plans for the day.

CHAPTER FIVE

Merry had been clear at every turn that she'd no wish for his company.

She'd apparently tired of protesting and instead intended to off him.

There was no other accounting for the gleaming saw she held in hand.

Just then, she brought the serrated blade up and made a slashing motion through the air, and for one instant, Luke, halfway down the winding stairway, contemplated surrendering the battle.

Alas, Merry made the decision for him.

As she whipped around, her skirts snapped loudly about her ankles. "Shall we?"

Did he imagine that she lifted her saw and pointed it in his direction for an overlong beat before turning and starting at a determined clip for the front door?

The butler, Blake, emerged from the shadows and drew the panel open.

Wind gusted through the front door with a blast of cold. She was mad. "We are going out in this?" He hastened his steps to catch her.

"I am going out in this," she called, her voice carrying in the winter quiet, made all the louder by the dearth of life in London at the holiday season.

He hurried to pull on his gloves. The leather articles, however, did little to chase away the chill, and in a bid to bring some warmth to his freezing digits, he rubbed his palms quickly together.

From out of the corner of his eye, he caught the sideways peek Merry stole in his direction, and he forced his arms back to his sides.

Why... why... the chit hadn't anticipated he'd accompany her. She'd *expected* he'd find the frigid temperatures and the threat of snow hanging in the early morn sky reason enough to return to the comforts of his familial residence and set himself up with a paper and a glass of brandy to warm him.

And in any one of the thirty-four years before this, Merry would have been correct in her postulation.

But that had been before he'd gone and made a mess of his life and his happiness. Now, he didn't give a jot for propriety. "I'll hand it to you, Merry Read," he said as they locked in a matched pace to whatever destination she'd planned. "You are nothing if not determined and tenacious."

She smiled. "Th-thank you." Her voice trembled slightly from the cold.

"I didn't intend it as a compliment."

"Well, it w-would be hard to take it any other way. What is the al-alternative? That I'm indecisive and given to vacillating?" She gesticulated wildly with her saw as she spoke, and he ducked sideways as that gleaming metal came entirely too close to his left arm.

"Well, I have no intention of leaving."

"Hmph," she muttered, her huff of annoyance stirring a little cloud of white.

Unfortunately, the pair of young footmen following close at their heels also had little intention of leaving.

And he didn't know why their presence should so annoy him.

Liar. You know. You know very well. The last thing he'd anticipated or wanted was to share his and Merry's outing with anyone, particularly gossiping servants. Quite simply, he found himself enjoying her company, and her barbs, and challenges, when he hadn't enjoyed... well, really anything since he'd tried to repair his relationship with Josephine Pratt.

Only, the pain that usually came from the memory of his folly and her and what could have been... didn't come.

"You've not said where we're going," he noted as they moved at the steady clip Merry set through the streets of Mayfair.

"Because you've only just asked. Green Park," she said, continuing to swing her arm as they walked.

"Here." Luke reached for her saw. "Let me carry that."

Merry's steps slowed, and there was a softening in her eyes.

"It is mostly an act of self-preservation." He immediately wished to call back that admission, for just like that, he'd quashed all the previous warmth in her eyes.

With a roll of her eyes, Merry held out the saw. "You're in-s-sufferable."

"I'd wager that's not the first time that charge has been leveled at me," he conceded, raising the edge of the blade to his brow in mock salute.

A sharp bark of laughter escaped from her, the expression of mirth tinkling and bell-like. "Have a care, or you're going to c-cut yourself."

"Ah, so that was not your intention, then?"

She laughed again.

He'd never been responsible for another person's mirth. Not like this. Not free and unrestrained and fulsome and sincere. Even with his former betrothed, their exchanges had been restrained. The lone embrace they'd shared had been equally restrained. Now, he found himself wondering what it would be like to take Merry Read in his arms.

No doubt she'd be a woman who kissed and made love with the same abandon she showed at their every interaction. And through the cold of the morn came heat that spiraled through him, a desire to discover those truths for himself.

"I don't recall you like th-this," she said as they entered Green Park, and for one horrifying moment, he believed she'd seen the wicked path his thoughts had traveled, thoughts that included her and him, together.

"And how is that?" Unnerved by how much Merry Read's opinion meant to him, he kept his gaze trained carefully forward.

"Teasing. Lighthearted. Cheerful."

They reached the entrance of Green Park, and he was grateful when she looked to the footmen who'd reached their sides. She favored the pair with a smile. "Here you are." Reaching into the pocket sewn along the front of her cloak, she withdrew two small sacks and placed them in their hands. "Some flat chocolate discs covered with nonpareils," she whispered. "I snuck some from my mother's kitchens before I came to London."

For the adoration in the young men's eyes, she might as well have handed them the moon and a sprinkling of stars to go with it.

"Thank you, ma'am," they said in unison.

"Thank you, Lawrence and Eaves. We shall call for you when we require your assistance."

Luke proved himself a bastard once again, for resentment burned in his belly at those shared smiles.

Luke stared after the young lads as they took themselves off. "Lawrence and Eaves," he murmured. "You gathered that after less than a day in my household." He'd not known their names in the years the young men had served in his employ.

Merry shrugged. "The better question is why don't you know?" She looked squarely at him. "There's always time to learn about the people around you. Why, you know my name," she pointed out.

He frowned. "You're not..." *A servant.*

"*Just* a servant?" She glanced his way.

Phrased that way, he heard the smugness in it. "I didn't mean... What I was saying..." Only, what *had* he been saying?

"Yes?" she prodded.

Yes, her father was his family's steward and her mother his family's housekeeper, and both her siblings were employed by his family. But she wasn't at all the same. "You played freely with my brother," he said on a rush. And how he'd envied them both. "You had free rein of the estates."

"And you think that somehow makes me different than Lawrence and Eaves?" she asked, amusement lacing her tone.

It did.

"It doesn't," she said, as if hearing his silent protestations. "It does not change that I'm still just a servant. I'm no different than Lawrence or Eaves or my mother or father or any other man, woman, or child in your employ." She stopped and put herself in front of him, halting his forward strides. "People do not cease to be people because they are born outside your illustrious ranks, Luke," she said with a matter-of-factness that stung more than had there been malice. She spoke so pragmatically, as if she merely recited the simplest of facts that the whole world should be in possession of but which he'd somehow failed to gather. "Just because people serve you doesn't mean they don't deserve to be *seen*."

Her earnestly delivered words brought Luke to a slow stop, and he stared off sightlessly into the distance as a long-distant memory whispered forward.

"But I like Willis, Mother."

"There are no buts, Lucas. Willis is a servant, and you don't play with servants."

"He's a boy."

"He is a servant," his mother insisted tersely.

Luke glared at his mother and his silent father. "Ewan plays with him."

His father at last spoke. "Ewan will not be earl one day."

"You are correct," he whispered, and it was hard to say who was more shocked by that quiet admission, him or the woman beside him. Back in the moment, he looked to Merry. "My father and mother schooled me early on in my responsibilities." A lone snowflake floated past, followed by another and another, until a soft swirl of white filled the air and dusted the ground. "Every expectation, every rule, everything from what I was to eat or not eat, on to who I was able to interact with was carefully specified." Those born of his station would have likely received a similar elucidation. There were those who existed within the nobility... and everyone else. As such, he'd been reared on that principle. It had shaped him and his every interaction. Never before had he questioned the wrongness of it... until Merry. However, blame didn't belong to his parents, it belonged to him for having blindly followed. "I've been a fool, listening and following expectations without ever thinking for myself."

Her eyes widened into enormous pools that put him in mind of warmed chocolate.

Luke slashed his spare hand in the direction of where the footmen had stood when Merry had temporarily relieved them of their responsibilities. "They've been part of my household staff for two and a half years now," he said, his words tumbling quickly over each other. "Two and a half years. Nine hundred and twelve days. And how do I know that?"

She opened her mouth, but he finished over her.

"Because I'm the one responsible for the finances and the ledgers detailing matters of business. Business, Merry. Business." His voice crept up. "And I've not known their names." He rocked back on his heels. "I've moved through life focused entirely on estate business and matters before Parliament, and well, there's never been time for those details." Even as that admission left him, he caught the conceit and self-absorption behind it, and along with that came an increasingly familiar sentiment—shame.

As she led them from the graveled path, through the grass, onward to a copse of trees, his strides grew quicker and more frantic. "And what has my devotion to rank and status gotten me?" His elevated voice carried throughout the gardens. "One brother whom I no longer speak with, the other brother whom I almost never speak to except for discussions on familial business." It wasn't every day that a man looked at himself, truly looked at himself, and saw that he didn't like who he was. He didn't like who he was, at all. And yet... closing his eyes, he tilted his head up toward the sky.

How very invigorating it was to simply own who he was and what he'd allowed himself to become.

Merry lightly squeezed his arm, bringing his eyes open. "Most noblemen will go their whole lives without changing," she said quietly. "Without seeing servants as people or seeing any worth in those born outside their ranks, and yet you have."

He laughed bitterly. "You heap praise where it's undeserved."

Her lips twitched at the corners, and she tightened her hold upon his forearm once more. "If you consider that praise, then there's been a dearth of compliments in your life." She softened that with a smile. Then the earlier seriousness returned to her expressive features. "I only speak the truth, Luke."

Luke. She'd called him by his Christian name, and how very right it felt wrapped in her deep contralto.

"I daresay this is the beginning of a friendship between us."

She laughed softly.

"You find that so very amusing?" he asked on a frown, equal parts hurt and offended. He'd not had a friend in his life, and having hung himself out there, vulnerable as he now was, left him with a strange little ache in his chest.

"Forgive me," she said, her smile promptly dying, and he fought to keep his features immobile as she ran an astute and piercing gaze over him. "I'm not laughing at you, but rather, at the improbability of knowing one another for nearly the whole of our lives and only now choosing to begin a friendship. Why... you didn't even know I was alive until yesterday morn," she inaccurately pointed out before striding off toward the neat row of evergreens twenty paces ahead.

You didn't even know I was alive.

Let her to her opinions. Luke beat the handle of the saw against his thigh and stared after her. He'd already hung himself out there, and all he'd managed to garner was a healthy degree of embarrass-ment. So why was it so very important that she know the truth? That he'd not been a total bastard. At least not as a young boy, he hadn't. That aspect of his character had come later, with years of tutelage at the hands of his father and tutors.

"You and Ewan always played battledore. He was rubbish at it, and you never wanted to beat him on three, so you played to five sets." He paused. "And you always won," he called after her. The winter quiet exaggerated the volume of his voice.

Merry's forward steps continued, but slowed and then stopped altogether.

"You hated playing spillikins on the mahogany floors," he said, "because there was not enough challenge in it, so you always played in the gardens, just off the graveled path that led to the boxwood maze."

Stop talking. Just stop this instant. So why did the words keep coming? "You and Ewan played hopscotch along the watering foun-tain, and both tried to get one another to miss a step and tumble into the fountain." He stared over the top of her head. "You never did," he said softly to himself. A sad little chuckle rumbled in his chest. "Ewan always did. And I was and remain certain it was intentional. That he loved taking a swim..." *Stop. Just stop.*

This time, he managed to quell the flow of memories.

Ever so slowly, Merry turned and faced him. The expression she wore was stricken.

Another blast of wind gusted around them, pulling at her plait and dusting her midnight tresses with a faint coating of white that gave her the look of some magical, winter wonderland creature.

Luke clenched and unclenched his hands, his left palm gripping the handle of the saw hard enough that the wood bit through the thick fabric of his leather gloves.

He'd been wrong.

With her lips parted and her wide-eyed gaze upon him, he'd

never been more exposed and vulnerable than he was in this very moment.

EVERYTHING MERRY HAD BELIEVED about Luke Holman, the painfully serious Lord Grimslee as a boy, had been a lie.

Of their own volition, her legs drew her back over to him.

She stopped with just two paces between them so she might better see the slightly heavy, angular planes of his face. His lips were tensed and strained white at the corners. His clear blue gaze was guarded. Wary.

"But... but... you never played with us," she said.

"No." Doffing his high, fur-trimmed hat, Luke beat it against his thigh.

Every expectation, every rule, everything from what I was to eat or not eat, on to who I was able to interact with was carefully specified.

It hit her with all the force of a fast-moving carriage.

"You weren't allowed," she whispered. "That is why you didn't speak to me. Or play with me. Because you were instructed not to."

A muscle rippled along his jaw, the tension there palpable, and her fingers ached with the need to smooth it away.

"I wanted to," he confessed.

And her heart buckled.

How wrong she'd been about Luke Holman. So very wrong.

For she'd thought he felt himself above her. She'd thought him too serious and studious to partake in the children's games she'd played with Ewan.

Only to find she hadn't been invisible. Rather, Luke's parents had insisted he live a life devoid of a child's pleasures.

Now, she thought of him in a new light, as a lonely boy whose entire existence had been dictated to and for him. A boy who'd never been able to simply be a boy and who'd instead dutifully followed the rules set down by his parents, while wishing for more. Wanting for more.

She thought of herself as she'd been just two days ago, chatting and laughing with her siblings about Luke, all the while failing to see him as a person... and worse, not considering what had shaped him into the person he was.

Mayhap that was why he wished to join her, then. Mayhap he wanted to steal moments from now that he'd been denied for his thirty-four years before now. In this moment, with all he'd revealed, she found herself seeing him in a new light. Or, really, seeing him for the first time. Mayhap that was why, despite her earlier resolve to be rid of his company, she found herself relenting.

"Christmas trees," she said.

Luke cocked his head, sending a lone curl falling over his brow, softening him.

"That is why we're h-here." She gestured through the whorl of snowflakes to the rows of evergreen ahead. Merry huddled deeper into the folds of her cloak. "When your brother and I were small, we came upon a story of Martin Luther and how one Christmastide season he decorated the branches with candles."

Luke looked from her to the trees and then back to her. "Are you saying we are here... to decorate a *tree*?" He spoke slowly, one trying to puzzle through the peculiarity of that telling.

Her lips twitched reflexively. "No, we aren't decorating the tree here." She gestured to the saw in his hand, and he followed her pointed glance. "We're going to cut one down and decorate it at your family's household."

His mouth moved, giving him the look of a trout out of a water. With a soft laugh that stirred a breath of white from the cold, she beckoned him forward. "Come." She started through the rows of trees, eyeing the options around them. The viscount she recalled would never dare enter Green Park to cut a tree down. He would have seen not only the process, but the intended result, as inane.

The crunch of snow and gravel indicated Luke intended to join her.

Not for the first time, she wondered at just what accounted for the drastic change that had befallen him in her absence. The only certainty was that she enjoyed this newer version of Luke. Around him, she didn't feel as if she was nothing more than a servant, which was what she was and what she'd been treated like by every lord or lady she'd come across in her travels of the Continent.

"I confess to not understanding it all," he said as he fell into step beside her. "It's hardly logical."

She glanced over, and he launched into a lecture. "Trees have no place in a household. They exist outside and are hardly an article to be decorated."

"Says who?"

He opened his mouth. "Says... everything the world knows about trees."

How very much like the sober little boy who'd called out Merry and his brother for one of the many games they'd played outside his schoolroom.

She stopped and put herself in his path. "Ah, but that is the point, Luke."

"What is the point?" he asked, looking hopelessly perplexed.

She took mercy. "Cutting trees down isn't logical. It doesn't serve any purpose but one"—she lifted a single finger—"to bring pleasure." Merry held his gaze and tried to will him to understand. "That which is fun or enjoyable is not bound by or created in logic. It is simply a matter of finding pleasure without any purpose required." Merry marched off, and this time, he accompanied her onward in her search without hesitation.

Merry passed her gaze around the copse, eyeing the trees as they went.

"How did you learn of this?" he asked.

"I've been traveling these past years. Your family was generous enough to send me abroad to visit households throughout the Continent." Shivering, Merry rubbed her palms frantically back and forth in a bid to bring some warmth to some part of her body. "I spent time with one noble family, where the lady of the household was from Portugal. The Regiment of the local high-Sacristans of the Cistercian Order wrote of Christmas branches that, upon Christmas Eve, were adorned with the brightest oranges. The other servants secretly derided the lady for that tradition, and I?" She smiled wistfully, remembering the eccentric older woman. "I was just so very fascinated, I wished to know everything about it."

Her skin tingled in a way that had nothing to do with the cold. She glanced over and found Luke's hooded gaze upon her. She cleared her throat. "I trust you find it silly."

"Quite the opposite," he said swiftly, and with his spare hand, he claimed one of hers. "I find myself..." His eyes moved over her face. "Riveted," he murmured.

At that slightest of pauses, her breath quickened and her chest rose and fell quickly, for in that moment, she could almost believe he spoke of her.

Cold as she was, she didn't want this moment with him to end. For in this very instant, she wasn't working or serving in the role of future housekeeper charged with the task of organizing the family's festivities. She was simply a woman conversing with a man about knowledge she'd gained in her travels and had shared with no one... because lords and ladies didn't speak to maids.

Wind whipped through the trees, stirring their branches. The frigid winter air sent snowflakes battering her cheeks, stinging her with their cold, and yet, his eyes upon her face, a heated look that bespoke desire, sent warmth radiating from her belly and fanning out, touching everyplace inside her.

It couldn't be desire... and yet, if it was not that which held them frozen here within the abandoned grounds of Green Park, what *was* it?

She wet her lips, and his eyes slipped a fraction lower as he took in that distracted movement. "Luke," she whispered, capable of nothing more than his name.

He lowered his mouth toward hers, and closing her eyes, Merry tilted her head back to receive his kiss—a kiss that did not come.

She struggled to force her lashes up.

His heavy features were strained. "I'm a gentleman," he said hoarsely. "I'll not do anything that you do not—"

Merry leaned up on tiptoe, erasing the space between them, and claimed his mouth for her own.

He froze and then, with a groan, devoured her lips, slanting his over hers. Again and again.

Thump.

She dimly registered the fall of the saw, and then his hat tumbled to the ground at their feet.

Clutching the fur-lined collar of Luke's cloak, Merry pressed herself against him and returned his kiss with unfrenzied abandon.

It was her first kiss. The first in the whole of her nearly thirty years. Not a young footman or village boy or bold son of any employer had ever even so much as attempted to steal an embrace. As such, she'd wondered what it would be like... and had believed herself incapable of inspiring desire so that any man would want to kiss her.

Only to see that belief proved to be a lie, here and now in Luke's arms.

His arms came around her, and she melted into him.

She moaned against his mouth, and he slid his tongue inside, stroking that bold flesh against hers, a brand that scorched and marked her as his. Her legs weakened under her, and he caught her hard to him and guided her back. Her back knocked against the wide trunk of a tree, and with his body as an anchor, he pressed her lightly against that tree and continued making love to her mouth.

"Luke," she moaned against his lips, and his name, breathless and weak, seemed to drive him into a frenzy.

He deepened their embrace. The moment proved fleeting,

however, as he continued his exploration, placing kisses on her cold cheeks, his breath warming her, his touch setting her afire.

Merry panted, and her hips took on a rhythm of their own as she undulated and moved against him in a bid to get closer.

The branches swayed noisily overhead, dancing in time to nature's fury and Merry and Luke's own passionate waltz.

Craaaaack.

Luke wrenched his mouth from hers, and with a curse, he hurled them out of the way. A small limb tumbled down a mere fraction of an inch from where they'd stood.

With that, reality came crashing in, an unwelcome, despised visitor in what had been the singularly most erotic, magical moments of her life.

Merry stood, her breathing coming hard and fast, as she fought for some semblance of a normal cadence.

The thing with having never been kissed was that a woman didn't know what to say after her first one.

In the end, she didn't have to say anything.

Clearing his throat, Luke swept up his forgotten hat and the saw. "Shall we?"

Shall we *what*? Continue their embrace? Find another place that was warmer and—

He was already scouring the grounds. "I think I have one," he said triumphantly.

Dumbly, Merry followed his gaze to a ten-foot evergreen that was perfectly rounded and had a perfect point at the top.

He had... simply moved on? To Christmas trees? While she was here, her heart threatening to pound out of her chest and her body still burning?

"Merry?"

"Of course. It's perfect," she blurted.

That morn, when they'd set out to Green Park, she'd been determined to be free of his company because she'd not wanted him around while she saw to her work. Now, everything had shifted... and yet, it had also remained the same. The last thing she wanted or could afford was having Luke Holman, the Viscount Grimslee, about. Not because she didn't want him near, but because she did. And that desire could only be dangerous.

As they settled on the evergreen tree, Merry committed to not taking any more help from Luke after this day.

No matter how much she wished to.

CHAPTER SIX

Luke had always been one to rise early.

Little rest for those of rank was the mantra his father had ingrained into him as a boy of four, when he'd been mastering his letters before the sun had even started its climb into the sky.

Since then, by three every morn, he was awake and groomed to face the day of business dealings and responsibilities.

It was an hour that most members of Polite Society would call ungodly.

Of course, as one who'd lived a life that wasn't licentious, he'd had no long nights of drinking or revelry, and so rising so early had never been a chore, not even as a young man just out of university. No, aside from the past four-month deviation from those norms, after the end of his betrothal to Josephine Pratt—now Josephine Everleigh —he'd risen before the roosters.

He'd never known a single soul to rise and face the day so early...

Until yesterday.

Until Merry.

Merry Read, who kissed without restraint and tasted of ginger-bread and orange and mint, a confectionary treat more intoxicating than any of the spirits Luke had drowned himself in these past months.

She was the reason he now waited in the same corridor he'd run into her when she was on her way to organize the holiday festivities.

Today also marked the first day he'd not awakened seized by the sting of regret and misery over the decisions he'd made in the name of honor.

Now, as he stood with a shoulder resting against the silk wallpaper, he felt only an eager anticipation to see her. Collecting his gold watch fob, Luke consulted the timepiece.

She'd be punctual.

If after her day of travels, she'd been awake and moving about yesterday at four o'clock in the morn, she'd be here now.

Restlessness filled him as he craned his head, searching for a hint of her.

And then he heard it.

> *"Bring a torch, Jeanette, Isabella!*
> *Bring a torch, to the stable call*
> *Christ is born. Tell the folk of the village."*

That slightly off-key contralto came softly down a nearby hall. He'd been a patron of London opera for some years. He'd attended performances throughout each Season, witnessing the performances of some of the most magnificent singers. Not a single one of those flawless, on-pitch voices held so much as a glimmer next to Merry's lively voice.

And he found every muscle in him straining toward that approaching songstress as the lyrics grew clearer and clearer.

> *"Lovely cakes that we have brought here*
> *Knock! Knock! Open the door for us!*
> *Knock! Knock! Let's—"*

Merry turned the corner and came to an abrupt stop.

His heart knocked against his chest, and as his lips curved in an effortless grin, he knew he was smiling like a lackwit, but he couldn't bring himself to care. He, who always donned a careful mask among all and guarded his pride with the same ferocity the king did his crown. "I believe the word you're looking for, Merry, is *celebrate*."

"How...?"

Luke pushed away from the wall and strolled the twenty-five or so paces toward her. "How do I know the lyrics?" Before she could speak, he broke into his own discordant song.

> *"Ah! Ah! Beautiful is the Mother!*
> *Ah! Ah! Beautiful is her child*
> *Who is that, knocking on the door?*
> *Who is it, knocking like that?"*

A smile dimpled her full cheeks. Had he even once made his former betrothed smile in this way, with a vivid brightness reflected in her expressive brown eyes? "I was *going* to ask how you continue to find me as you do, but hearing you break out into song has been vastly entertaining."

He pounced on her words. "Ah, so you have been seeking to avoid me?" Folding his arms at his chest, he gave her a pointed look. What accounted for the crushing disappointment her admission wrought?

"On the contrary. I was seeking to begin my work for the day."

On the contrary? Luke was unable to suppress another smile. Nor did he wish to. It felt surprisingly good to smile. Who would have imagined?

Merry shifted the sizable stack of books and journals in her arms.

"Here," he said, already reaching for her burden.

She took a step back. "What are you doing?" The proud minx fixed a stern frown on him.

"Helping?"

"I don't require help," Merry said so quickly, her words rolled together.

This time, unlike before, she didn't attempt to soften that rejection.

"Ah, but everyone requires help now and then." He again reached for her precariously balanced stack.

She merely adjusted her protective hold, angling her books out of his reach. "This would be one of the *then* times, then."

A laugh burst from him.

He couldn't help it.

Because she was so damned honest, and he was so damned accustomed to people not speaking freely and openly with him. And it felt so good. So very, *very* good.

Merry eyed him like he'd gone mad, and perhaps he had... but it was the absolute most wonderful form of madness, one that filled him with a lightness and joy.

Her. It was because of her.

"You're mad," she said, her eyes wide.

She'd called him mad. Luke laughed all the harder, doubling over from the depth of his amusement. "Yes, more than a bit, I s-suspect," he managed between great guffaws.

Merry inched closer and peered up at him through narrowed eyes. "Or is it that you're drinking again?" She sniffed at him.

"I'm not drinking." Nor had he craved so much as a sip to lose himself in since she'd stood over him, ringing that vexing bell.

She eyed him for a long moment. Tapping her right serviceable boot on the carpeted floor, she contemplated him.

He flashed his greatest attempt at a winning smile.

Did he imagine that her own mouth pulled in an answering smile? "You're not going to relent," she said.

"I'm not." He gave his lapels a tug. "I'm quite unrelenting, you know."

"I'm starting to gather that," she said under her breath in tones that could have never been construed as praiseworthy. "Very well. Come with me."

And he rather thought he might follow her anywhere she would lead.

They entered the greenhouse, and he took in the indoor gardens. He rocked back on his heels. Vibrant of colors, from emerald-green leaves to crimson-red flowering plants, there was something almost otherworldly about the place. As if it was a world devoid of the clutter of man and existing only with nature's perfection.

"Lovely, isn't it?" she asked, following his thoughts with an unnerving accuracy.

"Quite," he murmured in the greatest of understatements. Alas, he'd never been the wordsmith his two younger brothers were. "They are... lovely." How had he never set foot inside the greenhouse before?

Because you've been too busy attending the familial finances and estates and maintaining the proper connections among Society's most elite.

That was what had been expected of him since boyhood, and all he'd known. As such, he'd never considered any deviation from that.

"Now, why don't we begin with an inventorying of all the..."

As Merry spoke, Luke took in the enclosed space constructed of glass, from walls to ceiling. Even at the early morn hour, the moon bathed the room in a soft glow.

The frosted panes and snow-covered grounds outside served in vivid contrast to the tropical blooms surrounding them. In here, he could almost believe himself insulated from the cold and ice of the winter season. It conjured imaginings of far-flung places he'd studied but never visited because he'd been too busy being everything he was expected to be. For the first time, he imagined a world far from this place, away from his responsibilities, where he lived only for the joy and pleasure Merry had spoken of yesterday.

"Before we do, however," Merry was saying, drawing him back to the present, "we should take a moment to review the greenery." She glanced over her shoulder at where he stood at the entrance to the room. Her eyes sparkled. "Have you changed your mind about assisting me this morn?"

He'd changed his mind on many things these past days. But being with Merry Read, being near her and helping her, had not—nor would ever—be one of them. "Not at all," he said.

He needn't have replied. She'd already set her stack down and proceeded to organize the materials within a fraying old folio. Next, Merry dragged out a stool and seated herself.

There was a no-nonsense aspect to her control and command, one that he'd never seen any woman in so possession of, and it proved headier than the spirits he'd lost himself in these past weeks. Months? It was all blurred beyond his focus on her. Like the flicker of the lit braziers that lined the corridor outside, desire sparked to life.

And here he was lusting after her, as he'd been since yesterday, when she should be so unaffected. Disgusted with himself, he hurried to take the seat across from her.

"Now," she continued. "There are many steps that go into organizing a household party." She turned a paper out toward him. "There is even more so when it comes to holiday festivities. There are games to be decided upon for the guests, meals to be planned and in collaboration with the housekeeper, the halls to deck."

A memory trickled in of boisterous voices coming from the grounds fifty feet below his schoolroom window, two voices joined in song. "Joy to the World; the Lord is come!

Let earth receive her King!" he sang in an exaggeratedly deepened baritone.

Merry slapped a hand over her mouth, covering her laugh. Her narrow shoulders quaked.

He dropped an elbow on the table and rested a chin atop his hand. "Are you laughing at me, Merry Read?" Once, he would have been filled with indignation at the idea.

How was it that this tall, spirited woman had shown him in just a handful of exchanges that there was no peril and only good in finding happiness in life around him?

Merry leaned over so only a foot separated them. Close as she was, he could see every twinkle dancing in her eyes. "I wouldn't dare."

He inched closer, so close their noses nearly brushed. "And what if I said I don't believe that?"

She closed the remaining distance so that their noses did touch. "I would say you always were a clever one."

This time, they both dissolved into laughter.

As one, Luke and Merry stopped.

That same intangible shift between them reared itself once more, as real as a life-force.

Their eyes worked in concert, moving over each other's face.

Luke swallowed hard.

He wanted to kiss her.

I'm going to kiss her.

He tipped his head, the pull, *her* pull, too much.

Merry proved far stronger. "Where were we?" she squeaked, breaking eye contact and redirecting her attention to her materials, leaving Luke blinking slowly at the abrupt loss.

"As I was saying, we have to sort through which inventory of the greenery and flowers we have to be used for the holiday décor. Now, here." She slid another sheet across the wood table, and as he picked it up, Merry proceeded to fire off instructions. "If you could search out the following items and somehow list them so I know what I have to work with and what I might still need to order." With that, she set to work on whatever other task commanded her attention.

He was forgotten.

Just like that.

Giving his head a shake, determined to put her from his thoughts and channel his energy into the task before him, Luke looked down at the paper in his hands. Name after name of plants and flowers and trees and shrubs all stared back. Luke looked around the expansive gardens. How in blazes did she expect him to make sense of any of those—

"Here," she said. Not lifting her head, she slid a notebook and a small leather tome across the desk.

Picking up the latter, he skimmed the title. *A Guide to Proper Plants, Shrubs, Greenery, and Floral Works for all Seasons for Every Noble Household.*

He flipped through the leather volume. Illustrations of various plants and flowers and their names filled the pages.

"I'm never without it," she said, scribbling furiously away at her notes. "I trust you'll find it helpful. Oh, one more thing." With her spare hand, she held out a small pencil and notebook.

"What am I to do with those?"

"Inventory."

Inventory? He, who'd not be able to pick out lilac from lavender, would be tasked with identifying and listing them? And yet, pride prevented him from humbling himself any more than he already had. Particularly to a woman who'd been trying to rid herself of his help. For the first time since he'd gone and broken his own heart in the name of propriety, he focused not on a scoundrel's pursuits, but on the unlikeliest of tasks.

Neatly stacking the two books Merry had provided him with, Luke consulted her list and then checked it against the leather volume. There were no fewer than—Luke silently counted the unnumbered columns—twenty-three items.

"What are you doing?"

Ah, this proved an interesting development. He wasn't so very invisible, after all.

"I trust it should be fairly obvious," he said, noncommittal in his reply, deliberately evasive, and he found an unholy glee in the little frown he caught from her out of the corner of his eye.

"It's not at all."

Luke briefly looked up. "I'm developing a strategy to complete the assignment you've given me." He paused. "Unless you'd care to join me."

"No!"

That denial exploded from her with such ferocity, he grinned wryly. "I daresay I'm offended." And he would have been, had the virago, in her honesty of reactions and responses, been like all the fawning *friends* his family kept company with.

A pretty blush stole across Merry's cheeks. "Forgive me," she said unconvincingly. "It has nothing to do with not wishing to work with you."

A strangled laugh shook his chest, that rumble of mirth so unfamiliar these days, so unexpected.

"What?" Merry asked defensively.

He strolled over to her workstation and froze. Odd, for all he'd noted about Merry Read through the years—her tart-mouthed tongue, her spirit, her laughter, her penchant for exploration—never had he noted the whispery hint of apple that clung to her skin. Had she always smelled of an orchard at summer? Or had it been sometime after she'd gone traveling that she'd adopted that exhilarating fragrance? Even in the greenhouse, surrounded by lush scents, hers stood out. And enticed. Tempted. Fighting that quixotic pull, he set down his small pile. "It is the law of 'the obvious.'"

Merry cocked her head at a little angle that put her confusion on endearing display. "What?"

"It is universally known that there is truth to every word spoken," he murmured. As such, she'd all but confirmed she didn't want him around. Luke laid his palms upon the table and leaned forward, erasing more of the space between them. "Given your statement, I'm to take it you wish to have nothing to do with me."

To the young woman's credit, she didn't deny it. "If you're to be here—"

"Underfoot?"

"That is your word, not mine, my lord,"

Ah, so she sought to erect formal barriers between them. Why?

Why, when after yesterday he felt closer with her than he ever had... anybody. "Surely we've already established that we should call one another by our Christian names?"

"I'd at least ask that you do not distract me from my task, my—Luke."

My Luke. Even with the slight hitch in the flow of Merry words, he felt warmth stir at the intimate endearment—no matter how inadvertent it happened to be.

"And is that what I was yesterday?" he murmured, taking another step closer. "A distraction?" A memory surged forward, of her claiming his mouth in a kiss that had shattered his soul and rocked his reason.

Her cheeks exploded with color. "Yes." Her voice emerged slightly breathless. "No." Her eyes formed round circles.

He waggled his eyebrows.

"Not in that way," she said quickly.

Luke lowered his lips close to her ear. "And what way is that, Merry?" he teased. Or he'd meant to.

A great shift occurred in their exchange.

Merry wet her lips, drawing his eyes to the perfect bow of her mouth. "Not... not... in the way you are implying or suggesting," she whispered, and yet her body arched toward his in a natural sway that belied her protestations.

He'd been betrothed, but never had there been any grand passion between him and Miss Josephine Pratt. She'd been exciting and made him smile because she was an unconventional lady, but the air hadn't come alive between them as it did in this moment. With this woman. And yet, her words... were her words.

"I will leave you to your work," he said quietly. Did he imagine the spark of disappointment that blazed to life in her eyes? Or did he simply see that which he wished to see? He returned to the task she'd charged him with. Gathering up his materials, he wandered deeper into the greenhouse. As he walked, he circled off the more obvious plants and flowers he was familiar with.

Ivy
Holly
English boxwood
Red and white roses
Mistletoe
Pear tree

Of her list of twenty-three, there was a total of five—six, if one wished to count the various shades of roses she sought—that he was certain of.

Over the next hour, he wandered the expansive room, marking off the items as he found them and learning about new-to-him flowers. As he wandered each row, perusing his mother's gardens, he occasionally stole a glance back to where Merry worked.

Wholly engrossed in her task, she sat perched on the edge of her stool, her shoulders bent forward as she frantically recorded her words.

As he watched her, he searched for some hint of the playful girl who'd been unable to sit still. Because of that natural exuberance, she'd always been a perfect pair for Luke's brother Ewan. With the passage of time, she'd matured. She'd found a balance between playful and no-nonsense work, and both proved equally entrancing.

"Are you always this intent as you work?" he called out.

"Yes," she said, not so much as breaking in the pace of her writing.

When he stopped before her, she looked up questioningly.

"I've located your flowers."

Surprise lit her eyes, transforming them from an otherwise ordinary brown to one that sparkled and gleamed.

And then it hit him.

Another droll grin brought one side of his mouth up. "You were giving me work to distract me, weren't you?"

"I wouldn't say it *quite* like that," she mumbled, shifting damningly on her stool.

The minx.

He folded his arms, her books, still in his hand, dangled at his elbow. "You didn't trust I'd complete it either, did you?"

Her blush was bright enough to match the red roses that grew along the back of the greenhouse.

"Why are you so determined to reject my help?"

"Because you're a lord," she said, not missing a beat. "Because gentlemen do not join servants coordinating household affairs.

Why did the idea of her serving in some lord's household fill him with outrage and other emotions he couldn't identify in that tumultuous moment?

"And why shouldn't I be with you? Because I'm the stuffy, proper Holman brother?" He'd simply accepted that was his makeup. It was how he'd been born, and then he'd been all but fed reminders of those expected qualities all his life, as if they had been food to sustain him. And they had.

Until now.

"Well, let me tell you, Merry Read. I don't give a bloody damn if you're the Queen of England or... or..." *A servant in my employ.* Only, he couldn't bring himself to say it, even as that was what she was.

Merry stared at him questioningly.

"Or a pickpocket from St. Giles," he said instead. "I am having a damned good time being with you and don't intend to leave." Suddenly, the fight went out of him. Because he didn't want to be with her *like this*. He wanted her to want his company. "That is... unless you'd rather I leave you alone. In which case, I'll honor that request."

The idea of leaving and not sparring or engaging with her any further left him hollow. Because with her, he came alive inside, which was altogether different than the past months he'd spent in mourning over losing the woman he'd admired. With Merry, he was, for the first time, alive.

And he didn't want this feeling to end.

CHAPTER SEVEN

Merry had offended him.

That realization came not from anything he'd said, or even anything that had been underscored in his tones.

Rather, it came from the slight tension at the corners of his lips, which bespoke... regret.

I am having a damned good time being with you and don't intend to leave. That is... unless you'd rather I leave you alone. In which case, I'll honor that request.

He'd given her the out she sought.

Because he would. Because he was the honorable, responsible, respectable viscount.

I'm the stuffy, proper Holman brother.

Luke had spoken as a man who knew well and what he was. He'd spoken as though his character were the greatest of flaws.

And yet...

Regret was a sentiment she was all too familiar with for her own yearnings in life, and as such, she easily recognized it in another. It wasn't, however, pity or regret that accounted for this weakening inside. This need to go against all her better judgment came from one simple, but not insignificant, truth—Merry wanted to be with Luke.

"Forgive me," Luke murmured. He dropped a deep bow, one better suited for a lady of his station than the daughter of a servant and the woman who'd one day serve in his household. "I will leave you to your efforts." He turned on his heel and started for the front of the room.

She briefly closed her eyes in a bid to keep up her barriers around this man.

Do not.

Let him go. For the more time she spent with him, the deeper and deeper under his spell she would go.

It was best that she was nowhere near a man like Luke Holman, the Viscount Grimslee, whose embrace she'd dreamed of since their lips had first met.

All her efforts proved futile.

Unleashing a silent stream of steady curses, she forced her eyes open.

"I wouldn't say you are the stuffy, proper Holman brother," she called after him, and Luke abruptly stopped. As he turned back to face her, her heart did a leap in her breast. "You *were* the stuffy, proper Holman brother, though."

They shared a smile, and it was as though the impasse was broken, and a wall came down between them. One she feared would never, and could never, be put back in place.

Nor do I want to go back to the aloof strangers we've been to each other over the years. There'd come time enough for panic and fear at the implications of that truth, but she'd not have that intrude on their exchange now.

When he reached her side, Merry motioned to the other stool, and held a hand out for his completed work.

"Have we reached a truce, then, Merry?" he asked as she looked over his notes.

"It depends on how helpful you remain and whether you interfere with my work here," she said and softened that with a wink. Merry opened her mouth to deliver some other flippant reply, but her gaze locked on his face, and all coherent thought fled.

She'd known Luke nearly all her life. So how had she failed to note the cleft in a deeply squared jaw? Or the perfect slash of his noble nose, better suited to the stone renderings of David in homes she'd worked in over the years? And more... how had she ever failed to note the beauty of his features? Feeling his questioning stare, she swiftly directed her attention to his completed notes.

And found herself knocked off-balance not by the realization of his masculine beauty, but by the work he'd done.

She flared her eyebrows. His record-keeping was nothing short of meticulous. Knowing the impeccable student he'd been, that, however, was not the reason for her shock.

In an hour's time, he'd not only identified the flowers and greenery she intended to use for the holiday décor, but he'd also created a keyed map so that she might locate each item in question.

"I trust it meets with your approval?"

From another man, those words would have come as smug. "Very much so." And yet, looking up from his work, there was something so very endearing about him and that question he posed, as if he were still the exceptional student of his younger days around whom she'd never known how to be. Only this... there was a vulnerability to him that made him very much human and not the icy, aloof figure she'd taken him for.

"And what have you been seeing to while I was otherwise distracted?"

"It wasn't solely meant to dis—" Merry stopped at the playful glimmer in his eyes. That twinkle did the strangest thing to her heart's natural cadence. "Oh. You're teasing."

"A bit, I was," he whispered and favored her with a wink.

That sweep of long, midnight lashes from this man had no right to send her heart knocking another frantic beat. Why must he be teasing? It was altogether impossible to keep her wits about her when he behaved thusly. Her cheeks fired several more degrees. What madness was this? A thirty-year-old woman, and here she was blushing like a schoolgirl—because of her employer, at that.

Luke availed himself of her notes, that presumptuous commandeering of her materials a necessary reminder that she sat beside the future head of this and every household held by the Earl of Maldavers.

Only, seated before him now, Merry didn't feel like a servant. Rather, she felt as though she sat beside someone who saw her as an equal.

It is merely because you knew each other as children.

When he didn't say anything, and the silence stretched on to the length where awkwardness rose up, Merry sought to fill the void. "I'd only a short while to decide how to organize the household before your family's guests arrive," she explained, evoking that reminder of his rank for the part of herself that enjoyed his company and knew the dangers in that closeness.

"In the hour I found twenty-three flowers and plants, you coordinated seating arrangements for a dinner party, assigned the servants responsible for decorating which rooms, and assembled a list for the Yuletide feast?" He glanced up from her notes, and at the admiration in his gaze, she shifted in her seat. "Is there nothing you cannot or do not do?"

"I've simply seen to my responsibilities."

"Your responsibilities?"

And with the genuine confusion underscoring that question, it occurred to her. "You do know why I've returned to England?" she ventured.

"I... no." Several lines creased his brow. "I don't."

For a moment she hesitated, because when he found out her ultimate role here... in his household, surely this beautiful exchange would come to an end. And with it, an end would come to the teasing and being treated not as one there to serve, but as one to speak to as an equal. Her heart ached because she'd not realized how very much she'd missed simply being a person and not just an employee.

"Merry?" he asked when she didn't answer.

"I'm to take on the role of housekeeper."

His mouth moved, and it was three attempts before he got words out. Or, as the case would have it, one word: "What?" He cut in before she could speak. "For whom?"

He didn't...know? "Why... *you*."

"*Me?*"

She might as well have taken the family broadsword down and cut his legs out from under him for the shock in his tone.

Merry nodded again. "As such, you shouldn't be working with me. I'm to be working for you."

And there it was. The discovery and, along with it, this sudden, blasted urge to weep. "My mother is to retire soon, and I will step into the role of housekeeper."

Merry's body tensed, and she braced for Luke's abrupt departure.

Only... he didn't abandon his chair. His expression darkened. "You'll be my housekeeper."

She tried to make sense of the displeasure that burned within his eyes.

For what reason should he take offense?

Taking advantage of his distraction, she plucked her pencil from his fingers and started upon her plans for the music room.

Luke covered her hand with his own, staying her movements. She stared at their hands practically joined, her palm callused and ink-stained and his immaculate, though there could be no doubting the strength and power in his long digits. They radiated heat. Nay, their practically joined fingers burned like the bonfire she'd danced around as a girl upon his family properties. She looked up, and that same fire blazed from within the fathomless depths of his blue eyes.

"Is that something you want, Merry?" he asked quietly. "To become a housekeeper?"

That query proved sobering, shattering some of the spell cast by his touch.

Was that something she wanted?

No one had ever dared asked her that before. Why, that was a question she'd not even put to herself. To those born outside the ranks of the nobility, there were few options and only one certainty for all—men, women, and children would all work.

The very best any woman could ever dare hope for was serving in the esteemed role as head of some nobleman's household.

But was it what she wanted?

"Your silence hardly serves as a confirmation."

Merry swiftly drew her palm back, displacing his hand and leaving her fingers cold. "I want to serve as housekeeper." That insistence emerged halfheartedly to her own ears. "It is what I've been trained to do."

He gave her an all-knowing look.

Damn him for the perceptive, clever man he'd always been that he should see so much.

Despite her earlier hungering to have him remain at her side, she now, coward that she was, found herself wishing he'd go. For then she'd not be besieged with questions she didn't want to think about, ones that forced her to look at her life in a way that left a void inside.

Nay, in a way that *revealed* a void. One she'd never before known existed within her. Merry cleared her throat. "I... there's no more reliable future a young woman could hope for than to be head of a nobleman's household." Unnerved by the directness of his probing gaze, she grabbed for her pencil.

He intercepted her efforts. "That isn't an answer."

She bristled. "Of course it is."

"Fine," he allowed. "But it's the answer you likely received in your training that you've simply regurgitated back."

Merry's jaw came together with enough force that her teeth rattled. Damn him for knowing that. How did he know that?

He brushed a knuckle along her cheek, that touch so very effortlessly erasing the tension in her jaw, and briefly closing her eyes, she found herself leaning into that slight caress. "Do you want to be a housekeeper?" he repeated.

The question served to shatter his hold upon her.

When he still refused to relinquish her things, Merry tossed her arms up in exasperation. "Would it matter either way?" What did he want from her?

"Yes," he said quietly, with a sincerity that nearly brought tears to her eyes.

Which was preposterous. She didn't cry. And she certainly didn't cry about her future—one that was very secure, at that. But she almost did, and all because a gentleman challenged her with questions about her existence.

"I've not given thought to any life but this one," she finally admitted... to them both. "This is the best I could hope for." As soon as those ungrateful-sounding words left her lips, she wanted to call them back. "What I mean to say is—" Luke touched two fingers to her lips, silencing the lies she'd been about to hand him.

"What would you want?" he asked as he drew his hand back, and she hungered for that gentlest, and yet most intimate of caresses.

What would she want?

"I don't know," she confessed wistfully. What was worse, she'd never given thought to... really anything beyond the day-to-day of her life.

Over the years, she'd worked in various roles in various households throughout Europe with but one purpose to her travels—to prepare for the day she'd serve the Holman household. She'd taken notes for her future role the way a scholar might record lectures.

"I don't believe that," he said, folding his arms at his chest.

Yes, he was so blasted insightful that he should see those details.

They locked gazes, engaging in a quiet battle.

As the silence marched on, and he gave no hint of relenting, she pressed her lips together. She mumbled a word and grabbed her book.

He leaned closer. "What was that?"

"I said... travel," she said tightly. "Are you happy? I'd like to visit the museums in Paris and Rome, not with the intention of learning and recording design aesthetics for other people's households, but simply taking in those sights." Embarrassed by all she'd shared, those intimate pieces she'd denied even to herself until this very moment, Merry shoved her stool back.

It scraped noisily upon the stone floor as she hopped to her feet.

Luke shot an arm out, catching her at the waist, tightly enough to stir delicious shivers from that decisive point of contact, but loose enough that she knew she was free to leave if she wished.

Her throat moved.

How very different he was from all the noblemen's sons who'd attempted to steal kisses and take that which she'd no wish to offer.

Luke lightly pushed her heavy plait back over her shoulder and cupped her cheek. "You deserve that," he said quietly. "You deserve to go to those faraway places and see the world as you wish without any encumbrances."

As she and Luke settled back to work, she couldn't help but imagine that very life he'd painted for her...

But with him in it.

CHAPTER EIGHT

It had been one week of seeing to the holiday preparations. From before the sun rose, until many hours after it set, Merry was rushing about seeing to her responsibilities. From coordinating arrangements with servants, to drafting the menu for the Christmastide meal, to creating decorations to hang about the household, hers was not an unfamiliar role she'd taken on in numerous households. There was, however, one difference between this assignment and all the others to come before it.

Luke.

All the times prior, her sole focus had been on work. There'd been little time for laughter and celebration. Oh, she'd always loved the holiday season, but the pleasure and enjoyment of it was not something the servant class had the luxury of. Nay, servants were too busy transforming households for the lords and ladies of the *ton*.

Since she'd come upon him sprawled in the foyer, and he'd insisted on taking part in the day-to-day goings-on of holiday preparation, he'd risen with her and worked well into the night beside her. Long after the rest of the household had fallen asleep.

He was the first—and only—gentleman to ever help her.

And having him beside her as they saw to those tasks never felt like work.

Side by side in the nursery, with garland and the adornments laid out before them, she threaded a string of gold beads through a long branch of evergreen.

From the corner of her eye, she peeked at Luke.

Muttering to himself, he jabbed a piece of red velvet into an untrimmed branch at the middle of his *creation*. "Close your eyes," he said for the eleventh time since they'd begun.

"I cannot close my eyes, Luke. I'm working," she reminded him, neatly winding the remainder of her adornment and then tying it off at the end.

"Very well. Then stop peeking at mine. I told you at the start, it is a surprise."

A surprise.

There could be no greater one than the gentleman beside her. The teasing, thoughtful, and proud viscount who had put the same effort into their preparations for the holiday season that he had his studies.

Only, there was so much different from then to now. She didn't recall so much as a smile from the somber little boy. Now, whenever they were together, he wore a perpetual grin. An infectious one.

Despite his warning from moments ago, her gaze drifted unbidden to him.

Everything about him was real and warm and human, from the relaxed lines of his features to the looseness of golden curls he'd once kept slicked back in place.

Her heart fluttered in an all-too-familiar quickened tempo.

He paused in his task and glanced over at her.

Merry hurriedly dropped her focus to—

Her lips twitched.

"I see you laughing," he mumbled.

"I'm not laughing." She winked. "I was smiling. It's not exactly the same."

"It's not entirely different either," he said, all of his attention trained on that oddly shaped arrangement.

No, it wasn't. Nor did that adorably imperfect garland he'd worked tirelessly at since they'd arrived that morn account for the perpetual smile she'd worn that morning. With Luke distracted as he was, Merry freely studied him while he worked. It was simply him. He made her smile. And laugh, he did that, too. And how very wonderful it felt.

Her garland forgotten, she dropped her chin atop her hand.

How singularly odd that the man who would one day be her employer, the same man who'd been relentlessly devoted to his rank, should have opened her eyes to the truth that she was far more than a servant. She'd not been placed upon the earth with the sole purpose of serving.

Oh, that was how she and her family and the majority of the world survived.

But work was not all they were. She'd as much right to her happiness as any lady of the peerage. She'd as much right to her dreams. Dreams she'd not even realized she'd carried in her heart until Luke had forced her to look inside herself.

Not for the first time, Luke broke into a quiet, cheer-filled song.

> "I saw three ships come sailing in
> On Christmas Day, on Christmas Day;
> I saw three ships come sailing in
> On Christmas Day in the morning.
> And what was in those ships all three..."

Her smile widened.

He abruptly cut off that joy-filled tune. "Do you know, Merry? Laughing again, you are," he said with a faint thread of teasing in his voice.

"It's simply that I'm happy," she said softly. And she was. So deliriously, unapologetically happy. On the heels of that, her cheeks bloomed with a blush. Alas, he remained engrossed in his task. All the while, he continued working on... on... Merry squinted and, this time, couldn't even attempt to hide her smile. "What are you creating?"

He stole a sideways peek her way and hurriedly placed the greenery in his hands behind him.

"Close your eyes," he said. "I'm nearly done."

Yes, perhaps he was. But it also begged the question: "With *what*?" she asked as gently as she could.

He held the jumbled, misshapen ball aloft. Beads and red velvet ribbons hung down, a garish display that all but covered every inch of green.

Merry bit the inside of her cheek, but a snorting laugh escaped her anyway.

"*Hmph*." Luke gave it a slight shake, and the beading jingled merrily. "I'll have you know this is perfectly splendid."

She laughed all the harder. "It is perfectly lovely," she conceded, reaching for his masterpiece, but he held it out of her reach. "But what is it?"

"Ah, I shan't tell you. It's a secret." He waggled his eyebrows. "Until you're able to properly appreciate my work."

He merely teased, and yet...

"Does it matter so very much?"

He paused.

Catching the sides of her stool, she dragged it closer to him and then angled the seat so their legs met. "Why do you worry what I, or the world, or anyone else in between should think or feel? Isn't it enough that you should simply be happy and damn everyone else's opinion?" In that moment, it all became very blurred as to whether she spoke of him... or herself.

His finger smoothed the velvet ribbon distractedly, and he sat in silent contemplation. "I was raised early on to believe Society's perception of me mattered more than anything," he began slowly, his tones introspective. "I've measured my responses to... everything.

Every decision has been made first and foremost with my family's name in mind." His jaw flexed. "Even..." His words trailed off.

"Even?" she pressed, needing to know everything there was about him. Because he was the most real man she'd ever known, and in this short time together, he had become a friend.

"Even the woman I would wed."

Her heart missed several beats, and when it resumed a steady cadence, the rhythm was quickened. "You are betrothed?" Odd how three little words—four measly syllables—should sit like a pit in her belly.

"No."

Some of the tension eased, leaving in its place a giddy relief.

"I *was* betrothed, however." His lips twisted in a bitter smile. "Past tense. At my parents' urging, I broke it off."

There was a woman who'd very nearly been the Viscountess Grimslee... and who would have been Merry's employer.

Perhaps it was fatigue from the long hours she and Luke had kept, or perhaps it was an illogic thought that simply could not be rationalized away, but the idea of him with his Society-born lady left her bereft.

This is where you are to say something...

"I'm... sorry," she said softly, resting her hand on his. "She is the reason you..."

Luke stared at their almost-joined hands and then lifted his face. And in those perfectly carved features, there wasn't a hint of pain or regret. Only wry amusement. "She is the reason I was sleeping in the foyer when you arrived?" He wore a faintly sheepish expression. "Yes, she is the reason, and yet..."

And yet?

That question screamed around her mind, and the lessons on patience ingrained into her early on were all that kept her from demanding he say more.

"I regret that I let my family's concerns drive my decision. I regret the dishonorable way in which I conducted myself. I'll always regret that I let my worry about Society and what they might say matter more than what I wanted."

What I wanted. The sharp blade dug all the deeper. She stared down at the obscenely shiny objects littered about them.

"But I won't regret not marrying her," he said quietly, bringing her head jerking up. "Not because she wasn't an honorable or good woman, nor because my life with her would have been content, but because had we married, I would have never realized I wanted more than being *content*. You, however, Merry Read," he said, lightly caressing her left hand. "It was you who showed me I wanted more. That I want passion and joy, and I thank you for that."

"You needn't thank me, Luke. We are... friends."

Friends.

Aside from her relationship with her brother and sister, there'd been a dearth of friendship in her life.

And you cannot very well go on being friends with him when he is your employer. Not when he would eventually wed and Merry would answer to that lady of the household.

Luke looked up, and he searched his eyes over her face in a slow, delicate caress, and she held her breath, more than half afraid of what emotion he'd see there. But he gave no indication that he had detected the undercurrents of feelings she had no place feeling for him. Luke set his garland down and spoke with an earnestness she'd never remembered from him. "You've challenged me to see the world and live in it in ways that I never have. In ways I suspect will always be foreign, and yet"—he caught one of her hands, tangling their fingers as one—"I've never felt more alive or freer than I have this week with you, Merry."

Merry's heart lifted and then soared as Luke's words gave that organ flight. Only to come crashing down in a blaze of reality.

As much as she loved the Luke Holman he was before her, he would, by his very admission, forever remain a man worried about Society's opinion. Such men didn't have friendships with maids or other servants. They didn't tease their housekeepers, and they certainly didn't marry them.

They wed women such as the honorable and good one he'd been betrothed to. And even with a like social connection, his parents still had not approved of the match.

Her stomach flipped, as it had when she was a girl aboard a packet to France in a violent storm that churned up the waters, leaving her sick.

A light palm came to rest upon her forearm, and she jumped. "Merry?" he asked.

Suddenly, she was besieged by an overwhelming urge to cry at the tenderness of his touch, at something that would never—and could never—be.

"I was... thinking of what you said." Which wasn't altogether untrue. For even as she reveled in this new freedom he'd allowed himself and all the ways in which he'd changed, Merry proved selfish. "And how I'll miss this." Her voice faded to a whisper that she could not call back. With that, she made to return her seat to its previous spot so she could resume working.

Luke stopped her. "Why does it have to end?"

He didn't know. He couldn't know.

Her teeth snapped together with a ferocity that sent pain shooting from her jaw to her temple. "Come, Luke, by your very words here, you're aware of how Society is driven by its social order. Servants work."

He frowned. "That's not what I was saying."

"But it's true." She tied off the end of her beads and grabbed for another piece of evergreen to start on. "It is the way of the servant." Always working. "Always be working," she muttered. It was the mantra her own mother, as housekeeper, had ingrained into not just the entire female staff she was responsible for, but also her own children. Merry angrily dragged the gold beads around the vibrant strand garland. "And that is precisely what we've done this week, Luke. Work." Because no matter what illusion she'd allowed herself, or pretty dream Luke had put forward of her having a future beyond this, the truth remained—she was and always would be a servant. And this time here? Decorating the countess' London townhouse and organizing the family's festivities was still work. No matter how much joy she'd found with Luke as she'd overseen those tasks. Tasks were still tasks, and—

Tears blurred her vision.

Luke cupped her cheek and stroked it lightly. "Here," he murmured, his honeyed baritone as warming as the glide of his knuckles along her cheek.

She squeezed her eyes shut and gave her head a slight shake. She didn't want his touch. She couldn't afford the havoc it wrought on her senses any more than she'd already allowed this man. So why, as he complied, did she want to let her tears fall?

"The past days... this time with you," he quietly corrected. "They've not just been about my family's guests or what my mother or father expect for the holidays. It was about the time I spent with you, and the joy I found in it."

How was it possible for her heart to sing and weep all at the same? Merry released a ragged sigh and made herself face him once more. "But that is my very point, Luke," she said tiredly.

"You don't like decorating for the holidays?" His cerulean-blue eyes were as befuddled as his tone.

"Yes. No." She ran a hand down her face. Merry tried again to help him understand. She let her arm fall to the table. "I love preparing the household for the holidays. Every year since I was just a small girl"—and then before she'd gone off to be schooled in other noble households—"whenever my parents were off working on the eve before Christmas, I would rush about with my brother and sister, which, given their penchant for being at odds, was never an easy task." She laughed softly at the memory. "But on those days, we'd hurry to decorate, transforming each room of our little cottage, so that when our parents returned at the end of the night, it was bright and cheerful for the holidays. Then, on Christmas, we would all take turns sharing our Yuletide wishes." Merry caught hold of his hands. "I've loved every moment"—*spent with you*—"this week. I adore creating garland and hanging it and organizing festivities." She shook her head. "But when they are complete, then I will leave so"—*you and a household of ladies vying for the role of your bride*—"the world can enjoy those pleasures."

And she'd be left with a heart breaking for a future that would never be hers.

CHAPTER NINE

Luke's world view had been taught to him early on by his tutors and his parents.

Everyone had a place in it, be it a lord or a servant or a stable master, each person invariably had roles to fulfill. Or that was how he'd learned to look at the world.

But as Merry had said, as she'd helped him see, they weren't at all the same experiences.

Luke had made his life about his responsibilities, but as Merry had said, when they finished decorating the household, she'd go on her way, her work complete, and he'd remain behind to take part in the festivities.

Festivities that would be nothing and only empty without her here and a part of them.

These past months, he'd come to appreciate that he'd not liked himself... or the life he lived. But neither had he given proper thought to how everyone else lived. Not even his own damned youngest brother, who'd been all but exiled to the country by their parents. And it was humbling to be confronted with the depth of one's ego and self-interest.

God, and here he'd believed he could not be any more pompous than he was. Only to find, blind as he'd been to the great disparities in his and Merry's experiences, he was still the same narrow bastard he'd always been.

And he didn't want to be that man.

Just as he didn't want that to be the man she took him for.

"Come with me," he said, jumping up so quickly his stool toppled over.

He might as well have brandished a pistol for the shock that filled Merry's eyes as she gazed at the overturned chair. "Luke?

His garland in one hand, Luke took Merry's fingers with his other. He gave a determined tug that brought her to her feet. "Come with me."

"Where are we going?" she asked as he pulled her along, deeper and deeper into the greenhouse, bypassing vibrant shrubs and fragrant blooms as they went. Merry stole a look over her shoulder. "There's still more to be done."

"Yes. Yes, there is." Just not the work she referred to.

"We cannot simply leave." Merry dug her heels in, forcing them to a grinding stop. "There's the garland, and then we have just the afternoon to organize the games for your family's guests."

His family's guests. That was precisely who the expected parties were, and yet, that also delineated a separation between him and Merry, and fury and outrage blazed a path through him.

But it's true. It is the way of the servant. Always be working.

His mouth hardened.

Not on this damn day.

"To hell with the games."

Her eyebrows crept together. "That is... quite contradictory."

"Indeed," he allowed and gave her hand another pull.

She reluctantly followed him to the pair of glass doors that led outside.

The moon still hung in the sky, and with the fresh, untouched snow that blanketed the earth, it cast a vivid brightness over the grounds.

Luke reached for the handle.

"What are you doing?" Merry blurted, freezing him in midmovement. "It is... freezing."

Yes, she was right on that score. Just as she was correct on so many scores. And yet, he'd be damned if they didn't quit that blasted workstation and make their way outside. "Come," he scoffed. "It's not that cold."

As if Mother Nature relished in making a liar of him, a gust of wind battered against the glass panels. They shook and shuddered under the force of that blast.

Merry winged a well-formed eyebrow up.

"Yes. Yes. Well, perhaps it is a bit cold." Luke proceeded to unbutton his jacket.

Merry made a peculiar choking noise.

"Are you all right, love?" he asked, struggling with one of the gold buttons.

"Are *you* all right?" she countered, glancing up at the glass ceiling.

His lips twitched. "Ah, and here I'd not expect that the same woman who'd ring a bell over my drunken self would turn shy on me."

"I'm not shy, per se." Rising to the challenge he'd put to her, she slowly brought her gaze back down to him.

He widened his smile. "That's better." With a wink, he shrugged out of his jacket.

Merry nearly dissolved into a paroxysm and found that spot overhead that held her so fascinated. "That is not better. If anyone enters, well, it would be scandalous. It would..." He draped the cloak about her shoulders. She was taller than most women, but still several inches shorter than he was, and the heavy wool garment hung past her knees. "What are you doing?"

Starting around her, he grabbed for the brown wool garment hanging nearby.

"Luke, are you... wearing the gardener's jacket?"

He drew on the slightly snug jacket better fitted to the smaller, reed-thin Mr. Whitely. "I *am*."

"Why?" she asked slowly, like one trying to puzzle through a complicated riddle.

"Well, I cannot very well have you wearing it," he said as he made his way back over to her. Reaching past her, he pushed the door open and motioned her outside. "Merry."

She hesitated, glancing from him to that gaping exit to the grounds. "You've gone mad," she said and took a tentative step outside.

He grinned. Indeed, he had. Decorum and straitlaced living were highly overrated. How much he'd missed. How much emptier and lonelier and... miserable his existence had been until she'd opened his eyes to accepting happiness in his life. Closing the door behind them, Luke joined her.

The snow crunched under his boots, loud in the early morn quiet.

Hugging herself tightly, Merry rubbed at her arms. Small puffs of white escaped her full lips as she breathed. "Wh-what are w-we doing out h-here?" she asked, her voice trembling from the cold.

"I thought it should be obvious." He spread his arms wide. "We're simply having fun."

"Fun?"

He nodded once.

"You have gone mad. Come, Luke, there's work to do. Your family will awake soon in anticipation of the arrival of their guests." As she went on with her very lengthy argument, he bent down and gathered up a ball of snow. "G-guests whom, I sh-should r-remind you, will a-arrive at all manner of ti—what are you—?"

Splat.

Her words ended on a sharp gasp as his snowball found its perfect mark at the center of her jacket. His jacket. And how very right it looked on her. There was an intimacy to her wearing his article. Even if he'd been the one responsible for—

"D-did you hit me with a snowball?" she demanded, her arms akimbo.

He swiftly made up another and hurled it.

This time, she darted out of the way, and the missile grazed her hip. She glanced at the smattering of white upon his sapphire jacket like he'd fired a pistol ball at her. "What w-was *that* for?"

"Well, as I figure it, if you couldn't tell the first one was, in fact, a snowball, then you required another."

She sputtered and, bending down, stuffed her hands into the snow. A sharp hiss exploded from her quivering lips as she yanked them back. "Th-this is f-freezing."

He grinned widely. "It *is* snow." Had he ever enjoyed himself so? In the aftermath of losing Josephine Pratt, he'd taken a to-hell-with-it approach to the world, but that response had been born of resentment and anger... with himself and decisions he'd made. Never had he felt this freeness.

"F-furthermore, I-I'll have you kn-know," Merry continued as she scooped up a pathetically small ball of snow and tossed it at him, "it's not the size of the object, but how one wields it."

He choked.

Gasping, Merry made another snowball and hurled the projectile at his face.

He dusted off the moisture from his face.

"That was for having improper thoughts, Lord Grimslee."

"I didn't even say anything."

"You didn't need to. From your reaction, it was quite clear your thoughts had taken a wicked path."

He flashed a crooked smile and sidled closer. "Tell me, love. How is it that you recognized my improper thoughts?"

Her cheeks, already red from the cold, blazed three shades brighter from her blush. Then she gave a toss of her head. "I-I m-may h-have h-heard things a-among the other s-servants, my lord." She glided closer and dropped her voice to an exaggerated whisper. "Th-things that would sh-shock you."

He leaned in so the white puffs of their breath mingled in the night air. "And what would you say if I were to tell you I'm endlessly intrigued, Merry Read?"

Her bow-shaped lips formed a perfect moue.

Yes, not so very long ago, he would have been horrified at being part of such wicked repartee... and with a young woman, no less. Why, even the idea of being outside frolicking in the snow—in a borrowed servant's jacket—would have been a level of scandalous behavior beyond him. Luke touched a finger lightly against her mouth. "Now, I-I've shocked *you*."

"Y-yes," she said softly, hugging her arms around her waist. "You've sh-shocked me m-many times these past ten days."

Nine. They'd been together nine, and he felt he knew her better now than he'd ever known anyone. He felt he knew himself... because of her. And he knew one certainty: Nine days would never be enough.

A tender smile curved her beautiful lips up in the corners. "In the most wonderful ways," she added. Somberness chased away her smile as she worked her gaze over his face. "Do not ever change, Luke Holman. How you are now... who you've been these past days? Hold on to that."

I want to hold on to you. He wanted a life with her. Not with her solely as a friend, but as a friend... and more...

"We should r-return," she murmured.

Yes, they should. "To your work."

It wasn't a question, but an understanding that had come from all she'd revealed about her responsibilities as a servant.

It was also why they weren't returning inside. For, once they did, they would return to their roles, and this moment would end.

"N-not yet." Dropping to a knee, he lay down in the snow and stretched out his arms and legs. The cold pierced his garments, stinging his skin with the bite of it. From his threadbare jacket to his boots was soaked and left him nearly numb. He stared overhead at the star-studded sky, the moon hanging overhead, and just laughed.

Crunch-crunch-crunch.

Merry leaned over him, blocking his view of the unfettered landscape. The moon cast an aura of light around her dark tresses, burnishing them with shades of brown. "What are you doing n-now?"

Luke swiped his arms up and down. "I believe you used to call them a-angels?"

"Snow angels," she whispered.

He paused and stared up at her frozen over him, her expression both wistful and far-off. "I believe that is what I heard you call them. You and Ewan were outside my window."

"And he wouldn't join in," she said, finishing part of that telling for him. "Because he didn't wish to have his garments wet and miserable..."

"And I wanted to be down there with you, Merry. Because I'd never done anything so light or foolhardy or free," he said softly. The wind howled once more, lending a greater sound to his words and dusting flakes of snow around them. "And I wanted you to do this now because it isn't work or required. It's not even something that, when we finish, will remain long past the next gust of wind or snowfall." His eyes held hers. "It is something to do simply for the joy of it."

Her throat moved, and she clutched her hands reflexively in the fabric of his jacket.

He held a palm out, and she stared at his outstretched fingers before placing hers trustingly in his, and then she joined him on the ground.

Shivering, she lay so that only several paces were between them, and he reclaimed his position on the cold, unforgiving ground.

Merry stretched her arms and legs up first slowly, as if trying to remember those motions, and then there was an increasing zeal.

He stared on, unable to look away from her and the bright-eyed glimmer in her eyes. Or her wide, dimpled smile. Nay, he didn't want this to end.

Laughing, Merry found the rhythm, and her limbs glided in a perfect sweep, and that joy was so very infectious, he matched the pace she set until his laughter blended with hers.

They stopped and lay there, looking up at the night sky, their breath forming little clouds of white around them in the cold night air.

The snow crunched as she angled her head toward him. "Luke?"

He looked over. Emotion blazed from within the depths of eyes so vividly bright.

"Th-thank you," she whispered, twining her fingers through his like ivy. An electric current passed between them, heat when there was only cold around them.

Not breaking that contact, not ever wanting to separate from her, Luke held tight to her hand, and standing, he carefully drew her to her feet, guiding them away from the masterpieces they'd made in the snow.

They remained there, Merry's gaze locked with his, as time melted away.

Looping an arm about her waist, he drew her close and touched his lips to hers.

Merry melted against him as they devoured each other's mouth. Parting her lips, she let him inside. Heat. So much heat. How, as frozen through as they were, was it possible that there was this scorching hotness? He stroked his tongue against hers, and she met every bold, unapologetic lash. Gripping the lapels of his jacket, Merry pressed her trembling body against his.

Another gust of wind whipped across the grounds, battering the greenhouse doors.

Reluctantly, Luke drew back, breaking their embrace. He palmed her cold cheek. Her eyes remained closed as she leaned into his touch like a contented little kitten, absorbing the warmth he proffered.

I love you...

Incapable of feeling cold right now, he folded Merry close in his arms and just held her.

CHAPTER TEN

Since she and Luke had returned an hour and thirty minutes ago, the world had come alive. All around her, the music room bustled with servants rushing to and fro. With great care, young men and women carried about the garland made by her and Luke—and many of the other maids—and hung those brightly adorned evergreens throughout the gilded music room.

The staff was in the final frantic stages of preparing for the impending arrival of the household's guests.

Standing from the side of the room, overseeing the final arrangements, Merry was unable to keep from smiling.

Luke had pulled her away from her work and once more reminded Merry that she was as deserving of those moments of levity, compelled not by work, but rather by her own right to happiness.

And he makes me happy... Luke Holman.

Her heart quickened. Where there would be a time for horror and fear of the implications of that discovery, now there was only a giddying lightness that filled every corner of her person. It left her buoyant and—

"Her ladyship has requested your presence, ma'am."

Just like that, the announcement brought Merry crashing down hard to earth and, along with it, reality. "Her ladyship?"

"She awaits in the White Parlor." Did she imagine the faintly pitying look the butler, Blake, favored her with as he patiently waited for her?

Merry stole a last glance at the servants hanging decorations, and with a sickening dread turning in her belly, she forced herself to follow after Blake.

Each step sent her panic spiraling.

Stop it.

You are being ridiculous. Just because you've been summoned does not mean... what? That the countess didn't know Merry had gone and fallen head over heels in love with her ladyship's son?

Merry stumbled.

"Are you all right, ma'am?" the butler asked, and she struggled to so much as nod through the terror wreaking havoc on her senses.

When the butler looked a moment away from ringing for help, she forced her features into a calm mask. "I'm fine," she assured him.

Only, she wasn't.

Love Luke?

She couldn't.

Yes, she'd enjoyed their time together more than she'd enjoyed any other time in her life.

But love? It couldn't be. It couldn't be, for so many reasons. The least of which was the time in which they'd known each other and the greatest being the fact that he was a viscount and she his steward's daughter. A servant. She was a servant.

You deserve to go to those faraway places and see the world as you wish without any encumbrances.

Tears tightened her throat, and she struggled to swallow around them. No one had ever dreamed of a different future for her than that of servitude. Not even her own family. Not because they hadn't or didn't love her, but rather, because dreams such as those weren't permitted for servants.

Luke had spoken to her of more. And wanting more for her.

She loved him.

She—

Would one day soon become his housekeeper.

And never more had Merry been filled with this great need to cry. To curl up in a ball and give over to every last emotion a servant wasn't entitled to feel and weep until she broke from the pain of what could never be.

As they neared the White Parlor, Merry struggled to put order to her feelings and emotions.

After all, unless a situation merited her attention, the Countess of Maldavers didn't bother with servants aside from the head housekeeper and butler.

Oh, the lady of the household had received a reputation for being firm but fair.

None would ever dare accuse her of being warm. Neither did they speak unkindly of her.

Meetings were granted between the countess and a servant in only two circumstances: extreme pleasure on the lady's part, or displeasure.

"Here we are, ma'am," the butler murmured upon their arrival.

As Merry was shown into the White Parlor—the beautifully adorned White Parlor—just one glance at the countess' tight lips, pursed like she'd sucked the very lemon that had gone into Merry's special shortbread recipe, confirmed one fact—this was not to be a meeting where one was awarded the countess' *extreme pleasure.*

Merry forced a smile to her lips. "My lady," she greeted.

Seated on the ivory satin sofa with its gold piping, a tray of tea and a platter of shortbread neatly arranged before her, the countess made no attempt to rise. "Come in, Miss Read," she said coolly. "If you would, Blake?"

Merry stiffened as the butler hurriedly drew the door shut behind him.

Folding her hands primly before her, Merry remained at the doorway.

For all the warmth and joy of her meeting that morn with Luke, Merry was met with only a frosty cool from his mother.

Luke, who didn't treat her as if she were no more than a servant. Luke, who saw her as an equal. And, oh, how she hoped that when she left, and the only company that remained were the proud lords and ladies of London, he didn't lose who he'd been these past days.

"Come, come," the countess said, impatiently gesturing her over. "Sit."

It wasn't an invitation.

Drawing back her shoulders, Merry walked with the same dread Joan of Arc must have known. As she settled onto the indicated King Louis XIV chair, Merry noted the official-looking envelope that lay upon the table.

"I'm not a cruel woman," the countess began, snapping Merry's attention up and over to the lady of the household. Luke's mother.

Merry cleared her throat. "No, my lady. No one would ever say—"

The countess wagged a finger and with a tsking noise commanded silence as though she would a cat.

Merry flattened her lips. No, there could be no doubting that this meeting wasn't to be one in which the pleased mistress praised a servant for her work.

"I love my family greatly. I wish nothing for them but their happiness." She winged a thin, icy brow. "I trust you know something of that?"

"I... do," she said cautiously.

Fury snapped in the other woman's eyes in the greatest display of emotion Merry ever remembered from the woman, but when the countess spoke, there was only her usual regal calm. "The reason I asked you to oversee the holiday decorations was so that Lord Grimslee would be... *occupied.*" Merry stiffened. "And nothing more. I didn't want a friendship, because let us be honest with one another." She casually stirred a spoon in her tea. "Lords and servants? There isn't room for any relationships." She paused and glanced up. "Not one that is proper, anyway."

She knows. Balling her hands into fists, Merry kept her eyes directed forward. All the while, her stomach churned and twisted.

"*Of course* I know," the other woman said, as if speaking on the weather, in command of Merry's thoughts as easily as she was the moment. She paused that distracted stirring and pinged the residual drops on the spoon against the side of the teacup. "Imagine my surprise when I came to the nursery to speak with you regarding the final preparations."

Oh, God.

Merry's eyes slid briefly closed, and she concentrated on breathing.

"My son was frolicking in the snow, Miss Read. *Frolicking.*"

The reasons Luke had been aloof were clearer than they had ever been. What a sad existence it must have been, having a mother so horrified by his happiness.

The countess set her spoon on the edge of her plate. "And various forms of frolicking, at that."

Mortification brought Merry's toes curling tightly into the soles of her boots.

She'd seen them.

"I expect most employers wouldn't care either way. A young lord dallying with a servant isn't at all uncommon." The countess spoke through tightly compressed lips. "But my family does not need salacious stories. And Lord Grimslee does not require distractions from his future responsibilities. Not that I need speak to you about my reasons why or..."

While the countess went on, outrage sparked in Merry's belly, then fanned and grew until fury roiled in her chest. How dare this woman? She'd speak of Merry as though she were less than a person?

It was not at all different from how Merry had viewed herself. What had changed, however, was her. Because of Luke. Luke, who'd allowed her to see she was as entitled to her dreams and happiness and hopes as any person born to the peerage.

"As such," the countess was saying, "I'm left to determine just what to do now." *With you.*

Those two words didn't even need to be voiced.

If the countess expected she'd be cowed, the woman was to be greatly disappointed. Merry was not the same woman who'd arrived to oversee the holiday preparations. "With the meticulous care and thought you put into everything," Merry said, "I trust you've already arrived at an answer."

Surprise lit the older woman's eyes. "Very well." The countess reclined slightly on her sofa. "I'll cease with the games or dancing about the matter." So that was how Lady Maldavers would refer to Merry's relationship with Luke. "Having you here was a terrible idea on my part, for now obvious reasons. I'm not, however, dismissing you."

It was Merry's turn to try to mask her shock.

The countess arranged her skirts about her. "I'm not going to hold your family's employment or security over your decision."

She stiffened.

Stretching out perfectly manicured fingers, the countess slid the ivory packet across the table, moving it closer to Merry. "I am, however, suggesting it might be best for everyone if you chose to leave..."

Merry glanced down at the table.

"Go on," Luke's mother urged, picking up her teacup. Delicately sipping from that fine piece of porcelain, she stared at Merry over the rim.

Merry picked up the heavy packet and turned it over in her hands. All the while, her skin prickled with the burn of the other woman's eyes on her. Unfolding the article, she skimmed the contents.

And froze. "What is this?" she asked quietly, even as she knew, because of the words in front of her, just what Luke's mother offered... and intended.

"You went abroad working in households throughout Europe, Miss Read. I am merely presenting you with the opportunity to visit, not as a servant, but as a woman traveling as she would, with no requirements placed upon you. But you *are* leaving. Today."

Restless, Merry came out of her seat, and with the packet in hand, she wandered away from Luke's mother, needing space with which to think. With which to respond.

Merry stopped at the window and continued to study the gift at her fingertips.

I am merely presenting you with the opportunity to visit, not as a servant, but as a woman traveling as she would, with no requirements placed upon you.

The countess *offered* Merry everything she wished for—the opportunity to see the world, not as a servant, but as one without constraints.

And yet...

Her gaze fell to the ground below, the snow untouched but for a handful of footprints and a pair of snow angels, the tips of their wings touching.

As a servant, Merry well knew that households had ears everywhere. Yet, something in Merry's intimate exchange with Luke had been overheard and now was being used by this woman to manipulate her. It sent her flesh crawling.

Sucking in a breath, she faced the other woman. "As a girl, I did not much like Luke."

The countess went whipcord straight. Was it Merry's use of her son's given name? Or that insulting admission on Merry's part? She'd wager the greater offense to the other woman was, in fact, the former. "He was aloof and cold and pompous. Or, I thought he was. But do you know, my lady? These past days, I've come to find that it wasn't Luke I disliked. It was you."

Lady Maldavers' mouth fell open.

"It was how you and Lord Maldavers insisted your son, as the precious heir, be. You were the reason he was unable to smile or laugh."

The countess burst onto her feet. "How dare you, Miss Read?"

"How dare I speak the truth? Quite easily," Merry shot back. "I've come to appreciate I didn't know Luke in any way... until now. And the man I do know? He is a man who is honorable and giving." She scraped a gaze over the countess. "And he's certainly not one to find a person wanting for their birthright." So much love swelled in her heart, and she struggled to speak around the emotion clogging her throat. "Your son is a man who has made me think about my own life and what I want. Nay, what I deserve." Sadness pierced her chest. "And you may feel I do not deserve your son, my lady. You may find me inferior and less because of the status to which I was born." She crossed over to the pale, silent woman. "But for your ill opinion of me and your thoughts on my worth, I can leave this room with my head high, trusting that I've far greater convictions and honor than to accept a bribe." Fury lanced through her once more. "And I'll certainly never treat anyone thusly." With a disgusted shake of her head, Merry tossed that damnable packet down.

It hit the edge of the teacup, sending the brew sloshing over the edge, staining the table and the papers.

Merry made to step by the countess.

"What do you i-intend to do, Miss Read?" The countess' palms shook as she ran them over her immaculate satin skirts.

In other words, did Merry intend to tell Luke everything? It was likely the reason the countess hadn't ultimately resorted to sacking Merry and her family. "I intend to do that which you wish for most. Leave." Merry edged her chin up. "Not because of you." Because she'd not be a source of contention between Luke and his family. She'd not be a wedge in any way. And if she were being honest with herself, she was too much a coward to see Luke celebrate his holiday with a houseful of strangers who'd never dare appreciate him as he deserved, but who would command his attention forever anyway.

And not even an hour later, with her one bag packed and her heart breaking, Merry departed in the Earl of Maldavers' carriage for home.

CHAPTER ELEVEN

The guests had begun to arrive, and yet anticipation thrummed within Luke as he sought a glimpse of just one.

For the better part of the day, he'd skirted all company and searched for her. Where in blazes was she?

Merry had proven as elusive as she'd been as a child playing hide-and-seek with his brother.

Making his way to the greenhouse, he entered and did a search of the glass room.

It took but a single once-over and hearing the swath of silence to determine she was not there.

She was avoiding him.

It was all that made sense.

"Where in blazes are you?" he muttered. Quitting the gardens, Luke made his way back through the townhouse. Servants scurried about, seeing to the last-minute touches.

Which only increased his ire, because that was undoubtedly what kept Merry.

It is the way of the servant. Always be working.

By her own words, it was what Merry had always done and also, according to her, the entire reason for her being here in London. Never more had Luke looked at what life was for those born outside a life of privilege. And never more had he hated himself, which was saying a great deal, given the self-loathing he'd cloaked himself in after he'd failed to be there when his youngest brother needed him and after he had broken off his betrothal to a woman he'd deeply respected and admired.

Because all of it, every aspect of how he'd lived his life, pointed to one who'd never cared about the people around him: not his family, not those of the working class. And not Merry.

As he walked, his strides grew increasingly quick and lengthy.

Luke caught sight of the butler carrying a silver tray in hand and walking with an equally determined stride. "Blake," he called, his voice echoing down the candlelit corridor.

The servant hesitated, and for a moment, Luke believed the man intended to rush off, but then, ever the obedient butler, Blake faced him. "My lord," he greeted with a rusty, but deep bow.

The candles' glow cast shadows over the heavily wrinkled face, momentarily distracting Luke from his purpose, and he frowned. Blake had been on staff nearly twenty-two years. Nor had he been a young man when he'd begun working for the Holmans. He should be enjoying a retirement for his years of hard service. And Luke would see that he did.

Luke reached his side. "Hello, Blake."

The other man's pupils dilated in the light, his rheumy eyes revealing shock. "Good evening, my lord."

That's the manner of pompous prig I've been, that one of my loyal staff should be stunned by so much as a greeting. And Luke owed it to Merry for opening his eyes to that truth about himself... and also the desire to be and do better. "I was wondering, Blake, have you seen Miss Read?"

The older man's face grew shuttered. "I'm afraid I don't know what you mean, my lord."

Didn't know what he meant? What else could be construed or

misinterpreted by Luke's question? "Miss Read," he said once again. "I've not seen her since this morning, and I was wondering if..." A slow, horrifying understanding dawned and was confirmed when Blake's gaze dropped to the floor. "You don't know what I mean," Luke said, his voice blank, "because she's not here."

The servant gave a shaky nod. "That is correct, my lord."

Luke rocked back on his heels.

She's gone.

He went cold and then hot as his eyes slid closed.

"Where?" he gritted out, fury pulling that single syllable from him. A curse exploded from his lips. "*Where?*"

"Lady Maldavers is visiting his lordship's offices—"

Luke was already striding past the butler. And then he took off running. His chest rose and fell from a desolate panic threatening to swamp his senses.

For there could be no doubting just why Merry had gone.

He streaked past strands of garland they'd made, the gold beads twinkling merrily and bright.

As if to torment and taunt him with the visceral reminder of her, the one woman to ever bring him utter and unashamed joy. Her touch was all over what had been an otherwise, for him, sterile household.

The moment he reached the corridor that led to his father's office, he lengthened his footfalls, and not breaking stride, he grabbed the handle and threw the door open.

Matching gasps went up.

"Lucas Holman," his father said. "What is the meaning of—?"

Ignoring that question, Luke sharpened his gaze on his mother. There could be no doubting her guilt—she was pale and trembling slightly. "What have you done?" he bit out each of those four words.

"What is happening?" his father cried. "Are you drunk again?"

"Oh, no," Luke said frostily, leveling his mother with a hard look that drained the rest of the color from her face. "I'm completely sober."

"Lucas," his mother began. "It was for the best. This family certainly cannot survive another scandal."

"What is for the best?" the earl interrupted, looking hopelessly from his wife over to his son.

They ignored him.

"Why, with your brother's situation, we have to be mindful of our reputation and—"

"My brother, whom you've cut off from the damned family for mistakes made? For injustices carried out against him? Your own son?" Vitriol dripped from his voice.

His father's thick, white eyebrows formed a line. "What is going on?"

"Mother sent Merry away."

"Merry Read?" The earl's confusion deepened. "The steward's daughter?"

"Your son is carrying on an improper relationship with Miss Read."

His father's cheeks grew florid, and he sputtered, "What is this? I won't tolerate that from you, Lucas."

"You needn't worry. I'm not in and will not enter into a dalliance with her," he said quietly.

Both his parents' shoulders sagged with visible relief.

"I intend to marry her," Luke added.

Pandemonium ensued.

His mother erupted into a cacophony of tears and pleas. "You're doing this to get back at me for Miss Pratt, and I'll not allow it," she cried. Her husband rested a hand on her shoulder and spoke quietly to her, but she shrugged off his touch. "Do you hear me..."

"I said that will be all, Sara," his father said with an insistence that managed to silence her. His father caught his cane and thumped it on the floor. "Now, what is this about?"

"I'm in love with Merry Read," Luke said quietly, ushering silence into the room.

His mother fluttered a hand about her chest before clutching at her throat. "Don't be ridiculous," she whispered. "Why, just ten days ago you thought you loved Josephine Pratt and were spending your days drunk because of her."

Luke flexed his jaw, biting back the scathing words and measuring them instead. "I respected Josephine Pratt. I admired her." But he'd also been at sea around her, never having the right words and more intrigued by her than in a true partnership. "I love Merry," he said once more.

And she deserved to hear that from him. And she would.

But would she, however, want him? A pompous, self-absorbed bastard who'd only just had his eyes opened to the world? His chest constricted.

His mother dissolved into another fit of tears. "He's doing this to upset me, L-Louis. Surely you see that. He—"

"Enough, Sara," his father ordered, in the greatest of role reversals in their marriage. "I trust Lucas knows his mind."

"You would condone this?"

"What right decisions have we made where any of our sons are concerned these past years, Sara?" He looked sadly over at Luke. "Given... everything that has unfolded in our family, it is hard to say anymore what is right and what is wrong."

His mother's lower lip trembled, and she lifted her palms beseechingly. "I've not been cruel where Miss Read is concerned. Why... I... I even offered her passage to Europe and funds with which to travel."

"You...?" Luke went still. His mother had attempted to send Merry away. Nay, not only had she ordered her gone, she'd attempted to bribe her with the one thing Merry wanted out of life. A secret his mother would know only if she had been listening at some point to that most intimate exchange he'd had with Merry.

Luke saw, breathed, and tasted the red-hot rage that burned through him.

"Did she take that... offer?" his father ventured hesitantly.

"Of course she didn't," Luke snapped.

"No," the countess said at the same time.

No, a woman as proud and honorable as Merry Read would never accept such an offer, no matter how much she wanted or deserved it.

Luke unleashed a stream of black curses.

His mother bit her trembling lower lip. "Please, Lucas. I've only ever done what is best for my children."

"No," he said tiredly. "You've only ever done what is best for the Holman name. Those aren't the same things, Mother."

She jerked like he'd struck her, and then dusting the tears from her cheek, she gave her head a slight shake. When she again spoke, she was fully in command of her emotions, as she'd always been. "I do not expect you to know anything of the decisions we've made. When you are a father—"

"When I'm a father, I'll not put rank and status above the happiness of my own children." With that, Luke started for the door.

"Where are you going?" his mother cried.

"I think it should be fairly obvious," the earl drawled.

With his mother's wails trailing after him, Luke quit the room.

A short while later, he was horse-bound for Leeds.

CHAPTER TWELVE

One of the benefits of having two siblings who always sought to outdo each other was that, over the years, it had afforded Merry the ability to sit on the sidelines and be alone with her thoughts.

Or that had been the case.

"You've not said anything about what his lordship's Mayfair residence is like," her sister pressed.

Nay, she hadn't. Since her return that morn, she'd not wanted to think of that place or what had unfolded with the countess. And Luke. She especially did not want to think about Luke, and just how very much she missed him, and wished to be with him. And... Fighting back a swell of tears, she stared down at the roast beef on her wooden plate.

"Come," her mother chided, rescuing Merry. "Leave your sister alone. She's no doubt exhausted from the work she did and in such a short time."

"Overworkers, they are," her brother muttered as he sliced into the roast on his plate. He wielded it on the edge of his fork, brandishing it about like a cudgel.

"Shh," their parents commanded.

"What?" Diccan asked around a large mouthful of his roast. He swallowed forcibly. "They're all away, playing their merry festive games." He waved his fork around once more. "No need to worry about them hanging about and overhearing."

His father thumped the table. "We've all enjoyed a comfortable existence and steady work, which is more than most can rely upon, because of Lord Maldavers." He pointed across the table to his son. "You'd do well to remember that."

"Do well to remember that the very minute Merry returned from studying abroad to benefit their fine households, they ordered her onward to London?"

As Diccan launched into a long diatribe, Merry's gaze drifted over to the windowpanes and the flakes of snow faintly visible through the frosted glass.

Any other time, Merry would have felt only warmth inside for her loving brother's defense, and yet... her heart wasn't here. It remained in London, in the household of the family her brother now disparaged with words she would have agreed with... eleven days ago. But everything had changed. She'd seen that Luke was not the man she'd taken him to be. He was so much more. Seeing her, encouraging her to have her dreams, and... She bit the inside of her cheek and welcomed the sting of pain. God, how she would miss him.

"And for what?" her brother was saying. "To throw together a hasty celebration when the entire world knows what the real purpose was..." Diccan let those words dangle as the invitation they were.

A captive audience to her brother's tirade, Matilda sat forward. "And that was?"

Diccan stared at Matilda as if she had two heads. "Why, to distract the *ton* from the scandal of their eldest son, the precious heir. Why, it was enough that the youngest was a traitor, but now the pompous Lord Grimslee?" He brought his shoulders back and pointed his nose at the air.

"He is not like that," Merry exclaimed, and four pairs of gazes whipped toward her.

"Not pompous? Not priggish?" Diccan snorted. "Those words are synonymous with Lord Grimslee's name."

"Just what do you know about the viscount?" Matilda asked Merry with far too much suspicion for one of her years.

She knew he wasn't the man they believed him to be. "He's..." Merry felt every last pair of eyes home in on her face. "He's not that man. He's kind."

Diccan gave another snort.

Merry glowered. "He is. He's nothing like Lady Maldavers." That miserable woman had sent her packing.

Their mother banged the table with her fist. "Enough talk of the Holmans." She shouted order into the room. "Can we please begin with our Yuletide wishes?"

A sharp rap sounded at the door.

The entire Read family went silent.

Mama's mouth hung open as she stared with horror-filled eyes at the front door of their cottage.

Their father glared at his son, who had the grace to at least sink lower in his seat.

"What?" he whispered. "Surely you don't expect a Holman to come here at Christmas, no less?"

"Unless they *need* something," Matilda said in like hushed, but still inordinately loud, tones. "Which is entirely possible as—"

Knock-knock-knock.

This rapping came more insistent.

Jumping to her feet, Mama rushed to the door. She shot a silencing look over her shoulder and then drew the oak panel open. Snowflakes gusted into the room, little flecks that fluttered and danced.

Luke?

Her sister threw her a sharp look.

Had Merry spoken aloud? She couldn't sort it out. She couldn't sort anything out.

Her heart ceased to beat.

It froze. Immobile in her chest.

And then it resumed an erratic rhythm.

The wind howled, and Luke doffed the elegant black Oxonian atop his head. "Hullo," he greeted when no one made a move to speak.

"M-my lord," her mother stammered, sinking into a curtsy.

As one, the Reads belatedly shoved to their feet. The legs of their chairs scraped in noisy discord.

Except Merry's.

Merry remained fixed to her seat, unable to move. Unable to so much as take her eyes off the towering figure who filled the doorway. Because she was certain she'd conjured him. How else to explain Luke being here, on Christmas night?

Her sister kicked her under the table.

Grunting, Merry jumped up.

In the end, her father proved to be the single Read capable of reason. "Good evening, my lord. Is there something I might be of assistance with?"

That servantly query returned Mama to her usual composed self, and she was once more the in-charge housekeeper. "Please, please, come in," she stepped aside, allowing Luke to enter.

Luke stepped forward, and Merry's mother reached for his belongings.

He hesitated a moment and then handed over that elegant hat. The quality befit a nobleman and was of far greater value than anything in the Read's modest cottage. "Uh... thank you," he said, retaining his hold on the satchel he carried. "I was wondering... if I might"—his gaze slid over to Merry—"speak to your daughter?"

Her family all looked in her direction.

Merry's pulse pounded in her ears. "*Why?*" It took a moment to realize she'd spoken aloud.

The ghost of a smile played upon his lips, those very lips that had claimed hers in a kiss that burned in her memory still. And always would.

She cleared her throat. "That is—"

"Of course," her parents said for her.

With all the uniformity drummed into servants since birth, her family fell into step behind one another and filed past the now forgotten Christmas feast. The kitchen door closed behind the last Read, and Merry and Luke were left... alone.

There was surely something for her to say.

Only, she'd not thought to see him again and so had not bothered to prepare anything for a moment such as this. In the end, she fell back on the repertoire of words available to her as a servant. "Is there something I can do to help you?"

His thick lashes came down. "I'm not here because I want anything or expect anything, Merry," he said softly, and her belly fluttered as he started forward.

His lengthy strides made quick work of erasing the distance between them.

She wet her lips. "Th-then why *have* you come?"

"I learned of this..." He reached inside his satchel and withdrew a packet.

A very familiar packet.

"Oh," she said dumbly.

He set it on the edge of the table alongside her abandoned cutlery. "My mother informed me of... what she'd done." Next, he looped the strap of his satchel over the back of the yew wood chair her sister had abandoned.

Merry's eyes fell briefly to those hated pages his mother had wanted her to take not even two days ago. Now, it made sense why he was here. And her chest ached, because hopelessly and foolishly, she'd wanted there to be entirely different reasons that had brought him here. That he'd missed her as much as she'd missed being with him. The silence stretched on. When Luke made no attempt to fill it, she drew in a deep breath and met his gaze squarely. "Luke, you don't need to come here and apologize for—"

"Is that the reason you believe I've come? To apologize?"

She wavered. "Isn't it?" Why else would he be here... and at Christmas, no less?

"Well, that is one reason. My mother behaved unforgivably toward you, and I'll not make excuses for her heart or coldness, nor ask you to forgive such treatment. You deserve better, and I'd not ask you to accept less than the respect you deserve."

Tears clogged her throat as she fell in love with him all over again. Madly. Deeply. Head-over-heels, devoid-of-all-reason in love.

Luke cupped her cheek, and she leaned into his gloved palm, wishing away that still-cold and damp leather barrier between them, but content to take what she could. "I know this day is a special one," he murmured. "It is that favorite time where you share your Yuletide wishes." He dropped his arm to his side, and she silently cried out for the loss of that caress. "And I know what wish you've carried in your heart." Not taking his eyes from her face, he picked up the ivory packet. "You want this, Merry. You deserve it, and I've come here to tell you that it is yours, unconditionally."

She made herself accept that *gift*.

And her stomach flipped for altogether different reasons.

This was what he believed her wish was?

Only, why shouldn't he? That was what she'd shared with him. Merry turned the package over in her hands, studying it. It wasn't, however, what she wanted now. She wanted to travel... and so much more. *I want to travel with him at my side.*

Luke brushed his knuckles along her chin, bringing her eyes up to meet his.

"However, as it is the time for revealing one's Yuletide wishes, I thought it fair to share mine with you, Merry," he murmured. Reaching inside his satchel, he fished around and pulled out another packet.

"What is this?" she asked as he placed it in her fingers. Merry unfolded the pages and froze.

They were for a second passage.

"I want you to have the life you deserve, Merry," he said, his voice hoarse with emotion, and with every word, his tone grew more and more impassioned. "But I want to share it with you, as my wife."

As my wife? She struggled to follow the words, beyond those three, falling from his lips.

"I want you to travel and see the world and wish that I might do that with you." His throat moved. "But more? I love you, Merry Read." Her heart swelled and soared. "And because I love you, I want you to ultimately decide, and if you choose to go alone, then—"

With a sob, Merry launched herself into his arms.

Luke staggered and stumbled, but catching her at the waist, he kept them both upright.

"I l-love you," she stammered between great, gasping tears.

Wonder lit his eyes. "You love me?" he whispered.

How could he not know? Both laughing and crying, she took Luke's unshaven face between her palms and gripped him lightly. The light beard tickled her fingers, and she giggled. "Traveling to the Continent was only part of what I dreamed of, Luke. I want those experiences, but I want to share them with *you*."

Emotion paraded through his eyes. "I love you, Merry Read," he repeated, and then reaching around her, he scrambled around inside his bag.

She angled her head in a bid to see what he did, and then a startled laugh escaped her.

Luke withdrew another familiar item. Crushed and limp, but still recognizable. The garish ball with its gold beading and red bows.

"It is mistletoe."

"Ah," she said, catching sight of the sprig of white berries at the center of his arrangement.

"And this is my other Yuletide wish," he confessed, displaying the evergreen he'd worked so hard at. "To kiss you under the mistletoe, Merry Read."

Joy filled every corner of her being.

Gasps sounded from the kitchen.

"*What* did he say?" Diccan's loud whisper spilled out into the living quarters. "Did he say he wants to—?"

"Shh," Mama whispered.

Luke faltered, and an adorable blush climbed his cheeks.

Plucking the lovingly made decoration from his fingers, she stretched it above them. "Then let us make all our wishes come true this Christmas season."

As Luke lowered his mouth and claimed her lips in a kiss, that was just what they did.

The End

THE MINX WHO MET HER MATCH

Book 4 in "The Brethren" Series by Christi Caldwell

If you enjoyed The Viscount's Winter Wish be sure and check out Christi Caldwell's latest, _The Minx Who Met Her Match_, which features the story for Miss Josephine Pratt, Lord Grimslee's former betrothed!

Duncan Everleigh, barrister, widower, father. Accused murderer... Found innocent in the death of his wife, Duncan's reputation is ruined, his law practice is nearly destroyed, and his daughter hates him. He's content living for his work. Until one day he meets...

Miss Josephine Pratt...Her life is in tatters. Her oldest brother has brought them to financial ruin. Her betrothed has broken their engagement. Looking to escape, Josephine loses herself in her real passion—her other brother's law books. A chance meeting in the London streets soon finds her employed by the last man she should, the barrister who'll be opposing her brother in court.

Soon, Duncan and Josephine, two people who have vowed to

never love again, find the protective walls they've each built, crumbling. When past secrets threaten to destroy their future, they'll have to decide if love is enough.

Order your copy of ***The Minx Who Met Her Match!***

Made in the
USA
Middletown, DE